Happy

Libby

ALL GOOD THINGS

Penny

ALL GOOD THINGS

Perry Prete

GSPH

GENERAL STORE PUBLISHING HOUSE INC.
499 O'Brien Road, Box 415
Renfrew, Ontario, Canada K7V 4A6
Telephone 1.613.432.7697 or 1.800.465.6072
www.gsph.com

ISBN 978-1-77123-001-8

Cover: John Tkachuk and Magdalene Carson
Design and formatting: Magdalene Carson
Printed by Custom Printers of Renfrew Ltd., Renfrew, Ontario
Printed and bound in Canada

Library and Archives Canada Cataloguing in Publication
Prete, Perry.
All good things / Perry Prete.
ISBN 978-1-77123-001-8
I.Title.
PS8631.R468A66   2012 C813'.6   C2012-902224-1

DISCLAIMER

Medical protocols differ from year to year, region to region, province
to province, and county to county. Although I strive to be realistic,
the novel is a work of fiction and not meant as
a medical textbook for paramedics.

Binky and Munch

I ROLLED ONTO MY SIDE, opened my eyes, and gazed into the blue LED glow of the alarm clock. The light that broke through the curtains told me that the sun was just starting to rise. The heat from the late June sun was already hot. It was going to be a beautiful, sunny day.

"Shit!" The large, blue "6:12" beamed back at me. I'd screwed up setting the alarm again! I knew I had to be at work for 7:00 a.m. That left little time for much of anything. I usually left the house at 6:00 for the day shift.

I kicked the sheet off and jumped out of bed. No time for a shower. I ran to the washroom, turned on the tap, cupped my hands and splashed cold water on my face, dragged a comb through my hair. No time for a shave, but just enough time to brush my teeth. I found my uniform hanging in the den, got dressed, put on my boots, and donned my nylon windbreaker. Keys were already in the pocket, thank God! In the kitchen, I grabbed an apple, a banana, and a bottle of water from the fridge and entered the code to deactivate the alarm. After pushing * then 0 to reactivate the house alarm and hearing the alarm tones, I swiftly closed the door and dashed to my car. Unlocking it, I threw my "breakfast of champions" on the passenger seat and cranked the engine. I saw that "6:22" was brightly lit on the car radio. *Not bad*, I thought to myself. *I might just make it to work on time.*

CHEZ 106 and their morning team were playing the usual batch of classic rock to wake you up during the morning rush. I pulled out of the driveway, drove through the quiet neighbourhood streets, and headed east on the Queensway. Once I got comfortable with the commute, I scrolled down the memory on my cell to Maddy's cell number and pushed "send."

"Hi, Hon. Woke up late again, but I should make it to work

on time. I'll call later after three. Love you. 'Bye!" I had made it a habit to call.

"Some breakfast!" I took another bite of the apple, uncapped the bottle, and swallowed a mouthful of water. I was driving a bit faster than the normal flow of traffic. Even if I were pulled over, I knew most of the Ottawa PD. My "Ottawa Paramedic Services" stickers were firmly affixed to the front and back of my '92 yellow Porsche 968. The stickers were sort of a "professional courtesy" request. Once you were known, some of the friendlier cops might be inclined to warn you instead of giving you a ticket. Maybe! I was still taking a chance.

My Porsche was old, yes, but still a great car. And relatively cheap! That was the argument I had used to convince Maddy to let me buy the car. It wasn't too expensive, the car was a classic, and it was a cheap way to own a Porsche—there is no substitute.

Traffic was tight, but I was making great time. I slowed down to a more comfortable speed and finished my breakfast combination of apple/banana, washing it down with the last of the water. The late June morning sun was coming up fast in the east, blinding me. I put my sunglasses on and lowered the visor. The day ahead was going to be hot, humid, and beautiful—or so I hoped. I had no way of knowing what was waiting for me.

I've been living in Ottawa most of my whole life. When my family moved here, the city was not "The Regional Municipality of Ottawa–Carleton." It was Ottawa, Nepean, Gloucester, Vanier, and a lot of smaller cities, towns, and hamlets.

My family moved here from Sudbury, Ontario, when I was three years old. My time in Sudbury has long since faded from memory, replaced with tales and stories of Bytown. Over the years, we lived in a variety of Ottawa neighbourhoods.

I grew up in Ottawa, went to school in Ottawa, and now work with Ottawa Emergency Medical Services. Ottawa has one of the largest EMS agencies in the province of Ontario, probably the second or third largest. The call volume has been steadily increasing for years and off-load delays don't help matters.

I continued driving from the west end of Ottawa along the 417 east to the Walkley exit. My turn came up fast. It was only four kilometres from the 417. I turned left from Walkley Road and drove into the cul-de-sac parking lot of 2465 Don Reid Drive, home to the new Ottawa Paramedic Services HQ. The building is a marvel of engineering design and was awarded a LEED certification as a "green" building. With its abundance of windows, the lobby is awash in light. The new headquarters is much better than the old Ottawa ambulance building, which was nothing more than an old office building with drafty windows and way too many stairs. Glad we moved!

I parked the Porsche in the staff parking lot next to the bike racks. They are never used, so I knew my car was safe on one side, anyway. I grabbed my duffel bag and headed in. My analog watch showed 6:58—a new record! If this kept up, I could probably sleep in a few more minutes each morning. That is, if I ever learn how to the set the alarm properly!

I have never learned to keep up with technology. I enjoyed my old windup alarm clock with the dual brass bells on top. I had to wind it every night. Setting the alarm was as easy as turning the dial to move the hand to the desired time. It wasn't extremely accurate, but it was easy. Even if the power went out, the clock still worked. I owned that clock longer than I care to remember. Once it died, Maddy bought the digital dual alarm, dual time zone, auto DST settings, with a twenty-page operations manual. I have been trying to find another old windup clock for years. I liked my old clock! I like my old car! Even my cell phone is nothing more than a cell phone. No text messaging, no camera, no MP3 player, no GPS. Huge by today's cell phone standards, but it works. Unfortunately, I can't find a new battery for it, so when it finally goes, I will be forced to get a new multi-function model.

I swiped my ID card, entered through the employee entrance, walked down the hall, and, as usual, found my partner, Tom Lister, waiting for me. Again! I have a habit of doing this, but Tom always has my back. Tom is taller than me, with dark hair, big in a "body-builder on steroids" sort of way, which he vehemently denies. Hitting the gym five days a week is perfectly natural, he always says. Unofficially, he is also known as the Ottawa Paramedic Services' calendar boy.

"You forgot to shave again, eh, Nash? Don't tell me, you woke up late, didn't have time, and ate in the car."

"Am I that transparent?" My daily routine had become . . . well, just that. Routine.

Tom always called me Nash. I hated being called Nash. He started calling me Nash because I like the Nashville Predators. Not a very original nickname. I hate it and Tom knows it. To make matters that much worse, it caught on, and now almost everyone calls me Nash. Actually, I'm pretty sure no one actually knows my real name!

Tom is like my older brother, even though he is two years younger than me. We met in college in '97, graduated together after the two-year Primary Care Paramedic program, eventually becoming partners after we both went back to college to get our Advanced Care Paramedic certification.

"I'll book on; you clean up," he offered. I nodded in agreement.

Tom called dispatch, booked on, went to the garage, and was assigned a "bus" for the day while I went into the gym shower facilities to clean up. Some of the older medics still refer to an ambulance as a bus. Forgetting to shave was not something that was going to get me into trouble, but Tom believed you needed to look the part to be the part: clean and pressed uniform, shiny boots. Do your job well, go home safe.

"A dying breed," Maddy always said of Tom.

By the time I was finished, Tom was outside in the bus waiting for me. Our first call was to the Ottawa General Hospital ER. Tom booked 10–8 in service, and left the building. We had time to stop at Tim Hortons on Alta Vista before arriving at the OGH ER. Tim's is the quintessential police/EMS coffee refuelling centre. Only the young, elitist paramedics went for the "Mocha Grande Frappachino" and were willing to pay three times the amount for a coffee that you had to add the cream and sugar to yourself.

A quick stop for an extra-large double/double yielded a nice surprise. This was a Monday morning and Tim's was busy as usual. Mondays usually means long lines with a good chance of getting a call just after you pay for your drink and before you actually receive it.

Tom is too perfect for coffee. All he drinks is deionized water—four litres a day. Of course, we have to stop every half hour for a pee break!

"How are you adjusting?" Tom asked.

I turned quickly, looked at him, shrugged my shoulders, and returned to stare at the traffic in front. He knew not to ask twice.

"Did you feed the cats?" Tom's way to get me talking is to keep asking questions until he finds one I have to answer.

"Shit!" That pretty much gave it away. Luckily, I always leave out hard food and fresh water for my two boys. They would be okay for the day.

We drove along Smyth Road, pulled up the long ramp to the second level of the OGH ER, and parked under the canopy. We removed the cot and headed in for our first call, to take a patient back to a nursing home. Not the usual call for an ACP team. Tom and I are both experienced Advanced Care Paramedics, ACP for short, but dispatch knew we didn't mind doing transfers. If you treated the dispatchers well, they reciprocated.

Tom and I knew the emergency staff at all of the hospitals in Ottawa. It's easy when your partner is a bronzed, muscle-bound beach bum with golden locks that all the women—married or single, and even the occasional guy—will gravitate to!

This day was no different. We had time to chat it up with the nurses and doctors in the ER, giving the crews a chance to catch up on things.

Most of the morning was taken up by routine calls, nothing exciting. We had a few minor medical calls, but none that required any extensive medical intervention.

I am always amazed at how television portrays EMS. On TV, every call is life or death and all we do is run hot from one call to the next, saving lives every day. Truth is, most day shift calls are boring, and those lifesaving calls are the exception. We don't walk around the station with a trauma bag over our shoulders. Not every guy is tall and muscular with a square jaw. Not every girl is blonde with her shirt bursting at the seams, unbuttoned to her navel.

When we do run hot with lights and sirens to a call, friends and family think we get all excited and hyped-up. All we are really thinking about is that we should have gone for a leak before leaving, or are we going to get lunch at a decent time, or any lunch at all. This doesn't make us bad, it's simply the reality of the job. This is not the job for people who like to keep a schedule.

The morning flew by, going from basic call to basic call, dealing with off-load delays, no thinking involved. It was the most perfect, gorgeous day for driving around with the windows down and not doing a whole hell of a lot. We'd been able to grab a quick bite at a deli on Metcalfe Street, then dispatched back to the Civic Hospital ER. We went inside with our empty cot and no equipment. We'd been assigned a Code 1, the lowest priority call a crew can get. Most ACP crews don't do transfers. It has always been part of the job and still is, as far as we are concerned.

Three crews, two from Ottawa and one from Lanark EMS, waited impatiently in the halls of the ER to drop off their patients. All looked dejected and gave us nothing more than a passing glance. You could tell that they had been there for a while. It was too hot and muggy to be wasting the day standing in the emergency department waiting to unload your cargo. Their tolerance for delays was running thin. Tom and I knew better than to approach a crew on the edge of reason to engage in idle chatter when they had been waiting longer than they should. At least we were there to take one away and relieve some of the congestion in the waiting area.

This is where I'd met Maddy years ago. She was a new nurse in the Emergency Department and I had just completed my PCP program. Tom had introduced us, another reason, Maddy said, to hate Tom even more! I certainly hoped she was kidding.

The Civic ER was bustling. You could see into the waiting room as we drove past the glass walls. Every seat was full, with family members standing close by. Easily, half of these patients could have gone to their family doctor instead of going to the ER or using the ER as a family doctor. It was society's way of dealing with the impatient and the uninformed. If the Ministry of Health ever held an advertising campaign to teach the public what the ER was really for, wait times would drop and there would be more money for doctors, nurses, and equipment.

One of Maddy's fellow nurses handed me an envelope without saying a word. He didn't even ask whom we were there for. It was obvious he resented being at work today. Tom and I gave a quick glance to each other, made the face we've made a thousand times before to each other every time we meet someone who hates his job and wants to make sure his feelings are known.

After I verified the patient's name against the call information we received from dispatch, we followed Mr. Personality back to the bedside. No patient report, no introduction, just a quick hand gesture to inform us that we had the right patient. He kept on walking without saying another word.

Immediately, the frail, elderly woman's eyes found Tom and knew she had struck the jackpot. "Are you taking me home?" she asked Tom; I was not sure if she even noticed me.

"As a matter of fact, we are." He smiled showing too much teeth.

"This is my lucky day! You are quite the young man." I swear he blushed.

"Thank you. This is a nice break for us to take a lovely lady back home." He always knew what to say. "Ethan and I will get the stretcher ready and then take you home, if that's okay? And I get to be your guide for this trip." She smiled a toothless grin.

Tom felt it necessary to scoop her up in his arms. She put her arms around Tom's neck, and he turned and gently placed her on the cot while I stood by, looking at the smile beaming from her face. Tom had just made her day!

As we exited the ED, I gave a wave to the waiting EMS crews, who usually acknowledge by doing the typical head bob. Walking through the parking lot, I pushed the button on the remote to unlock the back doors to our rig. Tom opened the dual doors while I pushed the cot into the back of the rig and locked the swing bar onto the floor block. I lifted the foot end of the cot as Tom lifted the carriage up, and we pushed the stretcher into the locking position against the floor antlers and the locking bar.

The ride to the patient's apartment complex was uneventful and took only a few minutes. We booked 10–7—arrived on scene—and unloaded our patient, taking the elevator upstairs to the third floor. Tom led the way from the elevators, pulling the cot by the foot handle. We rounded the corner and searched the hall looking for apartment 320. Tom knocked on the patient's apartment door and waited for the family to answer.

Suddenly, a low, dense thud came from behind the door of apartment 318. Startled, Tom and I looked at each other. No words were said. We just continued to stare. No other sounds could be heard. We waited. Nothing more! Instinctively, I reached for the door handle of 318. "NO!" Tom whispered between clenched teeth.

I don't listen very well. Curiosity got the better of me. I slowly wrapped my hand around the handle. I gave it a gentle turn, felt the door open, and carefully pushed it open a crack. The door was unlocked! I peered into the apartment against the darkness, allowing my eyes time to adjust to the lack of light. The room was ominously black; heavy drapes were drawn against the sunshine outside. A quick look back at my partner was all that was needed to confirm that I should not be doing what I was about to do.

"Hello!" I called out.

No reply.

"Hello!" I repeated.

Again, there was no reply or sound from inside the dark apartment.

"Ottawa Paramedics."

I released the Velcro cover from my LED flashlight on my belt, depressed the thumb switch, and held the flashlight in my clenched fist at eye level with the light splitting the darkness. I opened the door just enough to let myself in. I left the door open to let the ambient light from the hallway illuminate some of the apartment. The darkness still dominated the room.

Tom remained with the patient in the hall. Tom had the portable radio with him. He was the driver on this call, and the driver always carries the radio. I swept the beam of light back and forth, slowly and methodically, attempting to distinguish the forms in the darkness. I followed the light to the right, walked a few feet, and moved the light to my left into the living room. I shone the light high to the right then slowly moved it across the room to the left. The drapes were pulled closed with only a thin strip of sunlight forcing its way through at the top. The light went across furniture that suggested someone in his or her thirties or forties: elegant, not too comfortable, and rigid. I stepped into the room. My heart was pounding so hard I could feel the pulse thumping in my ears. I was not supposed to be here and I knew it. This was not our job.

"Hello?" Nothing!

My light swept across the room and moved across the floor to the left then to the right. A hall went to the right, against the outside wall. The circle of light moved across the floor and lit the edge of the hall and a single running shoe that was pointing straight up.

An empty shoe doesn't balance on its heel!

I couldn't make out a leg or anything else. If there was a foot inside the shoe, the leg it was attached to was hidden behind the wall. No choice, I thought to myself. I am in this far—I might as well finish it. I followed the light through the maze of furniture to the edge of the hall, turned right, and found the rest of the body on the floor in the hall.

Now it *was* our job! I took two steps, knelt down on the patient's right side. I reached for a carotid pulse, found none, but felt something warm on my fingers in the darkness. I was ungloved.

"Shit!" I knew better.

I moved the light to the patient's face. My fingers were covered in blood and you could see the impression in the blood where I pressed against the left side of the neck, searching for the carotid pulse. I wiped my fingers quickly back and forth on my right pant leg with all the grace I could muster. My pupils were blown wide open now and, even in the darkness, I could make out more than when I first entered.

I moved the light down and saw the reason why there was so much blood. The entire right parietal lobe of the patient's head was missing. Dark hair and blood were mixed in the cavity of the wound. Blood had pooled around the patient's head as he lay there. Tissue and brain matter were hanging on the jagged edges of the skull. The bright white of the bone created a halo effect that circled the outer aspect of the wound. I turned the patient's head and noticed a small entrance wound over the left temple. Dark speckles surrounded the entrance wound; possibly gunpowder. This was a "through-and-through" gunshot at close range. I followed my light up to the right against the wall and saw where the blood had splattered brain matter, and skull fragments had left their mark on the wall. I moved the light back to further examine the wound. The size of the wound and the damage indicated the calibre of the gun that obviously did the damage.

"Gun?" I said to myself, realizing we'd actually heard the murder take place. That meant the killer must still be here.

My right knee was in the warm blood, which was soaking through my pants. I tried to stand but my knee slid in the blood. I was about to turn and call for Tom when something hard pressed against the back of my head.

"Don't move, please!" The voice was calm, sincere, and almost apologetic.

"Shut off the flashlight, get up, and turn around." This was not a request but a command. I thumbed the switch killing the light and holstered it. I kept my head down to show my understanding of who was in charge. I stood up slowly, so he would not confuse my fear with an attempt to attack. I could feel my foot sink deep into the wet, blood-soaked carpet like a foot in wet sand on the beach. Slowly, I turned.

The killer stood before me. He—I assumed it was a man by the commanding voice—was wearing black: black shirt, black pants, black shoes, a black toque showing only the whites of his eyes, and black leather gloves, which were holding what I thought was a very large handgun. Any gun pointed at me would be large. Even in the darkness, I could tell the pistol looked like an automatic, similar to what the police use, except the barrel was much longer. A silencer! That explains why we didn't hear the shot.

"You are not one of them!" His voice was more aggressive now. He pressed the barrel of the silencer against the middle of my forehead. I looked down the barrel of the gun and stared him in the eyes.

"Do not interfere with me again!" His tone changed. This was not a threat but a promise. The hammer of his handgun was cocked back. I closed my eyes, not wanting to see what was going to happen. He pulled the trigger! Click! Nothing! Nothing happened. I opened my eyes questioning why I was still standing.

"Next time," he paused, "the chamber won't be empty!" He turned and bolted for the door. Tom was still in the hall with our patient. I tried to yell for Tom to stop him. My mouth was dry. I couldn't say anything. I was going to give chase, but my legs felt heavy and thick, like day-old oatmeal. I forced myself to move and then felt the floodgates open. I felt my entire body jolted with more adrenaline than I have ever felt before. My whole body jumped into action. The attacker pulled the door open, and light flooded in from the hall.

I turned, leaped over the coffee table, and gave chase. I was already breathing heavily. I hit the entrance door with my right shoulder, sending it crashing into the closet door behind. The hollow closet door collapsed under my weight and the momentum of my run. Tom and the patient were still outside in the hall. Tom was mesmerized by the chaos that was unfolding before him.

"Call the police, 10–2000! Now!" I ordered Tom. 10–2000!—"Call police, no questions asked." If any medic calls dispatch with a 10–2000, all rigs stop transmitting, and the dispatcher radios back requesting a confirmation for an "All Clear." If no "Alpha Charlie" is given, the police respond, period. Tom knew something was up. This was not like me.

I hit the hall running, my feet were on fire, my heart pumping. The killer was a good twenty feet in front of me as he turned left toward the elevator foyer. I heard the stairwell door open. By the time I got to the door, it was just closing. Up or down? Down! He would want to leave. I would if I were him.

I leaned forward, slid my left hand down the rail, braced my right hand against the wall, and jumped from the top step to the metal landing half a storey below. My steel-toed boots hit hard, the metallic sound echoing in the stairwell. I turned and repeated my jump. I looked right and saw a painted black number two on the wall. I jumped again and again until I reached the first floor, pushing the door open, entering the lobby. I saw the black figure now. He had gained distance and was already outside the building, running past the ambulance parked in front of the building, and down the street.

I pushed hard through the glass double doors, fearing they would break from the force of my run. I looked right then left. The assailant was running down the street and had turned between two small buildings across the street. Without pausing, I picked up the pace and heard the sounds of my feet slap the interlocking paving stones that made up the apartment buildings' turnaround. I failed to look before running across the street. Drivers slammed on their brakes and leaned on their horns, as tires screamed against the hot pavement. The sun was high, and the humidity only made it worse. Sweat was pouring off my forehead. I turned between the buildings. The killer was gaining more distance. My heavy boots were slowing me down. My heart was pumping. My breaths were deep and burned my lungs. I followed the figure as best I could, but he was in better shape. He rounded the building and disappeared between two cars. He was not getting away. My pace quickened. When I reached the cars, I fell into one of the car's fenders, braced myself, pushed off, and continued the pursuit. When I emerged from the front of the building, my prey was closing a car door. The engine over-revved, and the tires squealed as they left rubber on the asphalt.

I ran back to the ambulance parked in front of the apartment building. I didn't have keys for the rig on me, but was determined to stop him. I found the hidden external electric door switch, pressed it, and heard the electric locks disengage. I jumped into the driver's seat and located the second set of keys. I was not going to wait for the glow plugs to warm up. It was June, and the bus had been running all day; the plugs would still be hot. I turned the key, and the large V-8 Ford diesel roared to life. I slapped the gear selector down to "D," hit all three toggle switches bringing the emergency lights into action, and stepped on the accelerator hard—and then promptly hit the brakes, making the nose of the ambulance dip down. I jammed the gear lever back into Park and killed the engine.

"Fuck!" I slapped the steering wheel in frustration. I couldn't chase him. Could I let him get away? It was a moot point. He was already gone, I rationalized to myself.

MULTIPLE SIRENS COULD BE HEARD fighting for dominance over the sounds of traffic on the hot June day. Several Ottawa Police cruisers arrived at the same time, while I stood looking in the direction the killer's car had gone. The cruisers came to a fast stop, parking in front of and behind the ambulance, preventing us from leaving. I didn't object, since we weren't going anywhere for a while. Now that the police were here, I land-lined dispatch to clear the 10–2000 and asked for a supervisor on scene. One of the officers came over and asked why I called in a 10–2000. After a quick briefing, we all headed upstairs to apartment 318.

Tom looked puzzled when I came walking down the hall with four Ottawa police officers in tow. My shirttails were hanging out, and sweat stained the front, sides, and back of my navy blue uniform shirt as a result of my sprint with the killer. My pants were stained with dried blood. Our elderly patient was still lying comfortably on the cot, waiting to be released into the care of her family, who stood beside her.

After I went inside apartment 318 with the police and directed them to the body, I excused myself to assist Tom in transferring our patient. When I returned, the police were in full investigative mode. The drapes were still drawn, but the officers had their flashlights on, penetrating the apartment with beams of light that crisscrossed each other. Several officers were speaking on cell phones, others scrambling to take notes, while another was looking over the body for clues. Tom and I went straight to the body. Tom bent over to examine the body.

"You sure he's dead?" he asked the officer, who had his face only inches from the open wound. "Do you want me to double check for you?" The officer looked back with disgust.

"Yah, I'm pretty sure he's dead!" he replied condescendingly.

One of the police detectives finally turned on the apartment lights to illuminate the crime scene. As Tom was patronizing the cop, something odd about the body struck me, something I didn't notice earlier. It must be my imagination! Blood splatter is seldom if ever uniform, yet a distinctive cross or plus sign was apparent on the victim's forehead. How could I have missed that? There was no possible way the blood could have pooled like that. Even with the apartment lights on, I used my flashlight, illuminating the victim's face. I was right! You could make out the streaks in the blood. The killer had drawn a cross on the victim's forehead with a finger or instrument. *Why?* I thought to myself. *What is the reason to paint a cross on the person you've just killed?*

More officers arrived as each minute passed. Tom and I were getting in the way, and we knew it, but we still had to take notes for our reports. We pulled back into the hall, attempting to find a spot where we would limit our presence.

"Can I speak to you?"

I didn't recognize the officer making the request. More officers were exiting the elevators, carrying bags and cases filled with forensic tools. They passed us without acknowledging our presence. Whatever the significance of the cross on the forehead meant, the cops would certainly find out.

A plainclothes officer began to question Tom in great detail about the recent events in apartment 318. Tom was the lucky one; he had nothing to tell.

I was kept out of the mix, to keep our stories our own, but I knew that my actions would be considered either heroic or idiotic. Only time would tell. At this very moment, I was thinking that idiotic was leading the charge. As I unfolded my story to the officer, an Ottawa Paramedic Services Supervisor stood patiently behind him, waiting for a pause in the conversation to interrupt. Realizing that I would eventually have to face my superior, I provided as many details as I could recall in hopes of delaying the inevitable.

After giving my statement, it was time to face our own supervisor. She had been standing close by, patiently waiting her turn to make sure we were okay!

"Officer?" she asked.

"I'm done for now," he replied.

She excused us, got permission for us to leave the scene, and began walking down the hall. She curled her index finger, indicating that we should follow.

Before joining Tom and Supervisor Carole Geffen, I peeked inside the apartment to see the progress of the investigation. The drapes were now open, permitting the sun to enter and brighten the entire room, revealing more details and possibly more clues to the crime. Little orange numbered pylons littered the room. The pylons stood upright, protecting vital pieces of evidence or body parts that were scattered around the room. Those officers who weren't squatting and straining to see every last detail were standing, feverishly writing in their leather-clad binders. Digital camera flashes were popping every few seconds recording clues and crime details on SD cards. One officer was responsible for recording the entire scene with a digital video camera. Like a skilled director, he made observations, recorded the victim, the scene, and every last detail all to review later. The room had the distinctive, metallic smell of fresh blood, an odour that really can't be duplicated elsewhere, thank God! Working as a medic for so long, you learn to recognize the smell, even to tolerate it.

I eventually joined the supervisor and Tom at the end of the hall for yet another narrative of the day's events. The story was beginning to sound boring even to me, with my actions seeming less and less justified with each version. This time was different. I couldn't be disciplined by the police for chasing the killer. However, I couldn't wait to find out what was going to happen when the EMS brass found out what I had done.

Supervisor Geffen had moved up the ranks fast. She hadn't been on the road long but knew her way around the political arena. Both Tom and I had been working longer than she had, but neither one of us had the desire to do her job. The nice thing about still working the road was the ability to end a shift, call it a day, and go home. A late call at the end of your shift was normal and part of the job, so overtime was a great way to bank your time for extra days off. Supervisors, however, had the delicate balancing act of dealing with both crews and management, trying to keep both happy—no easy task.

Geffen took notes as I recounted my events of the afternoon.

This was not your normal incident report that could be filed away and forgotten by the end of the shift. This could come back and bite me. I had entered a residence without permission, possibly contaminating a crime scene; left my partner alone with a patient; chased a suspected killer out of a building; and almost gave chase with an ambulance!

Tom glared at me each and every time I made a statement he felt was better left unsaid or in need of sugar coating. After the story had been told and notes taken, Geffen called one of the deputy chiefs on her cell. Geffen offered us counselling if we felt it necessary. Tom and I looked at each other, shrugged our shoulders, declining the offer. She had just made an appointment for me to go over the incident again tomorrow morning at 10:00 a.m. sharp. Someone would cover Tom's and my shifts, I was told. Either I was going to be in meetings for a long time or I would have some free time to myself.

We were done for the day. The rest of our shift was spent filling out incident reports, repeating, yet again, the same details of the day's events. After completing the paperwork, I reviewed them before we signed our names to them and submitted them to management. It wouldn't be long before the reports would be read, bringing more questions from management.

Tom and I finished our shift, cleaned up, and decided to go our separate ways instead of grabbing a beer and dinner. The day had been long enough, but I doubted I would get much sleep.

And I hadn't called Maddy like I had promised. Truth be told, in all the excitement, I had forgotten to call. Molly and Snickers were waiting for me when I got home. They took their independence from Maddy. In the summer, the cat door gave them free rein of the backyard. Their water and hard food bowls were always full, but their special treat was a can of moist food at breakfast and dinner. We ate dinner in front of the television, falling asleep on the sofa. I was surprised and relieved to turn my mind off for a few hours. I needed a good night's sleep to help relieve the stress and to shut out the dread of having a gun pointed at me. Unfortunately, I had to go over it all again tomorrow.

3

I HADN'T BOTHERED to set the alarm. Even if I had, it probably wouldn't have gone off anyway. I had been given the day off in order to prepare the explanations for my actions. The incident had left me a little more shaken than I thought. My sleep had been restless, so I figured I was owed a little extra sleep. Maddy was still unaware of what had happened and I wanted to leave it that way until after my meeting with management today.

I had taken my time getting ready and had a relaxing drive on the Queensway. Traffic had thinned by that time, and the sun was high in the eastern sky. Tim Hortons was on my way, so I stopped for my usual and still managed to pull into HQ well before ten. I walked in carrying my coffee and the notes that I had prepared the previous day.

Supervisor Geffen met me at reception, guiding me to a private room and telling me to wait. Wait! I hate waiting. Great . . . It was pure torture to sit alone in a bare room with nothing more than a table and a couple of chairs. It felt too much like a police inter-rogation room. Paranoia was not like me. Amazing how fast one's thinking can change when events alter perception. The room was white. White walls, white floors, white ceiling, even the chairs and table were white. The chairs were obviously designed to limit com-fort and/or to increase your anxiety level. The air conditioner was set at much too low a temperature. It would be uncomfortable even under the best of circumstances.

The wait was little more than ten minutes but felt like hours. An elderly man wearing the cliché white manager's shirt with four gold stripes on the epaulettes entered the room with a binder, a folder, and two coffees. The City of Ottawa ID card clipped to his epaulette introduced him as Dave Green. He placed all the items carefully on the table, opened the binder to the desired location, and pulled a pen from the sleeve, keeping the file folder strategically hidden under the binder. The label of the folder was partially visible and you could make out the name "Tennant, Ethan" in black on a white P-Touch label. The tray supported two coffees and a paper bag with creamers and sugar. He sat down, grabbed one of the coffees and slid the tray with the remaining coffee in my direction. He noticed I came prepared. My coffee was half gone so I graciously accepted the second that was being offered. He added sugar and cream, swirled the coffee, licked the stir stick and tossed it into the empty tray.

"How are you feeling today, Ethan?" he asked point-blank.

Ethan, he had actually used my name. Someone didn't know me as Nash! This was starting off better than I had thought it would. I added cream and sugar to my new coffee and took a sip. It was calming and helped me to relax a bit.

"Better than yesterday. Thanks for asking." This was not meant to be sarcastic, but rather a statement of fact. I was better today than yesterday. Another hot, sunny June day and everything seemed better already.

"So . . . ?" he paused. "You know this is not a disciplinary hearing but you can have a union rep present if you want." He paused again. "We just need to hear the facts directly from you and get the whole story."

I declined having a union rep present, once he had informed me that there would be no discipline. A huge burden was lifted, and I sat up straighter. I took a large sip and felt the coffee warm me from the inside. I no longer felt the breeze from the A/C unit blowing overhead. I didn't even open my folder with the report I had prepared the day before. I had told the story so many times and lived through it. There was no need to check my facts.

I recited my story almost verbatim to the one I gave to Supervisor Geffen. Dave kept his eyes on the pages in front of him. His pen was leading the notes in his binder as I relived the events of the previous day. My coffee was gone by the time I had finished the story. I now wished I had gone to the bathroom first. I fought the urge to go to the bathroom. When I was done, Dave looked at me to see if I wished to add anything. Nothing more was said.

Dave stood up, slid the pen back into its pocket, closed his binder, and extended his hand to shake mine.

"Off the record, I probably would have done exactly the same thing. I would have followed him, chased the bastard down and kicked the living shit out of him," he admitted in a quiet, co-operative tone.

I was pleased that management had decided against any disciplinary action but to actually condone what I had done was a shock. Before leaving, Dave offered me a few more days off, and counselling if I felt it necessary. He added that Tom had already agreed to take the next two days off with pay. Dave recommended taking the two-day break to collect my wits and come back to work with a level head. It didn't take me long to accept his offer of paid stress leave. I immediately started to think of what Maddy and I could do on our days off.

I collected my folder, deposited my cups in the recycling bin, and walked from the interrogation room. Tom was waiting for me in the lobby. We agreed that a round of golf on company time was in order and headed off to the Hunt Club Golf Course located out by the airport. Tom was a member at the "Hunt," and there was no getting in otherwise. Hunt Club Golf Course is a challenging course situated within Riverside Drive to the west, Paul Anka Drive on the east, and Hunt Club Road, which borders the entire southern section. Suburban sprawl has surrounded the course with magnificent homes that sit on postage stamp-sized lots situated on wavy streets. The Ottawa International Airport is directly opposite the course, but the beauty of the scenery overshadows the occasional roar of the planes as they take off and land.

We transferred my clubs to Tom's car and headed to the "Hunt" for the rest of the afternoon. A round of golf was better than talking to some counsellor about the murder, and I felt better than I had in weeks. Since I was losing so badly after the first three holes, I decided that I would buy dinner afterwards. It seemed only fair, since Tom was the member, and I was his guest.

The next few days were uneventful. After our paid stress leave, Tom and I returned to work.

THE ONLY ROUTINE PART of being a Paramedic is booking on each day and checking email and notices from the brass. Today, among the dozens of my emails, I had one from another medic who wanted to speak with me regarding my incident. Seemingly, the rumour mill had been kept busy on my days off.

Patrick Levac, a PCP—Primary Care Paramedic—wanted to see me immediately regarding my patient. He had news and had to see me in person. He left his cell number. I didn't know Patrick well, only in passing. We had never worked together, had never taken any classes together, but that wasn't unusual in such a large service. I replied to his email to let him know I had gotten his message and that I would try to touch base sometime during the day.

I rushed out to the garage. Tom had booked on and was waiting for me yet again. I tossed my duffle bag into the back before departing HQ. I quickly dialed Patrick's cell number, becoming more and more curious as time went on. The phone rang several times and went to voice mail. Patrick had a thick French accent. Curiosity was getting the better of me. I hit redial. Voicemail again! It would be several hours before I got to speak with Patrick about his email.

All of our calls that morning were routine and uneventful. Patrick was still not answering his phone. It was just before noon when Tom pulled out of the Queensway–Carleton Emergency Department and had turned north on the 416 Highway when we received a call for an MVA, Motor Vehicle Accident, on the 417, in front of Scotia Bank Place. The 417, a four-lane section of Highway 17 of the Trans-Canada Highway, snakes west from the Quebec border along the Ottawa River then across northern Ontario to the Manitoba border. In total, the Trans-Canada Highway traverses over 2,000 kilometres.

Ottawa CACC, Central Ambulance Communication Centre, knows our location at all times, just like Big Brother. The vehicle GPS system shows the dispatchers all vehicle locations in their catchment area. Scotia Bank Place is the home of the Ottawa Senators NHL Hockey Club. The building has gone through several name changes since the building was constructed in the mid-1990s: Palladium, Corel Centre, and now Scotia Bank Place.

The emergency lights on the rig were activated, and Tom accelerated fast through thick traffic northbound on the 416. We turned west on the 417. Traffic was already backing up on the westbound 417. The eastbound 417 had slowed due to rubberneckers trying to get their last look at the accident before leaving the scene. Surely, every single person who slowed traffic would have a great story to tell their family about the fatality they saw on the highway today.

Tom straddled the south shoulder and part of the fast lane in an attempt to get to the scene as fast and as safely as possible without causing any further accidents or becoming part of one. Dispatch updated the call information. Fire was already in service to the call, along with the Ontario Provincial Police. The OPP patrolled this section of the 417 highway. Fire was en route because the caller information indicated that the driver and passenger of one of the cars were trapped. Several more ambulances had also been dispatched.

Tom skilfully navigated our way to the scene. Even from a distance, we could see a large, white, four-door sedan resting on its roof. A small import SUV with severe front-end damage straddled the east lanes of the 417. Both air bags of the SUV had been deployed. Two occupants of the SUV were still sitting inside the vehicle. Several people had stopped to render assistance. Some were leaning in through the windows of the SUV speaking with the occupants, while others were peering into the white sedan. Tom and I had both donned our gloves prior to arriving at scene.

Tom booked us "10–7" scene as we arrived. The OPP officers had parked in the east lane and walked across the highway through the median. I heard more sirens in the background. I walked around to the back of the rig, grabbed the trauma bag, the oxygen bag, and a cardiac monitor and headed for the overturned sedan. Tom went for the occupants of the SUV.

I thanked the passersby for their assistance, knelt down, and peered inside. The car was too old for air bags. The windows must have been rolled down to enjoy the hot June weather, as there was no glass inside or around the car. The elderly male driver was belted in, hanging upside down from only a hip lap belt and was unconscious. He must have tucked the shoulder restraint behind his back. The female passenger was conscious, belted in properly, and was also hanging upside-down. She was screaming, tugging and pushing at the seat belt release button. Blood flowed freely from what could be a severe head wound, hidden by her long hair, and pooled on the roof liner below her. With her weight stressing the seat belt, the buckle would not release its grip on the hanging lady. I asked one of the OPP officers to crawl in the car to assist us to calm the lady down. I gave him some gloves and showed him how to hold her neck to keep her immobilized in the seat and prevent any further injury. Hair and blood on the "B" pillar on her right side between the front and back doors showed evidence of how she had sustained her laceration.

I felt for a carotid pulse on the male driver who was hanging upside down. No pulse. I checked his pupils. No response. I pulled out my scope and auscultated his chest for any possible lung or cardiac sounds. None! His chest was soft and moved freely. I opened his shirt, exposing a massive flail section. With the shoulder restraint behind his back, he must have struck the steering wheel hard and fractured his sternum and ribs. They were now floating freely and possibly causing severe trauma to his heart, lungs, trachea, and who knows what else?

I looked over the car to Tom's location. "Code 5!" I mouthed. The driver was dead. Tom nodded in agreement. Tom held up two fingers, pause, then one finger, pause, 3 fingers, pause, 1 finger, pause, 3 fingers. Two patients, both patients were a code three, serious injuries but non-life threatening. Thank God for air bags! Those two patients could go together in one rig. Under triage protocol, we couldn't waste time on a VSA (Vital Signs Absent) patient while we had three viable patients.

I saw my partner key the portable radio. I knew Tom was radioing dispatch for the ETA of the other ambulances. A quick glance down the highway revealed the fire crews attempting to get drivers to move their vehicles out of the way. Ambulances are much smaller and can get through traffic easier. Not so with larger fire vehicles. I returned to care for my upside-down patient. A complete primary and secondary assessment revealed no obvious injuries other than the severe laceration on her scalp.

I chose the equipment I needed and crawled inside the vehicle. I lay on my back on the roof of the vehicle, between the dead driver and the passenger.

"Hi. My name is Ethan. I and all these people are here to help you and we are going to get you out of here. Do you understand?"

She screamed.

I kept trying to explain what we were going to do but she continued screaming. I applied a quick dressing to stem the flow of blood.

"Can you tell me what happened?" I spoke in a slow, monotone voice. It seemed to work. Her screaming was replaced with deep, heavy breathing.

She replied that her father was driving her into Ottawa from Arnprior and just slumped over the wheel. The car then crossed the grassy median, was hit by an oncoming car in the west lane and rolled backwards into the ditch. She added that her father never wore his seat belt the way it was intended and that he seldom took his prescribed heart medication. She asked if it was possible that he'd died before the accident. There was no way to tell, but I nodded as if to give her the reassurance that he had probably died quickly. We weren't supposed to give patients our personal opinions on what may or may not have happened, but how a patient interprets a nod is open to interpretation. If a little white lie makes the patient believe something that lowers her anxiety, what harm is there in that?

I placed a non-rebreather mask with high-flow oxygen over her mouth and nose. It was easy to apply a cervical collar, then the KED, a vest device which immobilizes the head, torso and pelvis. Fire had arrived on scene and offered us assistance. I asked for a spine board along with another set of hands inside the car to help cut her down. A firefighter returned with the plastic spine board and placed it exactly how I had instructed. The board was under the patient, partially outside the vehicle. He tossed four straps into the car for me. Another firefighter came inside and positioned himself beside the police officer. After a brief set of instructions to the patient and my new first-response partners on how the next move would be completed, I grabbed my scissors and cut the belt on the count of "three."

I went from cutting the belt to taking control of her head and neck. The firefighter and police officer had her torso, pelvis, and legs held firmly in place with the aid of the KED. She was now free of her restraint, and we gently slid her down onto the board, head first. Her head went outside the passenger window into the waiting hands of another firefighter. The female firefighter made sure the oxygen mask was still in place. I released the leg straps from the KED, allowing her legs to straighten out. From inside the car, I placed all four straps on the board to keep my patient in place before any more movement could cause further injury. Black foam rolls were placed by each side of her head and were taped in place to maintain cervical spine immobilization.

We slid her out from inside and clear of the overturned car. The cot was prepped and lowered to halfway down. One of the firefighters and I hoisted the board up while the police officer rolled the cot under the board. She was strapped on the cot and secured. Cardiac monitoring leads were attached, and the NIBP feature on the monitor took her blood pressure. Her oxygen saturation levels were good at 99% with the oxygen running. My patient's vital signs were stable: pulse a little tachy at 108 but strong and regular, blood pressure was 146/94, respiratory rate was 22 and regular, temperature was 36.9 degrees Celsius, glucose 7.8. I started an IV of normal saline to keep the vein open.

When I looked up, Tom was assisting the other P-1 crew with his two patients from the SUV. Both patients were loaded into the other ambulance. We were fortunate that they had a double stretcher rig. Tom had both patients triaged, collared, boarded, and vitals done, with IVs running on both. The second crew loaded the patients and were on their way to the Queensway–Carleton ER, code three.

Tom came over and double-checked the male patient still hanging from the driver's seat. He was definitely dead! Tom asked Fire to cover the driver's door to prevent anyone from taking pictures or taping the event for the local news.

Tom and I loaded our patient for the trip to the Q–C ER. Tom booked 10–8, in service, to the Queensway–Carleton Hospital. Our patient was calm. She had accepted the death of her father. The bleeding was controlled with the dressing, no pain other than a sore pelvis from hanging upside down. We spoke on the way in, while

I monitored her status and did vitals every five minutes. She was a pleasant lady who had been placed in a terrifying situation. She had watched her father pass away in front of her and was then involved in what could have been a horrific traffic accident. She was alive and lucky.

We arrived at the Q–C, transferred our patient to the ER staff, gave our report, and completed our electronic ACR, Ambulance Care Report. Tom was cleaning up and getting the rig ready for our next call when Patrick Levac came in.

"Can I see you?" Patrick asked in his thick French accent. He was short, with thick, dark hair and wore old-style horn-rimmed glasses. The glasses suited Patrick perfectly.

We stepped outside of the ER for a breath of fresh air. I was more curious now than ever. Patrick seemed nervous, like he had a secret he was not supposed to tell anyone but was going to reveal it to me. The air was thick with humidity, the sun brilliant. I squinted to block the sunlight until my eyes adjusted. Patrick looked around to make sure no one was nearby. Even though we were alone, he grabbed my arm and pulled me farther away from the ER.

"Your patient, da one when you had da gun pointed at you, I heard dat der was someting strange on da forehead?" Patrick looked at me. He didn't blink. He was serious, scared almost. His thick accent prevented the "th" sound.

"Ya!" I replied. "He had a cross drawn in blood on his forehead. Why?"

"I had two patients, different detts!" I knew he meant "deaths." "Dey bot' had upside-down crosses on de heads, too! I put it on de ACR but none are being looked at by de cops!" There was a pause. The type of long unsteady pause that caused us both fear and apprehension.

Patrick and his partner had responded on a call to a house on Rue Beaudry off the Vanier Parkway, north of the Queensway. A young male had been struck by a car and dragged to his death while cycling. EMS arrived on scene first; fire and police were also called. Patrick and his partner noticed the point of impact on the road; the bloodstain was still bright red on the grey asphalt. The trail of blood was continuous from the impact to where the body had lain in the road. The end was evident! A blanket had been placed over the body as it lay by the south curb. No skid marks could be seen, and the trail continued for several hundred feet. A mangled mountain bike was casually tossed aside after losing the fight with the assaulting vehicle. A crowd had gathered not far from where the covered body lay, to console the friends and parents of the victim. People were yelling, crying, hugging and talking on cell phones. The morbidly curious were snapping digital mementos on their cell phones, surely to be posted on the Net before the day was out. There were no vehicles at the scene to indicate which one had struck and dragged the boy to his death.

Patrick had parked the vehicle in such a way as to protect the evidence and the body. Patrick had gone straight to the couple that were holding each other and crying. He'd asked if they were the parents. No words were said, just a nod in agreement. Patrick had turned to see his partner, who was carefully peering under the blanket to assess the patient. Patrick had gone over to assist his partner. The patient under the blanket was obviously deceased. The car had done excessive damage to the young cyclist.

Even a seasoned medic can be affected by the gruesome, visual effects caused by trauma. The body was no longer recognizable as a male or female. It was a blend of tissue, clothing, bone and blood. Arms and legs no longer had knees or elbows and were not in their usual anatomical position. The torso had severe avulsions that revealed the organs beneath. The light jacket and T-shirt were torn and imbedded into the wounds or wrapped around exposed bone. The helmet the boy had been wearing completed its task.

The face and skull were almost entirely intact except for a few cuts and abrasions. He had been a good-looking boy, maybe sixteen or seventeen, with a clean, fair complexion. In death, his eyes had remained open, looking eerily back at Patrick and his partner. With gloved hands, Patrick had decided to close the eyes and let him rest. Oddly, just below the brow of the helmet, a black cross had been drawn on his forehead. Never having seen this before, Patrick had considered it nothing more than a rite of passage for his group of friends or some other teen ritual.

Patrick continued telling me he and his partner had stayed behind to get as many details as possible to complete their ACR. It was only after the police arrived and all the details came out that the true story came to light.

A car had been following the boy and his small group of friends. Patrick came to learn that the boy's name was Chris Manners. Like a lion selecting the weakest of the pack, the driver of the car had picked Chris from the rest of the group, jumping the curb, riding the sidewalk and eventually running over the boy. One of the stunned boys who had been spared from the attack told the police that the driver had accelerated after the car struck Chris. It was only after the car was far enough away that the driver had stopped, reversed and stopped again. The driver exited the vehicle, calmly walked over to the boy he had just run over, examined the body, climbed back into his car and sped off, travelling south on Beaudry.

Patrick had asked the police officer if he could ask the group of boys if the black cross meant anything to them. Each shaken witness had denied having any knowledge of the strange drawing. With each boy, Patrick had watched carefully to see if a similar cross could be seen on any one of them. Nothing! He'd asked the youngsters if they thought the man who hit Chris could possibly have drawn the cross on him. The boys looked at each other, shrugged, and commented that he could have, but that they really didn't see what was happening and couldn't confirm what was done.

Patrick had stood close enough to eavesdrop on the police questioning of the boys to try to get more information. The description of the assailant had been vague and non-descript: a person dressed in black pants wearing a black hoodie pulled over his head and a dark ball cap pulled down low.

Patrick had made a comment on his Ambulance Call Report regarding the death and the cross on the victim's forehead. The ACR was submitted to management. If the police wanted or needed a copy of the ACR, they could request one.

Patrick had felt there was more to the case. It was an annoyance, the type of thing that tickles at the back of your brain, something that just doesn't sit right, but you just can't put your finger on it, until that tickle gets scratched. About three weeks ago, Patrick responded to a call that scared the hell out of him. And it scared him enough to prompt him to contact me about my murder call.

5

PATRICK BEGAN TO DESCRIBE the second call that bore a striking similarity to his first call and to my murder call. Patrick and his partner had responded to a house for a suicide attempt. It hadn't simply been an attempt, it had been successful.

The wife had come home after repeated attempts to contact her husband and found him in the basement, hanging from a rafter. The wife had immediately called 911, who instructed her to cut him down and start CPR. She had claimed that she couldn't touch the body. Not like that! A thick, yellow, cheap nylon rope had been tied tightly around his neck, the other end secured to a floor joist. The rope had dug deep into his skin creating a trench; his lips were swollen and thick. He'd been cold to the touch, and the skin above the rope was cyanotic, bluish in colour. At first glance, it appeared as if it had been deliberate. The man had only needed to stand up to prevent the rope from pulling the life from him. He must have let his feet slip out from under himself and let hypoxia take its toll. It would have been an agonizing few minutes. The fact that his pants were still on ruled out any sexual overtones to the accident. The man had been there for several hours and rigor mortis had set in.

Patrick went on to explain that the patient had a history of depression and had been diagnosed as suicidal. Patrick's assessment had revealed nothing remarkable on the body except for a small inverted cross on the forehead in black marker. He was startled to see something from a previous unrelated scene on this patient. The cross was not unlike the cross on the forehead of the mutilated boy a few weeks earlier. Patrick and his partner had performed a detailed exam of the body and the surrounding area. The cross continued to haunt Patrick.

A mirror! Patrick thought to himself. The patient would have needed a mirror to draw a straight cross on his forehead. You wouldn't think of putting a marker back in the drawer or wherever you got it from if you were going to go hang yourself immediately after. The marker would have to be in plain sight, he'd assumed, possibly next to a suicide note that was maybe even written in marker as well.

Patrick went to every mirror in the house: bathrooms, kitchen, bedrooms, living room. Nothing. Absolutely nothing! He hadn't been able to locate a marker close to a mirror, let alone find a marker anywhere in the house. Patrick had put himself in the patient's shoes: *If I were going to hang myself . . . draw a cross on my forehead before killing myself, where would I do it?* he mused. *Somewhere comfortable, someplace I call my own*, he deduced. A den!

He'd run through the house and found it. A small room, maybe fifty feet square, with a small desk and a computer. Pictures hung on the wall in an order that only the person who hung them would understand. Patrick had sat down behind the desk. No drawers! Therefore, no markers, no pens, nothing to make those marks! He'd moved papers back and forth, lifted the leather blotter and searched futilely. No suicide note anywhere! To Patrick's left, hanging on the wall had been a corkboard. One colour news photo on the board stood out from everything else. The news clipping had been partially covered over with newer and more current postings. Patrick had carefully pulled the thumbtacks to release the topmost papers, revealing an *Ottawa Sun* photo of a group of people standing in front of a burning car. It had been obvious the small crowd in the photo was frightened. He'd gently removed the article from the bulletin board; the headline said it all:

"Mother and daughter perish in tragic car fire"

The article beneath the photo revealed that a mother and her seven-month-old baby had perished in the tragic fire on August 19, 2007. Patrick had scanned the photo more closely. Second from the right! Second from the right was the man hanging from a rafter in the basement of this very house! Surprisingly and shockingly, there had been another person in the *Ottawa Sun* news photo whom Patrick recognized: the young boy who had been mercilessly killed on his bike was standing beside the man who was now also dead, hanging from a rope tied around his neck.

Patrick had made sure to give the article to the police and told them that no marker could be found at the scene. He'd told the officer of the similarity between the bike incident and this one. The police hadn't seemed too interested in Patrick's amateur investigative skills, especially since he had disturbed the scene by rummaging around the house and had pulled things from the bulletin board.

Since the patient had had a long history of depression and suicide attempts, Patrick felt that the police might possibly choose to close the case prematurely.

When Patrick had heard through the EMS grapevine of my brush with death, he sought me out. There was more than coincidence between the young boy's tragic death and the hanging, but I had to know if my murdered man was in that photo. I asked Patrick if he had a copy of the clipping. He didn't. The officer at the scene of the hanging had been given the copy from the bulletin board.

I thanked Patrick for getting in touch with me and for giving me the details of these two seemingly unrelated fatalities. There was a connection; I felt sure of it. There had to be more than just simple coincidence, with (possibly) three dead people in the same photo. All three of those people had died in mysterious circumstances. And all three died with a stupid cross drawn on them. Three dead people out of a group of six in the photo! I had to know more. At least two of the three had died at the hands of someone else.

I was now involved whether I liked it or not; there was no turning back now. I might possibly have found one of the victims—his killer had pointed a gun at me and pulled the trigger. That made it personal. I was still alive, but three people were dead. I wanted to know why!

I WOKE UP EARLY, rejuvenated and full of anticipation. I looked at the calendar in the kitchen. It was only two weeks until July 1, Canada Day. I love Canada Day. It was better than Christmas, better than my birthday. The whole country celebrated Canada's birthday. And Ottawa was the best place in the country to celebrate Canada Day. There are festivals, parties, bands, and beer everywhere! You can't go anywhere in Ottawa without catching the fever. This year, I planned on celebrating Canada Day on the Hill. Parliament Hill was hosting their usual Canada Day spectacular, and Ottawa Paramedic Services always did their best to keep the guests as safe as possible.

Canada Day on the Hill had a different feel than an ordinary outdoor concert or party at any other time of the year. People actually behaved on Canada Day. Everybody was there to have a good time and not act like an idiot. It could also be attributed to the huge police presence, but I like to think it was the sense of patriotism that kept everyone in line.

I hadn't felt this good in months. The sun was shining, and it was hot, really hot. It was the kind of humid heat that sticks to you and makes even the lightest shirt feel heavy and sticky, the kind of rare heat that makes Canadians appreciate summer more when we think back to digging out from under fifty centimetres of heavy, wet snow in February. Where else but Canada can you have temperature extremes of minus forty Celsius in the winter to plus thirty-five Celsius in the summer? Where else can you have snowbanks on the side of the road that prevent drivers from seeing oncoming traffic? Only in Canada do we have snow rage! Canadians truly appreciate the warmth and comfort of summer.

I checked on Molly and Snickers, making sure that they had enough food and water for the day. I had been ignoring them for the past few days, and they were letting me know it. In the basement, the dirty uniforms I had left on the floor were covered in cat hair. A little well-deserved payback from Molly and Snickers for the lack of attention.

Because it was so hot, I decided to remove the large roof panel from the Porsche, placing it in the rear hatch. I wanted to get as much sun as possible. It was almost like a Targa top 911. I had to drive down to the *Ottawa Sun* newspaper offices on Antares Drive to go through the archives and hopefully find that news clipping from August 19 of last year. I had no idea what was involved, but going straight to the source was likely the best course of action.

Queensway traffic was light, and I decided to take full advantage of the open road. I opened up the small Porsche engine and felt the rush as the revs increased. I took the long way to the *Ottawa Sun* building. I wanted to enjoy the sun and the city of Ottawa on my day off.

Surrounded on the north and east by the Ottawa River, the city of Ottawa is on the south shore, with the province of Quebec on the north shore. The Ottawa River separates the province of Ontario to the west and the province of Quebec to the east. The river was once a main transitway for the logging industry when the city was nothing more than a tiny settlement. Now, it saw more tourist and pleasure boats than logging.

Parliament Hill, Canada's political house, located on a high point in the city's north end, on the bank of the Ottawa River, looks south to the rest of the city. Across the river, on the north bank, sits Gatineau, Quebec. The Canadian government has many of their crown buildings and services divided between Ottawa, Ontario, and Gatineau, Quebec.

The area was founded by the Odaawaa First Nations people on the banks of what is now the Ottawa River. The first European settlement was founded in the early 1800s. In 1857, Queen Victoria chose Ottawa as the capital of Canada over Kingston, Ontario, and Montreal, Quebec. In wasn't until 2001 that the former city of Ottawa and all of the surrounding cities, towns, and hamlets in the area became the Regional Municipality of Ottawa–Carleton. Regardless of what it is called, Ottawa is one of the coldest national capitals in the world. Summers are warm, but not what I would call hot. Winters can and have been bitterly cold, with heavy snow accumulation that often brings the city to a standstill.

In the winter, the Rideau Canal turns into the world's longest outdoor skating rink. Funny how I have lived in Ottawa all but three years of my entire life and I have never once skated on the Canal. The same goes for visiting Parliament Hill. I guess it's true that people who live close to tourist attractions seldom visit them. That includes me.

I travelled east on the Queensway, south on the 416 then east on Hunt Club Drive. There were few traffic lights, as Hunt Club Drive has lots of green space instead of buildings. A decade ago, it was mostly fields, with few buildings. Now, it was more developed for industrial and residential use. I continued to travel east on Hunt Club, drove over the rail overpass, slowed at the lights, and turned onto Antares Drive. I pulled into the parking lot, passed several buildings on the left, and parked close to the *Ottawa Sun* newspaper entrance.

The *Ottawa Sun* newspaper offices were new, spacious, and computerized. I entered the building and walked over to the receptionist. I asked where I could go through the archives to find old newspaper articles.

She directed me to an office on the third floor. I decided to take the stairs; the exercise would do me good. The office was a huge open concept with desks everywhere. Phones buzzed constantly, with people typing as they spoke. People hurriedly walked about with papers rushing to meet deadlines imposed by the presses. "Organized confusion," I always called it. To the unknowing, it looked like chaos, but I am sure it was a typical day for those who worked here.

The young man behind the desk I stopped at looked up from his LCD monitor and offered me a meek greeting. I explained my problem regarding the article. The young man searched quickly for a form and, failing to find one, located the file on the computer and printed a new one. He handed me the form to complete. It requested the date of the article and any other information I could provide. I was told that it would take a few days and that someone would call me when the information was retrieved.

"A few days!" I exclaimed to the receptionist. "I really, really need this! NOW! Isn't there any way you could expedite my request?" I pleaded my case with a brief history of the incident to impress upon him the urgency of retrieving the article.

"You know, as a medic, Mr. Tennant, you must be used to rushing around and getting things done in a hurry!" He paused giving me the impression my request would be flatly denied. "For me, this will be the highlight of my day. Gimme that form." I handed the form to the young man, who promptly got up and walked to another computer terminal. A few quick keystrokes, a pause, his head cocked to one side from behind the monitor; then he asked me if I wanted the picture printed in colour. He stopped himself halfway through the question, raised his eyebrows, knew the answer without my having to reply. A few more keystrokes, then a low hum emanated from a large, grey HP printer on an adjacent table. You could hear the printer warm up and then slowly regurgitate the papers. He walked over to the table, pulled the pages from the printer and studied them for a moment, then looked back at me, puzzled, as if to question the urgency of my request.

He placed the two sheets of paper, the photo and the article, in a large manila envelope, pulled the plastic strip off, and sealed the package. He came back, handed me the envelope, and gazed at me. I was filled with anticipation, and he knew it. I had to slow myself down when I reached out to take possession of my new-found information. It takes a lot to get me excited, and holding this envelope was doing its job quite nicely. I wanted to tear it open before I left the young man's desk, but I had to maintain my composure. I asked if I owed him anything for the prints. He shook his head from side to side, squinting his eyes and furrowing his brow as if I'd said something offensive. I nodded politely, turned, and left. I bolted down the stairs, through the lobby, and out to the parking lot. I unlocked the driver's door and jumped in. The hot leather seats felt comforting, like a warm duvet on a cold winter's night. I left the door open to air out the car. My foot rested on the pavement to keep the car door propped open. I tore the envelope open like a child opening a long-awaited Christmas present.

The *Ottawa Sun* employee had been nice enough to blow the picture up and enlarge the article to make it easier to read. It was the picture that caught my eye as soon as I pulled it out of the envelope. One person stood out more than the rest. The picture was grainy, but his face was recognizable, even though the first time I had seen him, it was in the dark and with a large portion of his head missing. My mind was recounting Patrick's conversation word for word about the two victims he had seen and how he'd felt when he'd pulled the article from the corkboard. My stomach felt like a heavy tumour had suddenly grown inside and was now weighing on my thoughts. A wave of nausea hit me hard. My breathing stopped and I gasped to take in a long, slow, deep breath. There he was! I touched the print and circled his face with my index finger as if this action would give depth and meaning to the situation. I stared at the picture, drinking in the event and every last detail of the gruesome scene.

A group of six people, horrified, were standing on the sidewalk on the east side of Riverside Drive. On the west side, in the southbound lane, a car was straddling the curb, hood up. A wheel had come off and was nowhere to be seen in the photo. The car was still in flames when the photographer captured the event. Of the six people in the photo, four were men, two women. The four men included one young boy, most likely the one killed on his bike. One of the men was the hanging victim, who stood alongside my shooting victim. That was three men out of four. One man and two women remained. Were any of those women or men killed or dead that we don't know about yet? This was indeed the same picture Patrick had described that showed his two victims.

I pulled the second sheet from the envelope. It was the article that accompanied the photo from August 19, 2007. The article was short, with few details.

"Mother and daughter perish in tragic car fire"

Was there really a reason to read the entire article? The headline was pretty explanatory. I decided to read the news clipping.

Late yesterday, a mother and infant child were tragically killed when the car they were travelling in rolled and caught fire.

Lindsay Phillips, 32, and her daughter Andie, 7 months, were killed when their car left the road and rolled several times before the car came to rest on the west bank of Riverside Drive. Several bystanders came to the aid of the trapped occupants, but were unable to assist the mother and daughter. A leaking portable gas can had ignited and set the car ablaze. Several people tried in vain to extinguish the rapidly spreading inferno before the entire car, including Phillips and her daughter, was overcome.

The victim's husband, Aidan Phillips, 34, is currently stationed in Afghanistan with the Canadian Military, based at CFB Petawawa. He is flying home by military aircraft and will arrive at CFB Trenton in a few days.

Police state the victim had purchased gas for the lawn mower and was returning home at the time of the accident. Police are continuing their investigation, but few leads were known at press time.

I knew whom I had to go and see now!

7

I DROVE DIRECTLY to the Ottawa Police Headquarters on Elgin Street from the *Sun* newspaper building. Flew was more like it! I broke every posted speed limit to get there. I had to see Detective Galen Hoese, an old friend from high school. We were originally both going to become cops. Galen had decided right from high school to fulfill his fantasy. I, on the other hand, had been more inclined to find myself with mindless odd jobs and travel. It had not been a bad way to spend my youth, and I certainly don't regret how things worked out.

I pulled off the Queensway and went north on Metcalfe Street and around to the station parking lot. I parked in the employee parking lot under a surveillance camera. If they wanted to ticket or tow me, I wouldn't be hard to find: I would be inside the building raising hell. I got out, slammed my door, heard the loud thud, turned and regretted shutting the door so hard. No damage to my car. My walk had purpose, my gait was unmistakable, and I had a mission. I was pissed off. It showed by the way I walked. This was not a great way to walk into the police station. I could get shot for what I was thinking.

I grabbed the chrome handle of the glass door and yanked hard. The door swung open quickly. I walked through the foyer toward the desk clerk. I nodded without saying a word. She nodded back and buzzed me through security. I had been here dozens of times in the past few months, so I was known to most of the shift. I walked to the main centre of the floor and up the stairs to the second floor. The walk did me good. I calmed down a bit — just a bit, mind you. I was furious after reading the article in the *Ottawa Sun* and came to a quick conclusion; like my good friend Detective Hoese always said, "The most obvious bad guy usually IS the bad guy!"

Now I wanted answers. After all, I'd not only had one of the murder victims as my patient, but I'd also had a gun pointed at my head; that, I felt, put me square in the middle of this case. I wanted answers and I wanted them now!

I had calmed down by the time I got to the top of the stairs. Detective Hoese was sitting at his desk, his back to me. I walked straight toward him, around his desk, and stood before him. Galen didn't even stop typing or look up. He knew it was me. Perhaps the desk clerk had called upstairs and given Galen advance warning. My obvious attitude may have been a giveaway.

"What?" He didn't even look up.

"This is your case, isn't it? It has your smell all over it!" I tossed the envelope holding the copies of the article on Galen's desk. The envelope circled in mid-air before it landed over Galen's hands as he typed. With a flick of his right hand, the manila envelope fell to the floor. His eyes never left the LCD screen before him. Galen was definitely in charge and he just proved it.

I bent over to pick up the envelope and removed the article and photo that I'd retrieved from the *Ottawa Sun*.

"This is the same case as my murder, isn't it?" His eyes glanced up then back to the screen.

"It isn't 'your' murder! It's 'my' murder! My murder case, to be more exact! You're a fucking ambulance driver. I'm the cop, remember. You keep on forgetting that little fact. I shoot 'em, you fix 'em."

This was a long-standing argument that Galen always opened up with. The only time I controlled the situation was when I was working on a patient at the scene of a crime. Other than that, he was always in charge. Always! Even as kids in school. Galen had an unwavering desire to be a cop. He never changed his mind, not once.

"You knew I was the one who found the body. I chased the bastard down. Without me, you could have gone days without even knowing there was a body until someone called because of the stench! Cut me some fucking slack."

Galen finally stopped typing. He looked up. He had fire in his eyes. He pushed his chair back from his desk, pulled himself up, propped himself on his fists on his desktop and stared at me. I got his attention.

"Listen here! I don't need no fuckin' ambulance jockey coming in here telling me how to do my job. I don't need to inform you which direction the investigation is going just because you were involved. And if you were in shape, you should have caught the guy instead of letting him get away." There was sincerity in his voice and anger in his eyes.

The rest of the squad room had stopped their activities and focused their attention on me. I'd pissed off one of their own. I was now the bad guy in their house. Not a great position to be in. I decided to back down a little, just a little. I grabbed a chair, pulled it up to Galen's desk and sat down. Galen sat down and rolled his chair closer to his desk. He picked up the keyboard and moved it to the top of the pile of paperwork on the left side of the desk. Galen had positioned himself in charge, embarrassed me, and elevated himself in the hierarchy of the police squad room.

"You want a Diet Coke?" Galen asked me quietly.

He got up and returned with two cans. I knew better then to confront a cop in his own house, but this was a long-standing tradition between us. Galen would often question my patients on scene, and I got to stand up and put Galen in his place in front of my co-workers. We each got to show off in front of each other's colleagues.

I tilted the can and took a mouthful of cold Coke. I let it sit in my mouth to wash away my dryness.

The only difference between our usual cop/medic banter was the fact that this time I really was upset. This was the first time one of us actually was part of the other's case. I wasn't pretending when I came in, but Galen had no way of knowing this. Another big mouthful of Coke. I took a deep breath and sighed. Galen could see my apprehension.

Galen sat back in his faux leather office chair. It creaked under his weight. He ran a hand through his thick, wavy red hair. For a man in his late thirties, his freckles made him look much younger. We had known each other far too long. He didn't have to ask. He knew I was upset. There was no question of concern, no "How are you doing?" He paused and let me take my time. Galen grabbed the copy of the *Sun* article and the photo. He gave the pages a quick glance and put them back in the envelope. He moved the keyboard and rummaged through the stack of files on his desk. He pulled a case file, opened it, clicked the mouse to open a new screen, and typed in the case file number.

Within a few seconds, I could see the file appear almost like a PowerPoint presentation. Several pages appeared at one time on the screen with a file column on the left. Galen scrolled through a few pages, paused, read the information, and looked at me.

"Okay, what do you want to talk about?" This time he was sincere.

"You know about the fire and other murders?" I asked.

He nodded in acknowledgement. He pulled a few pictures from his file and handed them to me. "We linked the murders after the second victim. Ethan, we do know how to do our jobs. This town doesn't have enough murders that we don't talk among ourselves. The crosses were a dead giveaway. Pardon the pun. Your case gave us more information to go on but we are still in the dark about a lot of what is going on."

I questioned Galen about his philosophy that the most obvious suspect is usually the right suspect. The victim's husband certainly should be a suspect. As soon as I'd read the article, I had put two and two together.

"That was our first thought, too," Galen admitted. "We checked with the Department of National Defence about Mr. Phillips's whereabouts at the time of the murders. He has a foolproof alibi, buddy. DND says Phillips was back in Afghanistan with his troop before any of the murders took place. Can't be in two places at the same time, can you?"

So much for the obvious suspect theory! With the husband halfway around the world, the obvious suspect was no longer a suspect. I felt cheated somehow. But then again, how could this be resolved so simply? It couldn't. I knew it. But I wanted it to be this easy. Crime, clues, suspect, arrest, and that would be the end of this whole messy affair. I'd had too much turmoil in the past few months and I wanted this to be over quickly without too much of a mess. Galen didn't need to say anything; I knew what he meant without his even saying a word: "Stick to playing doctor—leave the investigating to me!"

"Feel like grabbing a hot dog? My treat!" Galen offered.

He pushed back from his desk, the wheels creaking again. He got up, pulled down on his tie until the knot slipped, yanked on the end and let it flow through his collar. He rolled it up, tossed it on top of the pile of case files.

"This is the worst thing about the promotion to detective. Brass makes me wear these stupid ties to make me look professional. Me, look professional?"

Galen had put on a lot of weight since the promotion from uniform to street clothes. He didn't even bother to buy new clothes. The shirt buttons just pulled to their limit across the expanse of his belly. His large cowboy belt buckle was hidden under his roll. The suit was at least two sizes too small. Galen always reminded me of a British, red-haired Colombo with just a hint of his parents' old-country accent. Galen had gone from a fit high school student to an overweight, smart cop.

I headed for the stairs, Galen for the elevator. He glanced over at me, threw his head back and joined me for a walk down the stairs. We walked through the foyer and met the wall of humidity. Galen squinted and looked into the cerulean sky. Like most Canadians, when we walk out into humidity, we look up at the sky, expecting to see the moisture. Galen took off his suit jacket and dangled it over his shoulder from his left index finger. He looked north, saw the object of his current dining preference, and started walking directly toward the hot-dog vendor in the next block. I followed closely. It was a free lunch after all.

"So?" I asked.

"So, we have nothing. Absolutely nothing. Zilch, zip, *nada!*" He paused. "Three murders all connected. That much we know. The problem is, we don't know why. After the second murder, when the medic found that article at the scene, we started to put the whole thing together. Is it a game for him? The chief put together a task squad to work this case. I called an old Ottawa Police buddy who went over to CSIS. We discussed the case over beer and he set me up with a behavioural analyst. He offered an 'off the record' CSIS profile, since this is our case. Four murders by the same guy will label him a serial killer. This guy is confident. He doesn't clean up after the murders, and he isn't trying to hide the evidence. The murders are either well planned, or he simply doesn't give a shit."

A look of frustration took over. He continued in more detail.

"The Canadian Security Intelligence Service gave us nothing that we didn't already know. Again, the problem is, we know next to nothing. We know the car accident was just that, an accident."

We stopped at the intersection, waited for the traffic to clear, then walked across the street. I listened to everything Galen had to say.

"The mother and child died in the fire. Foul play is not suspected at all. Witnesses said she swerved to miss a dog that ran across the road, she hit the curb, and rolled the car several times. This was confirmed from the skid marks at the scene. The large gas can that had been in the trunk broke open and leaked. We still don't know what sparked the fire. It was most likely just a freak accident. The fire was real intense. They didn't have a chance."

We arrived at the hot-dog cart.

"What do you want?"

"I'll have a hot dog topped with mustard and sauerkraut, and a bottle of water."

"And I'll take two large sausage dogs and drag them through the garden and a Diet Coke." Cop lingo for the works. He went healthy and picked the baked potato chips.

Galen paid the vendor, slipped the change into the tip jar and paused. He looked at his haul and offered me his jacket to carry. It's a small price to pay for a free lunch with an old friend. His pit stains ran down each side of his shirt, marking a contrast against the white poly/cotton blend.

We continued our walk north. Between bites and falling condiments that hit the sweltering sidewalk, Galen explained that the victim's in-laws live in Petawawa, north of Ottawa. The in-laws had a long military history, with several members of the family having served in the Forces. The husband, Aiden Phillips, had been serving his second tour in Afghanistan. His service record was spotless. After a military mandated grieving period, the husband asked to be returned to Afghanistan.

The victim's immediate family in Ottawa were hit hard by the deaths of their daughter and grandchild, who had been living in Ottawa with her family while Aiden was in Afghanistan. Lindsay had been their only daughter, and Andie, who was named after Aiden, had been the only grandchild. Galen stated that Lindsay's family were still grieving, and the father's health has been in decline since the accident. He wasn't expected to live much longer. This one accident had taken its toll on both these families.

Galen finished his first sausage dog, wiped his mouth with a napkin, pulled the tab on his pop can and had a drink. The pop can was wet with condensation, and he dried his hand with the last napkin. He looked around for a receptacle to deposit his trash, found none nearby, so he stuffed the napkins into his pants pocket. Galen took a bite from his second sausage dog and left a bright yellow stain on the corner of his mouth. I wiped the corner of my mouth with my finger while looking at him, the silent universal sign: "You have a little something there!" He didn't catch on. Great detective!

I finished my hot dog, cracked the top on the water, and chugged it down in one gulp. The water was already getting warm from the heat and humidity. I balled up the napkin, hot-dog sleeve, and plastic bottle and stuffed them in a pocket of Galen's jacket, which I still carried. We kept walking, and Galen continued to disclose details of the police investigation while he ate.

Police had checked on the six witnesses who saw the accident, and by all accounts, there was nothing that could have been done to help the victims inside the burning car. One of the women reported psychological problems since the accident after hearing the baby screaming as the car became engulfed in flames. Then the screams had stopped. One of the men had ventured close to see if he could help but the heat had driven him back. They'd all watched as Lindsay Phillips and her infant daughter Andie died in the fire.

After the second murder, the police had located the remaining four from the photo. The police had the names and addresses of everyone on scene from the accident investigation report, so tracking them down had been easy. Other than the accident, there was no connection between the six random people being at the same place at the same time to witness these deaths.

A loud belch emanated from my host. The sounds of warm Diet Coke forcing down the remnants of a barbecued sausage and bun with enough condiments to make its own salad could be heard from the other side of the street. All in all, a pleasant dining experience. He saved the chips for later.

Galen gathered his waste from our gourmet lunch and placed them in the appropriate city recycling containers—one of our city's finest doing his part for the environment. I gave him back his jacket. He noticed the bulge in his suit jacket pocket, reached in, felt the napkins and bottle and gave me a look that a father gives his child when they get caught doing something wrong. He pulled out the waste, separated it, and put this in recycling, too. We headed back.

Galen continued his story without missing a beat. "The lab was not able to accurately explain why the crosses were painted on the forehead of the victims."

Without any hesitation, Galen began a long description of the history of the Christian Cross and the possible significance it plays in the murders.

"The cross can be different sizes and shapes and possess many styles. Even the swastika is said to originate from the original cross. The Egyptian ankh is a hieroglyph for the sign of life. The problem remains that each religion has its own take on the cross and the significance it holds. The making of a cross on the forehead and or chest was done to safeguard oneself against evil.

"It also signifies the sacrifices Jesus made and his victory over sin and death. If the meaning is personal, the drawing of the cross on the forehead or eyes can have several meanings. Since the cross first represented a way of public execution that was extremely painful and grotesque, the murderer may have thought this to be the victim's public execution. It may have been a way for the killer to cleanse the body for something he had seen in life and prepare his soul for the afterlife. It could also have been the ravings of a madman with no clear religious symbolism at all and something that was done like a trophy on his victims; or a last-minute decision to throw us off. Who the fuck knows?"

Galen paused again, looked up at the sky, turned to me, and shrugged his shoulders.

"Shit! It is so fucking hot right now!" His sweat stains were evidence of his keen observation skills.

"We may never know why this prick does what he does!"

Pause. "We know from eyewitness accounts, yours included, that we are probably looking at a male suspect. Your testimony only verifies that. You said by the way the murderer ran and spoke, it was a man, or at very least looked and sounded like a man." Another long pause or Galen had cramps developing or bad gas from the two sausage dogs. "With so little to go on, we are thinking of calling in help or going public with some of the details to see if we can generate some leads."

This was good news to me. From the sound of it, the investigation was moving forward without my help, and I didn't have to worry about it anymore.

"So, Ethan." Another pause. "We are doing everything we can with what little we have at our disposal."

We arrived back at police headquarters. Before we parted ways, there were the polite handshakes, the thank you for lunch, and the promise to stop by for road hockey with his kids. Even with the weight of the large hot dog brewing inside, I felt lighter and relieved. I turned and started walking around the building toward the parking lot when I heard a loud, gut-wrenching belch with absolutely no hint of restraint from the person who generated it.

Yup, it was gas!

THE NEXT DAY WAS UNEVENTFUL. I changed Molly's and Snickers's litter box, cut the grass, raked the grass clippings off the yard, and washed and waxed the car. I cleaned the house and installed my new surround-sound system. Overall, things seemed to be getting much better. I called Maddy and left several messages, giving her updates on how things were going. Six days to July 1, Canada Day. Things were definitely looking up.

The day after, I woke up refreshed, ready for work. I made a nice breakfast, took my time on the drive in to work, and appreciated the beautiful morning sun. The weather continued to be unseasonably warm—a real treat after last winter, when the temperature was colder than normal and the snowbanks were so high, a driver in an SUV couldn't see over the frozen mounds of ice and snow. The city had run their snow removal budget dry within the first few months and wanted to add a surcharge to the residences of Ottawa to cover the budget shortfall. Even by the end of April, there had still been hidden snow piles somewhere in the city.

I stopped at Tim Hortons for my morning coffee and rolled the rim and won a free coffee in their contest. That free coffee would be for later in the shift when I was feeling a little rundown.

I actually beat Tom in to work and had a large bottle of Dasani water waiting for him. Tom was shocked to see me dressed, shaved, and ready for the day. It felt good to show Tom up once in a while. I was ready to book on as soon as he walked in. It was a real change for me, compared to the past few months. We walked out to the garage, got assigned one of the better rigs, hopped in, and drove out to meet the day.

The conversation was light and fun. The calls were easy; even wait times in the ER seemed to be less than the norm. The entire morning went by without incident, without stress. Tom and I had the opportunity to catch up and talk like old times. We were just able to talk; no death, no trauma, just talk. It was nice to chat about things other than me and my problems, so I shifted focus to two of Tom's favourite things: golf and working out.

The extent of my golf knowledge was what club to use (occasionally I was wrong about that, too), where the clubhouse was, and when to allow a group to play through. The topic of working out was way out of my league. My idea of working out was the walk from the front door to the Porsche parked in the driveway. But this was Tom's day. I wanted to let him pick the subjects and I played along. The conversation bounced from one thing to another between patients, moments of privacy, and waiting in the ER to drop off a patient.

Today had shorter delays in the ER, and our conversations sometimes had a third voice, courtesy of the patient on the cot who would often offer an opinion. Patients usually realize that the wait is not the doing of EMS but rather that of the hospital staffing. So when the patient wants to join in our conversation, Tom and I usually don't mind. It helps to pass the time. Our patient was triaged, assigned a room, and transferred to their charge. We cleaned our gear and loaded our cot.

We had cleared the Ottawa Civic ER and headed east on Carling Avenue when dispatch called with a high-priority, life-threatening call, a Code 4, directing us to the apartments on Prince of Wales Drive just north of Hog's Back Road. There is a group of three buildings. It was the building in the middle, closest to the road. We knew the building well. Low rent. High call volume. I activated the lights and used the siren as needed. I seldom drove like a NASCAR driver in the final laps of a big race. No sense in getting killed or killing someone else on the way to help a patient. Tom was the same, one of the many reasons we worked well together. Working twelve-hour shifts with a partner you don't get along with is difficult at the best of times. Working with Tom was always easy and comfortable.

Dispatch updated us: a single adult male, not seen in days. The concerned neighbours called 911. Police were on their way as well. Tom and I looked at each other. That pretty much always means they will be there within a few hours. If it was a D.B., dead body, they would let us check it out first. If the door is locked and no one lets us in, we can't enter anyway.

It was a straight drive south on Prince of Wales to the group of apartment buildings. Few lights along the way reduced our response time. I pulled left into the parking lot, stopping in front of the main entrance. I booked 10–7, arrival on scene. I removed the keys from the ignition, hanging them over the portable antenna. I opened the back doors, pushed to release the stretcher-locking bar, and pulled out the cot. We unloaded the cot, defibrillator, trauma and oxygen bags. I grabbed the foot handle of the cot, and Tom controlled the head of the cot as we entered the front foyer. I turned to look back through the glass doors. My head started to spin. Everything looked familiar. It wasn't the building where the murder occurred the week before, I knew that, but it was apparent I still had issues. The foyer sent me back. I paused. Tom's forceful push on the end on the cot brought me back to reality. We walked to the main lobby and stopped in front of the dual bank of elevators.

I pushed the UP button and waited. The light flashed its way down to the main lobby. A bell and the opening of the stainless steel doors signalled the arrival of the elevator. Tom raised the head of the cot, lowered the head bar and helped me place the stretcher in the small elevator so we could both fit in. I pushed the button for the sixth floor. When the doors opened, Tom looked at the sign facing us and turned toward apartment 608. We pushed and pulled our stretcher to the door of apartment 608. The smell was evident as we stood in the hall. It reeked like a litter box that needed to be cleaned, badly! Between the pungent aromas of ethnic food and the ammonia litter-box smell, it was difficult to know where one odour started and the next began.

I knocked hard on the door, identifying myself and expecting to hear a quick response. No response. I knocked again. Still no response. I was about to radio dispatch explaining our situation when we both heard a faint voice from behind the door. Tom knocked again. The voice from behind the door was faint, but audible.

"Help!" Not your normal welcome, but it was permission to enter.

We tucked the stretcher along the wall. I slung the main bag over one shoulder and the defib over the other. Tom grasped the door handle and turned it slowly. As the door opened, we were greeted with a rank odour. We now knew where the litter box smell was coming from. Tom quickly closed the door. The June heat intensified the smell from the apartment. We both closed our eyes. The stench burned our eyes like acid floating in the air. Tom closed the door and we took in a deep breath. He opened the door quickly again, and we both entered the apartment with our heads bowed. Our mouths were closed in a vain attempt to prevent the smell from causing nausea and our eyes partially closed to prevent them from burning. A few steps in, and we both turned and exited the apartment for the safety of the hall. Tom and I both kept N–95 respirator masks in our pockets. These masks were not intended for these types of calls, but in this circumstance, they would do in a pinch. We put on the masks and pulled the elastic tight around the back of our heads. We both donned our gloves, pulling them up high to protect our watches. We looked at each other, like warriors about to do battle. A nod. We were now ready for this battle. Once again, we inhaled deeply, opened the door and stepped in to the hazards of the patient's apartment.

The apartment was dark. All the bedsheets that posed as curtains were drawn, and the stench grew stronger the farther we went in. Unfortunately, the masks did little to quell the stench. Tom and I both reached for our small LED flashlights and illuminated the dark room. Dual beams pierced the room. Newspapers in plastic sleeves, books in shipping boxes, magazines, and unopened mail were piled high on tables and the floor. The sofa and chairs were covered in dust so thick it blended with the fabric to form a new material. Where they weren't covered with loose paper, the coffee and end tables had enough built-up dust to write messages in. Dust saturated the carpets enough to leave footprints in them. Random pictures on the wall indicated the tenant had no family—or family that didn't care. The pictures were from a discount store and were generic scenes of landscapes known only to the painter who'd created these works of art forty or so years ago. Even in the limited light of our LED bulbs, the paint on the walls looked old, faded, and cracked. The beam found a light switch.

Tom flicked the switch. Two lamps cast a bright light, and one immediately blew, dimming the room slightly, but there was still enough light to reveal more clutter. We holstered the flashlights.

The smell started to permeate our clothing, burning its way deep in our noses. We could actually taste the smell of urine and rotting food. I started to breathe through my mouth only, but it only made the taste worse. I pinched the metal band of the N–95 mask tighter over my nose to pinch my nostrils closed.

As we walked through the apartment, I turned to see our footprints in the dust and those of the patient as they tracked his path through the maze of magazines and books on the floor.

Tom called out for the patient. He answered with a barely audible voice. We followed the voice down the main hall past the living room on the left. The kitchen was directly across from the living room. The first bedroom was next to the kitchen. The door was open and revealed where the tenant stored the garbage that he had collected over the years. As we went past the bathroom on the right, I blindly reached in with a gloved hand, lifted the light switch and looked in to see the once white sink now permanently stained a dark brown. No amount of cleanser and scrubbing would ever extend the life of that sink. The single bathroom light fixture added much-needed light to the hall. The second bedroom door was to the left and ran adjacent to the living room. Tom went in first.

Tom surveyed the room for safety concerns. The stench was strongest here. It was so strong, even our shallow respirations caused pain in our lungs. Again, the light was turned on to illuminate the scene.

The patient was lying on the floor between the bed and closet. He was rolling from side to side, arms flailing, legs kicking, trying in vain to right himself like a turtle lying on its back. No spinal injuries here. The elderly male patient had obviously been on the floor for a few days. He was tall, slender, with sunken cheeks and matted salt-and-pepper hair, and he had not shaved in quite some time. His beard was almost white except for the few black hairs that remained. His fingers were thin and bony, and his nails were long with dirt under all of them. The tips of his fingers were clubbed, indicating possible COPD, congestive heart failure, or both. His pants were from better days, when he'd had more weight on him. The vinyl belt pulled the pants tight, locked in a hole punched with a pen or some other household instrument when he'd gone beyond the smallest setting. The pants material had bunched at the sides and rested on his pelvis. The long-sleeved flannel shirt he wore, possibly his only one, was so thin you could see the T-shirt underneath. The buttons that were missing had never been replaced. Even in this heat, he wore flannel.

The bed next to him had a peculiar shape to it. For some reason, the sheet was tented. The sheet had a unique pattern to it. It was a chestnut brown in the centre with the rings like an old tree stump, fading from dark brown to a light yellow. It appeared the patient would urinate in bed every night and attempt to dry the sheet and mattress by putting a box of tissue between the mattress and the bed sheet. It didn't work. I bent over and lifted the edge of the sheet. Even through my gloved hand, I could feel the cool dampness of the wet sheet. The mattress was so old it had a permanent depression where the patient slept every night. The smell was strongest here. The ammonia was burning my eyes, making them tear up. I had to stand and distance myself from the smell. I kept my hands far away from myself to avoid touching anything.

Tom was talking to the old man lying on the floor. We noticed the reason for the "new" smell the other tenants noticed coming from our patient's apartment. The man had defecated several times while lying on the floor. He was covered in his own feces from the chest down.

Tom turned, stood, and asked me to go look around the apartment for clues to the patient's medical history. Tom could handle him on his own for now. I left the bedroom, confident in Tom's ability to handle the situation. Tom is not only a great medic but most patients feel intimidated by his size and seldom put up much of an argument. Before checking out the apartment, I radioed dispatch requesting a second rig for assistance with this patient.

I went straight to the washroom. Not only was the sink in desperate need of sandblasting to clean it, but the toilet was disgusting. The bowl was solid brown with deeper hues of bronze where the rust stains had paved their path down from the rim over the years. Missed pee splatters on the wall and around the bowl and tank had remained untouched for equally as long. The shower had no curtain, no bath stain around the tub. How often did our patient clean himself? I gave a quick check to see if the bar of soap had fallen on the floor or was hidden around the edge of the tub. Nothing!

At this point, my gloves had touched more than I cared to mention. With my left hand, I pinched the cuff of my right glove and pulled my right hand out. I bunched my right glove in my left hand. With my right hand, I inserted my index and middle finger under the cuff of my left hand, careful not to touch the outside of the glove and folded the glove onto itself and pulled the glove inside out with the right glove still inside. The only exposed part was the inside, clean area of my left glove. I looked for a wastebasket to discard my used gloves. I was not surprised there was none. I placed them on the toilet tank.

I reached into the glove holder on my belt and pulled out another rolled pair of nitrile gloves. One pair remained. Usually, three would suffice. Not sure this time. We still had a patient covered in feces to clean up. I pulled an antiseptic towelette from my pocket and cleaned my hand first. My hands should be clean but I wasn't taking chances. I donned the new gloves, carefully avoiding any potential tears. Maddy would be proud of my procedures. She hated me bringing any germs home.

The mirror of the bathroom medicine cabinet was thick with, with, well, something! The reflected image was distorted. Taking my cue from the police, I used my company-supplied pen to open the cabinet. Not a bad idea. Now I really understood why they do this. The metal cabinet, once white, was now rusted in spots and dust covered what few items were inside. It was safe to move the items inside. I don't think the patient had been in here since the '80s.

A tube of toothpaste that looked like its cap was welded on with dried paste from years gone by sat alone on the bottom shelf. No toothbrush. I didn't see one on the vanity, either. I wasn't even sure if the patient had any real teeth left.

A white metal Nitrolingual Spray bottle was on the shelf above it. I hadn't seen an old white metal Nitro in years. I lifted the bottle, turned it over to see the expiry date stamped on the bottom: 07-97. The label, dark and faded but still legible, on the Nitro bottle gave us his name: Henry Roscoe. Great, more than ten years had gone by since the pump was prescribed. I pumped it once, nothing, twice, nothing. It was empty. No other Nitro Spray around. The patient had a cardiac history. He probably hadn't seen a doctor in over a decade, too. The rest of the cabinet was empty.

I went to the kitchen next. An ancient fridge was facing me. A good place to start! A large pull handle on the front released the lock and the rounded door swung wide open. Empty. Absolutely no food! No milk, no beer, just a vast cold expanse of cool air. At least the fridge still worked. Even the bulb that illuminated the interior of the fridge seemed lonely.

The kitchen porcelain sink was equally as dirty as the bathroom sink. Soiled dishes, plates and bowls with dried food lay in the sink and on the counter. Utensils, defying gravity on the plates, hung mysteriously from food long eaten and left for someone else to clean. One lone plastic glass was placed on the counter beside the taps. No dirty pots or pans on the stove or in the oven.

I opened the kitchen cabinets and was greeted with a sight I would only expect to see at supermarkets. I was stunned. I opened another and another. More of the same! Surely someone must be purchasing food for our patient. In each of the cabinets, there were granola bars, different flavours, different varieties; dozens, perhaps hundreds, of boxes of chocolate-covered bars, yogurt-covered bars, and fruit-filled bars; and every possible type of fruit and granola bar sold. I looked for the garbage can. Under the sink, the old garbage can was filled with granola boxes and wrappers. There was a plastic bottle partially hidden under some of the wrappers. I moved a few of the wrappers to reveal a couple of sports drink bottles. That's all this man lived on, granola bars and sports drinks. On a small table behind me, a plastic shopping bag with one side pulled down showed its inventory of sports drinks. Green garbage bags, full and rounded beyond their limits, had been stuffed under the table instead of finding their way to the chute.

I walked out of the kitchen to the living room. I guessed the dust-covered sofa was from the fifties. Something straight from the Cleavers' house in *Leave it to Beaver*. It had low, flat side arms, thick knit green material with large pull buttons to hold the material and padding in place on the back. Unread newspapers, unopened books, and mail were stacked high in several unstable piles. I picked up a box addressed to the patient from *Readers Digest*, and the postal stamp indicated it was mailed in 1969. The address label was for Henry Roscoe but indicated a different address. It looked as though Henry had brought everything with him from his previous residence.

I scanned around the room for more information. Along the far wall, a TV console sitting on the floor spread itself across the far wall. It was a combination TV with a record player and AM/FM tuner and speakers built into the sides. Above the TV was a series of framed black and white photos. I stepped closer and leaned over the TV console. All of the pictures were of military men from World War II. As I went from frame to frame, one face was repeated in each one. I hadn't had a good look at our patient's face, but there was some sixty-year resemblance. The young man who once wore his military uniform with pride was now lying on his bedroom floor in his own feces!

I picked a dust-covered, faded, black and white print off the wall, thinking it probably showed our patient in his younger days.

I went over to the front door and propped it open by wedging the dusty floor mat under it. I brought the stretcher in from the hall and positioned it close to the bedroom door. I prepped the cot by lowering it to waist height and removed the remaining bags, placing them on the floor. I pulled the sheet off the cot and I walked back toward the bedroom. Tom had finished his assessment of the patient.

"The only evidence of medical history is an old Nitro Spray that expired before Y2K! The patient's name is Henry Roscoe." I showed him the old-style bottle. Then I handed Tom the picture. I knew he would appreciate the history. Tom's father had been in the military for most of his life, and Tom was born on a military base. Tom took one look at the picture of our patient in his uniform, recognized his rank, and turned to the patient and asked, "Sergeant Roscoe, can you tell me what happened?"

The old man turned to look at Tom with a renewed sense of being. He remained silent but smiled a toothless grin.

"We have to clean you up before we take you to the hospital.

Is that okay with you, Sergeant?" Tom was always caring, but this time there was genuine concern for the ex-military man.

"Thank you, sir." Our patient was reminded of a better time and referred to Tom as "sir," seeing the stripes on his epaulettes. Tom smiled. You couldn't see the smile through the mask but could see the concern and respect in his eyes. My partner did have a way with people—old ladies, old men, kids, and puppies, Maddy always said.

Tom had placed an IV of normal saline to help hydrate the patient. The patient was on a nasal cannula at four litres per minute that kept his oxygen sats at 98 percent. Tom had already run a twelve-lead ECG and kept the monitor on. The sergeant's vitals were as stable as could be expected under the circumstances.

I tore the cotton sheet into strips to use as wipes to clean the patient. Tom and I had almost finished cleaning the feces off the sergeant when the backup crew arrived. You could hear the gagging from the hall. The two medics walked in, without gloves, without masks. I had never met either one of the medics before. They looked young, eager, and inexperienced.

"Crap, the guy is covered in shit!" one of the rookies exclaimed. His voice was high pitched. He was breathing through his nose and speaking at the same time.

"No shit, Sherlock!" the other replied. "The place reeks!"

"Enough with the 'shit' comments, okay, guys?" Tom was not amused. He felt a need to protect the ex-military man who obviously needed more care than he was able to give himself.

"Give us a hand cleaning this guy so we can load him. Nash and I will take him in so he won't dirty your nice, clean cot." Sarcasm from Tom.

Tom moved to one side to run another automated blood pressure on the monitor, double-check the IV, and see how much oxygen was left in the "D" tank.

The sergeant's vitals remained stable. He was still confused, but it looked like he felt more at ease since Tom had addressed him as "Sergeant."

"I am going to swap the 'D' tank," Tom said. "Our O_2 levels are getting low." This was not a request. Tom started to change oxygen tanks with the rookie crew. They knew better than to start arguing. They had already irritated Tom, and even kneeling down, Tom's size was still imposing. The two medics didn't put up a fight.

The four of us removed most of the sergeant's feces-saturated clothing, wrapped him up in a clean sheet, and log-rolled him onto the stretcher. We had him in the semi-sitting position and continued with oxygen and monitoring. Tom handed him the framed print to hold on to. Sergeant Roscoe relaxed, closed his eyes, and clutched the photo. He fell asleep almost immediately. The other crew cleared the scene and went down the elevator before we left the apartment. We rolled our sleeping patient out of the building, loaded him, and went directly back to the Civic ER.

After a short delay, Sergeant Roscoe was admitted. Even with our on-scene cleanup of the patient, the stench overpowered the ER.

We called dispatch and got permission to go back to base, disinfect, and change. We were both feeling more than a bit dirty after the call at Sergeant Roscoe's apartment. By the time we got back to base, had a quick uniform change, and booked back into service, there were only a few hours left in our shift. We cruised around, grabbed a quick meal, and finished our shift.

It was a beautiful night, and Tom and I decided to head over to Marshy's Pub at Scotiabank Place for a beer and chicken wings. We parked our cars in the nearly empty lot in front of the pub and went inside. People were taking advantage of the warm weather and going to restaurants with outdoor patios; or having barbecues. We were shown to a booth up front by the bar and we ordered a pitcher of draught and a large plate of wings. Only a few tables were busy. It was still early. The evening crowd would not arrive for a few hours yet.

"Oh, I almost forgot. I uploaded the four Senators games from the first round of the playoffs in April '07, the ones where the Sens lost four straight and were trounced from the playoffs. Why do you want to show them to Maddy?" Tom slid my iPod over to me across the sticky tabletop.

"Because we enjoyed watching them!" I shrugged my shoulders. "Even if they did suck."

The pitcher of draught arrived with two large glasses. Our server poured a glass for each of us from the pitcher and placed it on the table.

"The wings will be here shortly." She smiled, turned, and walked away. Tom leaned away from the table to get a better look as she headed back to the kitchen.

"Come on, you can't tell me that ass," he paused and tipped his head in the direction of the server, "is not worth looking at!" He smiled. "Maddy wouldn't mind, you know."

"*I* mind," I argued back.

"I have to take a wicked leak!" Tom got up and headed for the bathroom. I sipped the draught and wiped the condensation from the sides of the glass with my fingers and dried them on my napkin.

Our server returned with a large platter of crispy wings with small bowls of dipping sauce, honey garlic for me, suicide hot for Tom. I hate spicy, hot food.

"Where is your buddy?" she asked as she placed a huge wad of paper napkins on the table.

"The john."

She asked if there was anything that I wanted to see on TV while I waited for Tom's return. I asked for the local news. She used the remote and switched channels on the TV that faced me and left the rest of the televisions on the sports channel for the rest of the bar.

"Let me know if you need anything else." She smiled and left. She was either flirting for a bigger tip or was interested. She was good at flirting. I figured her tip would be more than the usual 15 percent.

I ate a few wings, dipping them in the honey garlic sauce. Daring, I tried the hot sauce. Big mistake! I had to take two large mouthfuls of draught to sooth my burning tongue. Beads of sweat formed on my brow. God, I hate hot food.

I watched the news, not really paying attention until I recognized my old friend. Detective Galen Hoese was being interviewed on the local news. Galen was standing with the precinct in the background. The interviewer was speaking. No sound was coming from the TV. There was no audio. I stood up. I looked around. Everyone in the pub was busy eating and talking. Our server was nowhere to be found. I wanted to hear this. I needed to hear this. I scrambled up to the flat-screen TV, pulled a chair underneath it, climbed up and turned up the volume. I stood on the chair, inches away from the TV, watching Galen being interviewed. He wore the same suit as he always did.

The volume was audible mid-sentence, ". . . asking the public for help. If anyone has any information, we are asking you to call Crime Stoppers. Again, here is a sketch of the person of interest in the deaths of at least two individuals." He held up a drawing of a hooded male face. "He is described as six feet tall, thin build, Caucasian. Please come forward if you have any information on this person."

Galen continued talking. They flashed the toll-free number to call if anyone had any information on the "person of interest." I stopped listening. "Six feet tall," he had said.

Six feet tall? There was no way the suspect was six feet tall. I am five-nine, and we stood eye-to-eye in that apartment where I found the body. There is a big difference between five feet, nine inches and six feet. I stood on the chair, not really looking at anything, but lost in thought.

"Would you mind telling me exactly what you think you are doing?" I looked down. Tom was standing there, looking up at me.

"Six feet tall. The other witnesses said our guy dressed in black was six feet tall. Galen has it all wrong," I said, looking down at him.

I climbed down, replaced the chair, and went back to the booth. I tilted back the glass of draught.

"The cops have our statement, Nash. Let it go. We can't do anything about it." Tom grabbed a wing and started eating.

I PULLED OUT OF THE PARKING LOT and dialed Detective Galen Hoese's cell number. Voice mail! He was probably manning the lines, taking tips from viewers of the newscast. I left a short message. Hopefully, Galen would call me back shortly. I directed the car east onto the Queensway toward the police headquarters where Galen was stationed. Traffic was light. The night sky was brilliant orange, dark clouds blending with the light. The night was bringing a cool relief from the heat we had been experiencing for the past week.

I continued east on the Queensway, turned north on Moodie Drive until Moodie ended at Carling Avenue. I stopped for the red light. Traffic was still light. In fact, there were no vehicles travelling east or west. This light was always long. Just as the light turned green, giving me clearance to continue into my neighbourhood, my cell phone rang. I was only a few hundred metres from my house. The settings on my phone gave me about ten rings before going to voice mail. I turned right, pulled into the driveway, killed the engine, and answered the phone.

I answered the phone with, "Galen?"

"Nash," he replied.

"Any tips come in yet? I have a question for you." I waited for a typical police response or at least a sharp warning telling me to mind my own business.

"What?" Galen seemed tired and not in the mood for our usual banter. He took me by surprise.

"My guy was not six feet tall. Why did you say the suspect was six feet tall?"

Galen went on to explain that the two other police reports both indicated that the suspect was approximately six feet tall. All the witnesses had given the same description. Mine was the only description that differed from the other witnesses who saw the suspect. Great, I was the delusional one.

I stepped out of my car and locked it as Galen continued talking. I unlocked the front door, stepped inside, and shut off the alarm. I would be alone again tonight except for Snickers and Molly.

"As far as I know, I was the only one who was face-to-face with this guy. Why would you dismiss my description?" The pitch of my voice was getting a bit high and I was beginning to talk a bit too fast.

"We got a lot of good leads tonight. Come in to see me tomorrow morning and we can go over some of them and see if you can help us out." Galen knew how to make peace with me. Going in to see him and hopefully clearing up some of these loose threads would make me feel a lot better.

I had lots of vacation time banked. Taking the day off tomorrow seemed like a good idea. I called the supervisor and booked a few vacation days. It was never a problem getting the time off. The supervisors were accommodating . . . well, most of them were, anyway.

I pulled my sweatshirt over my head, yanked my T-shirt out of my jeans, and kicked my runners out into the front hall. The shirt was tossed into the basement for laundry day. Maddy hated me tossing my clothes around the house. I walked downstairs, picked up the shirt, and put it into the hamper. The hamper was overflowing, and I had to force the shirt to fit in. *What the hell*, I thought. *I really have to start doing my own laundry.* White T's or socks made up one pile; the colour pile grew faster. Molly and Snickers ran around the basement watching me fumble around pretending to know how to do laundry. In their mind, this was Mommy's domain.

They would get a treat tonight for protecting the house. I walked back upstairs to the kitchen, retrieved and shook the aluminum bag of Whiskas Temptations cat treats and they came running. I still wasn't sure if it was the tuna-flavoured treats or me they loved more. Either way, having two, purring, hair-shedding poop machines made the time alone feel less, well, lonely.

Their hard-food bowl was still full, so I emptied and washed the water bowl. I added fresh water and placed it back on the floor. I opened a small can of moist cat food, emptied the contents on a plate, and placed it with the buffet feast on the floor.

I grabbed a Labatt Blue out of the fridge, twisted off the cap, and tossed it in the sink. I walked over to the sofa and fell hard onto it. I slid down until my butt was on the edge and my crossed feet were placed strategically on the coffee table before me so as not to obstruct the view of the TV. I hit the power button on the TV remote, and CTV *newsNET* came on. All the usual bad news was reported: war, earthquakes, and the environment; and, always high on the list, gas prices dominated the broadcast. I tilted the bottle back and let the Blue quench my thirst. I tucked the bottle tightly between the seat cushions beside the remote. This was another thing Maddy hated. I would have to remember to put everything away before going to bed.

I felt my eyes become heavy and I kept missing segments of the news broadcast between eye openings. With each passing second, my eyelids would stay closed longer and longer and I would miss more of the news. I pulled the Blue from between the cushions and put it on the table before me. I lay down with my head on the arm and let nature take its natural course.

Images, colours, sights, and sounds began to flash in random before me. Images that made no sense, images from the murder in the apartment, the broadcast, EMS calls. All these images tried to fit into my mind at once. Images that didn't fit. Like a square peg trying to fit in a round hole. My mind was the hammer hitting the images harder to make sense of them all.

The outline of the man in black, looking at me and pointing a gun, flashed before me. Patrick telling his story of the patient found hanging and the young boy on the bike. My chase with the murderer kept appearing and disappearing at random. I was looking into the darkness into the face of the man holding the gun at me. I would see myself walk around the apartment as if through the lens of a camera, finding the body, seeing myself standing in front of the murderer, looking into the darkness of his eyes, straight on as if his face were the same height as mine.

I shot up, sitting on the edge of the sofa, panting. I was out of breath but I hadn't done anything. Adrenaline shot through my veins like hot liquid burning me from the inside out. I could feel my adrenal glands pulsing, pushing the adrenaline through my bloodstream. I was just dozing off, dreaming of, of . . . the murderer before I woke up! I wasn't wrong. He *was* my height—*not* over six feet tall like Galen had said. Who was right? Who was wrong?

I reached for the beer on the table. My mouth was dry, my tongue thick. The beer was getting warm, but it still tasted good and did wonders to get rid of the dry feeling in my mouth. I took another big drink and finished off the bottle. I held the empty bottle before me. I swirled it around, hoping that miraculously more beer would appear if I swirled the bottle faster, turning the foam on the sides back into liquid gold. I put the bottle back down on the table. I paused, closed my eyes, and breathed deeply. I placed my elbows on my knees and cradled my head in my hands.

I felt the pressure of the events of the past few weeks taking its toll on me. Time would heal all wounds, or at least make them easier to deal with, but, right now, I needed to know things that the police didn't want me know. I needed to know things that the killer didn't want me to know. I was caught in the middle of something way beyond my ability to cope with or comprehend. In my position, I didn't have the ability to investigate the murders or the suspects involved. I could walk away from the situation and just let the chips fall where they may. But could I live with myself?

I already knew the answer to that question. I couldn't leave this business unfinished. I had to follow the events through to the end.

THE NEXT MORNING, I sat at Galen's desk holding two dozen Tim Hortons doughnuts and two trays of large black coffees, with cream and sugar in a bag. Police officers, sensing the doughnuts and coffee, walked past me enticed by the smell. If the bad guys all smelled like doughnuts and coffee, there would be no crimes unsolved! The police would seek them out in much the same way they found me sitting with the stash of goods.

I felt uncomfortable sitting alone with coffee and doughnuts in a police station. The police started to act like sharks as they circled their prey, bumping into them to sense if it was worth the effort. In my case, the fresh hot coffee and smell of the morning doughnuts were deemed worthy of a coordinated attack. Just as I felt an ambush was imminent, Galen walked up behind me and laid his hand on my shoulder. This was police body language to claim the prize as his own. Galen would pick through the prize, remove his share, and then let the lower members of the squad room have their way.

I laid the two boxes of doughnuts down and opened the first. Galen grabbed two doughnuts, a Canadian Maple and a Blueberry Fritter, and placed them on a napkin. He pulled a coffee from the tray, reached into the bag, and secured some cream and sugar for his drink. As soon as he sat down, the other officers in the squad room knew the time was ripe to jump in, scavenge the remains, and take whatever they could. Random hands reached in, grabbed anything edible and a coffee, and left. By the time the feeding frenzy was done, all that remained was some chocolate icing from a few doughnuts stuck to the inside of the box. Sharks could learn something from police officers.

I should have taken a doughnut and a coffee before deciding to share.

"Thanks, buddy! We're even now," Galen said, referring to the hot dogs the other day. "Even"? Galen hadn't bought hot dogs for the entire EMS squad.

Galen sat back, wiping the clear glaze from the corner of his mouth that the fritter left behind. He crumpled the napkin, made a perfect shot, a no-net, nothing-but-air basketball shot into the wastebasket. He stirred the coffee to blend the sugar and cream and took a careful sip so as not to burn himself. It was then that I noticed: he wore the same suit from lunch, same suit from TV the night before. At least he was consistent. I still don't think Galen owns another suit.

"Do you have anything for me?" I asked. I didn't even break a smile. I was tired from falling asleep on the couch and knew that anything I wanted would be difficult to get. Taking a serious approach and a stack of doughnuts and coffee didn't hurt.

"Come on, Nash, you have to be more specific than that. You call me up last night and give me shit because your version doesn't mesh with what we have. What the fuck do you want from me?" He pulled a file from the stack of files on the corner of his desk. He opened it and continued talking between sips of coffee.

"Listen, I appreciate the info you gave us on your assault, but let's face facts, the memory can play tricks on you." He flipped a couple of pages over and found the one he was looking for. He placed another file on top of the open file and turned the lower file around so it would face me. Galen stood up, placing both hands on the desk with one hand on the file.

"I want to go over your assault in detail. I need every little piece of information in your tiny little 'Ambulance Driver' head. If you are holding out on me, I want you to give it up now." He raised his voice just a little so that everyone in the squad room heard.

"Thanks for the coffee, Nash. Damn shit flows through me. Now I have to piss. When I get back, I want to know everything. Here, review your statement and brush up." He tipped the cup and finished the last of the coffee. He turned and walked away without saying another word.

I pulled the open file from Galen's desk expecting to see my statement. Instead of something familiar, I saw the police report from the murder in the apartment sitting on top of other police files. I realized Galen was letting me see confidential reports to help me deal with my issues. Instead of asking Galen questions, I could find everything I needed here. I flipped through the reports, found what I was searching for. I thought I could remember everything but decided I needed a pen and paper. I looked around the room. No one, absolutely no one was paying any attention to me at all. I found a pen, pulled a sheet of paper from the piles of blank paper on Galen's desk, and started writing anything of interest. Dates, times, names . . .

I found the names of the six witnesses who'd had the misfortune of seeing Mrs. Phillips and the baby, Andie, perish in the fire. The names of the six witnesses were: Chris Manners, the young boy on the bike; Daniel Tremblay, the man who was found hanging; Roger Fabian, the murdered man in the apartment. All three deceased. The three remaining witnesses were: Elizabeth Cooper and Terrence Russell, both from Ottawa, and Catherine Johnston from Brockville, Ontario. Everyone else was from Ottawa; only Catherine Johnston was from out of town. The small town of Brockville is only an hour south of Ottawa and is situated on the north shore of the St. Lawrence Seaway. The file was pretty thick with police-related reports, information from the Internet regarding crosses, information that I couldn't decipher, and copies of crime scene photos.

I wrote feverishly, barely legible at times. I would look over my shoulder to make sure I wasn't raising the suspicion of the other officers in the room. The officers were too busy to care about what I was doing. I continued to flip through pages, trying to find as much information as possible. I looked up to see Galen returning from the washroom. He wiped his wet hands through his red thick hair changing the colour to a darker red. The water spots on his jacket gave away the fact that he did in fact wash his hands. At least I hoped that's what the spots were.

I would have liked a few more minutes alone with the file, but I was happy with the opportunity Galen had given me. I kept the file open, reading as fast as possible like a student trying to complete a few more questions before the teacher has to pull the exam away. Galen sat down, coughed gently. I understood exactly what he meant. I closed the file, placed it back on his desk, and handed him back his pen.

"Thanks for giving me the opportunity to review my statement," I offered.

"Anything new you want to add?" he asked, knowing full well he would get an answer.

"On the news last night, you mentioned the guy was six feet. When the guy had the gun to my forehead," I used my index finger to point to the middle of my forehead and pushed hard to emphasize the fact that the event was as clear today as it was the day that it happened, "here, right here!" I added with more emotion, "I looked him in the eyes. Well, I couldn't see his eyes, exactly, but we were the same height."

Galen stood up abruptly, walked around the desk, and stopped before me.

"Get up!"

"What?" I was surprised by his actions.

"Get up, now!"

I stood up. Galen moved fast, very fast for a large man. He grabbed a stapler off his desk with lightning speed and slammed it to my forehead.

"What the fuck?" I screamed.

The other officers turned to look at the commotion. I was certainly becoming a regular distraction at the station.

"Where are you looking?" Galen yelled.

"What?" I didn't know how to respond.

"Where?" he shouted directly at me.

I couldn't believe it. He was right. I was looking at the stapler being pushed into my forehead. It was only a stapler, but I was fixated on it. It couldn't hurt me, but Galen was right. I wasn't looking at him; I was cross-eyed looking at the stapler. Galen was at least two inches taller, but I wouldn't know it. Could I have been that wrong?

I sat back hard into the chair. I started rubbing my forehead in an attempt to erase the indentation left by the pressure applied by stapler. My mind flooded with images of the man putting the gun to my forehead. Did I imagine the height because I was focused on the gun and assumed the assailant was my height?

"Sorry, Ethan, I had to show you the hard way. I know how stubborn you can be." Galen only used my name when he wanted to be sincere.

"It's okay," I replied. "I needed a wake-up call. How much more of what I saw was only imagined?"

Galen shook his head and shrugged his shoulders.

"The mind plays tricks on you and makes you see what you want to see. We like to rely on evidence instead of eyewitness reports. Evidence doesn't lie."

I grabbed my notes, stood up, and extended my hand. Galen stood, grabbed my hand and squeezed hard.

"Thanks for letting me come in and review my statement." My voice was quiet, almost inaudible, like a child caught doing something bad and forced to apologize. I turned and walked away.

As soon as I sat in my car, I turned the key, only to power the radio for some background noise. KISS belted out "Rock and Roll All Night." Three witnesses remain. If this was indeed a "death list," I wanted to speak with them to find out if any of the witnesses knew more than they realized. I stared at the papers that I'd placed on the leather passenger seat beside me. My mind filled with the option of whether to review my notes or let it drop. What the hell! I picked up the pages and flipped through them. Galen would get into trouble if anyone ever found out about the way I "stole" my notes from the case.

Most of the notes looked like code in quick scribbles that were hard even for me to decipher. I looked everything over, seeing each name of the remaining witnesses, some half-written jargon of scene notes and telephone numbers, finally deciding on Catherine Johnston for no apparent reason. The name just stood out, again for no apparent reason, none other than her name. I pulled the picture from the *Ottawa Sun* from my file to see what she looked like. The picture was too fuzzy to see anything other than a dark-haired woman standing in a group with everyone else.

Besides, the end of June offered great weather, and the excuse I needed to run the engine. I looked up at the sky through the sunroof. It was blue with scattered clouds. No rain in the forecast, so off came the sunroof, to go into the back hatch. I turned the key. The engine roared. I pulled out of the parking lot and turned east on the Queensway toward 416 south.

Brockville beckoned.

A FEW MINUTES LATER, I was cruising along at just under 120 kilometres an hour on Highway 416 south. The speed limit is 100 kilometres along the Queensway, the 416 and the 401, but I felt safe against the OPP stopping me as long as I stayed under the 120 mark.

I had the windows down, the sunroof off, and the wind blowing hard through the car. To prevent my notes from being blown out the window, I'd tucked the file in the fold of the passenger seat and placed my cell phone on top. A CD was playing, but I couldn't really hear it over the sound of the wind rushing in through the open sunroof. It was hot, very hot. Cars drove past with all the windows rolled up tight. Even with sunglasses on to protect themselves from the glare of the late June weather, I could see the puzzlement in the eyes of the other drivers on the road as a Porsche was travelling slower than everyone else and with the windows wide open instead of rolled up with my A/C on. It was obvious their air conditioners were on high to keep the cabs of the passing cars cool.

This is a practice I could never understand. All winter long, our cars are closed tightly against the frigid Canadian winters, heaters turned up high to defrost the windshield and warm and soften the hard seats. We quickly tire of using the ice scraper against the ice buildup on the front windshield, the back window, and the side passenger windows. We have to brush the snow off from the roof, the hood, and the trunk. Yet the moment the weather gets warm enough to enjoy the heat, most Canadians repeat the actions of winter by closing the windows and blasting the A/C rather than the heater. Instead of enjoying the hot and sometimes humid weather that we seldom get, people tend to shield themselves in a cocoon of chilled air, the very thing we bitched about all winter long. The only exception is that people are dressed in shorts, sleeveless shirts, and flip-flops. In the winter, the human form is barely recognizable under layers of nylon, insulation, big boots, toques, and gloves.

I enjoyed the drive. The noon sun was still high and the heat intense. Pit stains had formed under both of my arms, and my back was drenched from being pressed against the leather seat. I could feel the moisture gathering under my thighs. Leaning forward against the steering wheel, I let the wind blow dry my back. It felt good. I stayed in that position until the shirt felt dry and cool. Sitting back into the seat, I put my left arm outside the window and let the wind rush in through my short sleeve. It dried the moisture quickly. Unfortunately, I could not repeat the process with my right arm or my legs. Being a little warm and wet was a small price to pay for the comfort of summer.

Even though I could not hear the CD playing, I could see the display of the songs playing in vain against the sound of the rushing wind. "Blinded by the Light" by Manfred Mann was inaudible, so I hit the switches, and both windows rose quietly from inside the door. I hit the back button on the CD player and cranked the volume. The song started over from the beginning. I sang along. People in passing cars smiled as they looked in and saw me singing out loud with the band on the CD player. I didn't care. I was warm, driving my car, and feeling good.

By the time the song was over, the heat inside the car was getting close to unbearable, even for me. The sweat was rolling off the end of my nose, my back was wet again, and my arm pit stain extended to my waist. For a brief moment of weakness, I thought about turning on the A/C but decided against it. The electric windows descended into their respective doors. I repeated my drying process for my back and my left arm. I drove over the Rideau River overpass. I was just north of the town of Kemptville, a bedroom community of Ottawa. Kemptville was once a farming town that had turned into a thriving extension of Ottawa. Some people felt that Kemptville was losing its once small-town feel, but I'm sure it will take decades for that small town to grow large enough to ever get to that point.

The sky began to darken the farther south I drove on the 416. I peered through the sunroof to see the clouds growing thick and black. The air started to feel moist and it was definitely getting cooler. The drop in temperature was a welcome relief. The sweat stains on my shirt disappeared quickly. As I turned west onto Highway 401, where the 416 ended, rain droplets started to hit my windshield. I set the windshield wipers to the lowest intermittent setting. I looked at the rear-view mirror. There was almost no rain on the back window. An occasional wipe of the blades took care of the visibility out back.

I continued on Highway 401 toward Brockville past Prescott. The rain began to come down a little harder. I increased the speed of the wipers so that they now cleaned the windshield every ten seconds or so. I turned off the radio. The once-blue, clear sky had become dark with thick cumulus clouds that hung low on the west horizon. The dark skies and cool air seemed to stall over Brockville. Not the welcome I'd expected. The highway travel signs directed me to the Stewart Boulevard exit in Brockville. I turned north on Stewart Boulevard and continued north through several traffic lights until I reached Laurier Boulevard. I turned east on Laurier. Two streets later on the right, I turned right again onto Peden Boulevard. I looked to my right and left through the rain-soaked windows for 11300 Peden Boulevard. The slower I drove, the more the rain entered through the open sunroof. Found it—11300 Peden Boulevard.

I turned right again into the driveway. No cars. Was anyone home? I reached behind and found the spare navy blue nylon jacket I keep on the back seat. I donned the jacket, popped the large glass hatchback, and rushed out into the rain. I grabbed my sunroof and quickly installed it to prevent the interior of my car from getting wet. The rain began to come down a little harder, making it more difficult to assemble the roof. Once the roof was on, I ran to the front door.

The small overhang provided little protection against the rain, which had started coming down heavier by the minute. The mail-box had no name on it, just the house number. I turned toward the street to see if I was being watched. I noticed the front yard. It was clean, and the grass was burnt from the dry heat wave. Nothing remarkable that would stand out. Sensing I was in the clear, I opened the mailbox and peeked in. Either the occupants weren't at home or they received copious amounts of mail. I reached in, grabbed what I could, and pulled out several envelopes. The name on each envelope was Catherine Johnston. No Mr. Johnston. No other Johnston. Was she a single woman or a single mother? There were no children's toys in the yard or anywhere visible. My guess: single woman. I flipped through the envelopes for more evidence. Nothing stuck out and nothing seemed out of the ordinary. There were bills, flyers, and notices, but nothing personal to reveal anything about the person who lived inside.

I knocked at the door. No response. I knocked harder. Still no response! I pushed on the doorbell and strained my ears against the sound of the rain. The sounds of the chimes were audible inside. I waited. Was she even at home? I didn't even consider that possibility when I decided to drive down from Ottawa. I cupped my hands around my eyes and looked through the side window beside the front door. The frosted glass revealed less than the mail did. I could make out lights and distorted figures. None of the figures moved. Furniture! I turned and looked around at the neighbours' homes to see if anyone was watching me. The rain was coming down harder. No one in their right mind would be out in this downpour, except me. I wiped the condensation from the door glass, cupped my eyes again and decided it was worth one more look. Still nothing!

This was a wasted trip. I looked around again, somehow feeling guilty for invading this person's privacy. I was not sure why I felt guilty but I knew I would feel violated if a stranger were skulking about my house in the rain. I looked toward the sky. The clouds were still thick and dark. I closed my eyes against the force of the rain stinging my face. For a moment, the rain felt good and I forgot why I was in Brockville. Memories were being washed away. The rain was warm but still refreshing against the humid heat of the afternoon. I put my head down, spit out the water that had gathered on my lips, wiped my face with my hand and made a vain attempt to dry my hand on my wet shorts.

I was wet. Actually, I was drenched. I pulled my hands back through my soaking wet hair. The drive down from Ottawa in the afternoon heat had left my hair feeling thick and greasy with dried sweat. I looked around again, still feeling guilty. No one was out enjoying the rain. I surveyed the layout of the house and yard. I was at the main door, situated at the centre of the front façade. The attached garage was to the left of the house, the living room main window was to my right. Without thinking, I darted to the left, my feet slipping on the wet grass. I ran past the garage to the backyard. I quickly looked around. No toys—only a barbeque and a low-end patio set perched on top of a small deck. The backyard was well cared for. I grabbed the rail of the deck to avoid any mishaps on its wet painted steps and carefully made my way to the patio doors.

I cupped my eyes again to peer into the window. The kitchen spread out before me. The dining room table was bare. The counters had a few dishes scattered about, but again, I could see no evidence that anyone was at home. I turned around and slumped back against the glass door.

No one is home, I thought. No car in the driveway. All the lights are out. Should I wait? Should I go for lunch and come back? Since I drove all the way down from Ottawa, it made sense to give it another try and come back later. I pulled my jacket hood back up over my head. The rain was coming down a little harder, now. I looked up and, deciding to make a run for it, took a few steps off the deck and jumped the three wooden steps. I hit the wet grass hard, my feet sinking into the grass and earth. I slid with my legs leading the way as if I were sliding into home plate. My body went down, with my butt taking the full force of the rain-soaked lawn.

I attempted to stand and managed only to get more brown mud all over my shoes and legs. I got on all fours and carefully stood and made a dash for the garage overhang. I hit the garage wall hard, and let the back of my head bang against the garage wall.

"Damn!" I knew better than to jump from the deck like a ten-year-old. That was a stupid, childish thing to do. My feet, shoes, legs, and shorts were soaked through and covered in dark, wet muck. I didn't want to get all that mud in my car. Perhaps there was a rag or a towel or something inside the garage that I could clean up with.

The garage door was within reach. I prayed it was unlocked. The door handle turned without resistance. I pushed the door into the darkness, and the scent of a musty dirt floor and a humid wooden garage filled my nose. I fumbled for a light switch. Nothing! I reached for my light . . . wrong belt. I never carry a flashlight when I am off duty. A practice I would have to change.

The lone door window allowed limited light into the garage. A car was parked directly in front of me. That explained why no car was parked in the driveway, but why wasn't someone at home? I walked around the car with my arms outstretched, waiting for my pupils to adjust. I reached the driver's door and pulled the handle. I was in luck! The door was unlocked. The overhead light illuminated the interior. I pushed the headlight switch to brighten the area in front of the car. I fumbled to find the high beams and pulled the arm switch and the garage lit up even more. I stood and looked into the light. Plastic and cardboard boxes were stacked in front of the car. Rain dripped through a hole in the roof, casting an eerie dance in the yellow light of the car's sealed beam. Flies, dozens, perhaps hundreds of them, danced in and out of the rain, in and out of the light.

"Christ!" I said out loud. I know what this meant. I have seen and been to too many calls not to know what this means. Now I really wish I had that flashlight.

I walked closer to where the flies had claimed their prize. The buzzing became louder, and, as I entered their space, the flies viewed me as a threat to their domain and began to bump into me. As I took in a breath, one fly entered my mouth. I coughed and spit . . . spit again! And again, damn it!

I was fixated on what I would find in the darkness. I looked up. Even though it was dark outside, the contrast of the deep darkness inside the garage made the overcast skies outside brighter. The roof was riddled with tiny holes that allowed rain and light to enter. It was hard to imagine that the holes could have been made by anything other than what I was thinking. The angle of the roof made it difficult to see where the shotgun blast had come from. I followed the buzz. A small row of boxes approximately two feet high blocked most of my view, but the buzzing and the unmistakable smell of death held my attention.

"Come on! How many times is this going to happen?" I rarely speak out loud to myself; yet this time it felt natural.

The flies kept guard over their prize below as host to their future larvae. The host would be home to more than just fly eggs. If left alone, insects of all types would make the jumbled ensemble of bones and flesh their home.

I believed that I'd found Catherine Johnston.

CATHERINE JOHNSTON woke up late. No alarm clock. No need to get up early. No need to do anything at all. Her plans today included no house cleaning, no trashy magazines, no reading, no shower. She wouldn't even shave her legs! It was to be her day at home. She had just started one week of vacation and had no plans for the time off.

As she got out of bed, Catherine tugged down on the Winnie the Pooh T-shirt that she slept in. The T-shirt barely covered her buttocks. She liked the look and feel of being a little bit of an exhibitionist at forty-one, even if it was in the privacy of her own home. She walked to the bathroom, looked hard into the mirror, and saw an image that was becoming more unrecognizable every day. Her forty-one years had been hard. Catherine looked well beyond forty-one. She had never been married, never wanted to be married, never cared to be married. Catherine's life had not turned out the way she wanted. But she was happy. She smiled. The image in the mirror smiled back. The crow's feet around the eyes were deep, making the blue eyes in the reflection seem dark and mysterious. Her smile went wider.

Catherine was happy!

She ran her hands through her dyed hair. She pulled her long hair back around her ears and tied it back in a ponytail. As much as she liked her eyes, she hated her ears. Catherine never wore earrings. She didn't want to draw attention to her ears. She smiled again.

Catherine walked downstairs. She could smell the coffee. She loved the automatic start on her coffee maker. Catherine unlocked the side door and stepped a few feet outside to retrieve the *Brockville Recorder and Times* from the day before that she had not read. It was sunny out. They called for rain today. But that was predicted for later. It was just beautiful right now.

As she reached for the paper, the T-shirt rode up and revealed enough to send a chill up her spine. Secretly, she wanted to be seen. She looked around. No one was out, and, even if they were, the side garage would obstruct the view except for old Mr. Swenson's house directly beside her.

Mr. Swenson was not the type of man who would be up this early or would be looking out the window. The fact that Mr. Swenson would disapprove of Catherine's behaviour made the act that much more thrilling. There was no one at Mr. Swenson's she cared to show off to, anyway. Still, it made her feel alive. Catherine paused, opened the paper, letting the flyers fall to the ground. The act was deliberate. She bent over. The T-shirt rode up high, revealing everything from the waist down. She took her time scooping up the flyers. The morning air felt good. She smiled again. Wide! This was her private act of rebellion. Catherine stood up, shook her shoulders, and skipped back into the house. She was excited, very excited. Living alone had its drawbacks, and not having a man at this very moment was a problem.

The paper was laid on the table, coffee at the ready, the *Bob and Tom* radio talk show in the background for noise. She sat at the kitchen table, sipped the black coffee, and read the front page. The *Brockville Recorder and Times* is a local paper that highlights the regional news and just enough national and international stories to make the paper worth reading.

Catherine squirmed in her chair. She rubbed the back of her neck and strained her head back. Damn, she needed a man!

She skimmed over the headlines and found an occasional story to read in its entirety but mostly she was just wasting time.

Perhaps it was time to think about getting a dog. She passed the OSPCA every day to and from work and thought often about getting a dog. She would even bring dog food and cat litter in to donate to the shelter on a regular basis. The workers knew Catherine by name.

Is this what people do when they get old? she thought to herself. *They go out and get a pet to fill the void of loneliness?* As Catherine scanned the paper, her mind kept going back to the dog. What kind of dog? Would it interfere with her social life? What social life?

Catherine refreshed her coffee and continued to read an article that she wasn't really interested in. She was unaware of the figure that stood motionless in the hall closet. Every movement she made was being analyzed with military precision. The reconnaissance would lead to Catherine's death.

Catherine finished the paper within the hour, folded it up, and walked to the door to toss it into the recycling bin. She thought about walking outside again for another show but she decided that she would relieve the tension in the shower instead. Her toss was perfect in aim. The paper landed in the blue bin on top of all the other recycling.

"Nothing but net! Two points!" she cheered to herself.

She was talking to herself again! Another thing single people do when they live alone. At least if she had a dog, talking out loud would be permissible and not viewed as a sign of early senility.

Catherine walked upstairs to the washroom. She turned the taps and set the water temperature for the shower, then turned on the radio she kept on the cabinet over the toilet tank. Living alone, she liked the company of voices on the radio.

She reached over and pulled the T-shirt over her head. As her head emerged from the bottom of her shirt, she screamed. Catherine jumbled the garment in front of her to cover what little she could.

"Jesus! Who the fuck are you? Get out of my house!" she screamed.

Her voice was strong, assertive and demanding, but the figure standing before her did not move. Dressed in black from head to toe, the figure said nothing. For a brief moment, Catherine felt that maybe it was someone who just wanted to see more. Maybe her little show had caught the attention of the wrong guy.

"Get out of my house, you perverted little creep!"

Her voice was stronger, louder. There was no mistaking Catherine's verbal directions but the figure ignored her orders and stepped closer. Catherine did not scream. Instead she lunged at the figure with the full intent to kill this bastard who had invaded the privacy and sanctity of her home, knocking him back out through the bathroom door and into the hallway.

Catherine did not kick or scratch. A right cross, swung like a man, caught the intruder off-guard, hitting him on the left temple.

Growing up with three brothers had taught her well. She dropped her T-shirt, needing both hands free, and pounced on the dark-clad figure. She pushed the figure hard against the wall. Catherine heard the breath being forced from her attacker's lungs with a loud bark. As the trespasser paused, she brought her knee up fast with intent to maim. Her knee found its target and the would-be attacker fell to the floor. The sudden groan indicated that the male attacker had been caught in the groin. Catherine straddled the assailant and began to wildly punch just anywhere—anywhere she could land a hit. Punch after punch found their mark and the barrage did not stop.

The invader raised his arms, attempting to stem the punches from landing and causing any injury. He rocked from side to side to knock Catherine off balance as she continued to punch. A sudden swing from her attacker hit Catherine on the side of her head, causing her to fall and roll toward the top of the stairs. Dazed, she paused, shook her head to clear the stars. Before Catherine had the opportunity to regain her senses, she felt a sharp pain in her left side. Catherine fell sideways and tumbled down the stairs. She knew she was in trouble. She got on all fours, feeling a wave of nausea, but knew that she had to get up and continue the fight. She felt that she was winning, and that her attacker had simply gotten in a lucky punch. Now this was a new fight!

Catherine looked up the stairs. She didn't see anyone. Had her attacker left? Was she safe? Still on her hands and knees, she noticed the blood dripping onto the carpet and realized she'd taken a serious blow to the head. She felt the laceration on her forehead. Catherine felt the space between the skin and warm blood that flowed freely from it. When she brought her hand down, it was saturated with her own blood and hair. A renewed sense of anger welled up inside her.

The cordless phone was always kept in the foyer. Catherine was only a few feet away. Her head ached, her knees and shoulders were raw from the fall down the carpeted steps. She crawled a few feet, grasped the phone and dialled 911. As she was about to hit the talk button, her world went black.

The intruder stood over Catherine. A new wound opened on the back of her head where the Asp baton connected at the base of the occipital lobe of her skull. Blood surged freely and stained the carpet.

The intruder dragged Catherine's unconscious and bloodied body from the foyer out to the garage. In this quiet neighbourhood, no one noticed a dark figure dragging a nude woman from the house to the side door of the garage. Catherine did not moan and her attacker was not sure if she was still alive.

He perched her upright on a stack of boxes in the back of the garage. Her weight was difficult to position, but he finally succeeded in posing her. The shotgun stock was braced against the dirt floor, barrels pointing straight up in the air with Catherine's chin resting on the end. Her arms dangled at her sides.

Her killer lay on the ground out of harm's way, reached over and pulled both triggers.

13

THE LIFELESS BODY LAY between two boxes on its right side. The shotgun stock had been braced against the dirt floor, leaving its mark, possibly between her legs, and had fallen away from the body. I could make out hair, probably from the back of her head. My pupils adjusted to the limited light and were completely dilated.

I looked back and up at the front of the garage. I made my way back to the garage door. The old wooden door did not have an automatic opener. I fumbled for a lock. There was none. I reached down to the bottom of the door, dug my fingers into the dirt under the lip of the garage door, and pulled. The heavy wooden door lifted easier than I thought it would. Water dripped off the door down my arms. Rain blew in, washing some of the mud from my shoes and legs. Looking around, it was easy to see how a loud noise could be overlooked in this neighbourhood. Here I was, a perfect stranger in this town, walking around a home, opening a garage door without even a single person looking out for the safety of their neighbours. In Ottawa, I would have aroused suspicion long ago.

The garage filled with natural light, so I killed the lights from the car.

I patted my front pockets, back pockets, and belt, fumbling for my cell phone. Then I knew exactly where I'd left it. Scanning the back yard, I surveyed the area where I slid when I'd jumped from the deck. Sure enough, the phone was lying on the rain-soaked grass. I ran from the protection of the garage into the deluge. Rain continued to pour down in torrents. My right foot slid on the wet grass, stretching my leg muscles beyond anything they had done in years. I grabbed the phone and ran back to the safety of the garage. Under the right circumstances, a summer rain would be a welcome relief. Today, it was a nuisance that only made my day worse.

Hoping to dry the cell phone before using it, I looked around for a dry . . . anything! In the entire garage, I could not see a towel, a clean rag . . . nothing! I wiped the phone on my shirt and then blew on the phone in a vain attempt to dry it. This was analogous to the mother's kiss on the sore knee. It didn't do any good, but it was the attempt that mattered.

I usually leave the phone turned on, but I must have inadvertently shut it off while it was in my back pocket. I pushed the green power button and the lights lit up in the dim light of the garage. The glow had a warming effect on me. I really didn't want to go to one of the neighbours and ask them to call 911. It was better to keep things as low-key as possible until all the emergency services crews arrived.

I keyed in 911 and hit TALK.

"Nine-one-one. What is your emergency?" The voice was very professional, direct and unemotional.

"Murder," I replied.

"What city?" I forgot I was on a cell, otherwise they would have known.

"Brockville, please!"

"One moment, I will connect you."

Instantly, I was speaking with the Brockville Police Department.

"Brockville Police." The female dispatcher was no less professional.

"Can you send a car to 11300 Peden Boulevard, please?" Pause. "I think I found a Catherine." Stupid! "I think I found a body. Catherine Johnston." Another pause! "I *know* I found a body, I mean. It may be Catherine Johnston."

In all my years working in the 911 system, I had never actually *called* 911. I will never make fun of people who call 911 and get nervous. It is one thing to respond to calls as a profession—quite another to happen upon a dead body, especially if you are not used to seeing them.

"How do you know she is dead?" A valid question!

"I am an off-duty paramedic from Ottawa." I could feel the tension ease. I just went into work mode.

"I have already dispatched the cruisers to your location." I was relieved.

"Sir, can I get your name, please?"

The rest of the conversation was pleasant enough; that is, pleasant enough for discussing the details of a body found in a garage and currently acting as a buffet for the local insect population.

I went back to the body. Of course, it was still there. Nothing had changed. As I stared at it, the movement of the insects over the dried bits of flesh, hair, and bone was made even more eerie in the shadows. I looked at every detail, wondering if this could actually be a suicide, how anyone could do this to herself.

I'm not sure how long I stood there, but it felt like only seconds before the first cruiser showed up. The male officer got out of the car and sprinted over for the protection of the garage overhang. He stood before me, tall, looking down at me. We stood just inside the opening of the garage.

I was covered in wet muck. My shirt, shorts, and shoes were wet, dirty, and certainly not the image of the medic that I wanted to portray.

"Did you find the body?" There was no second-guessing his tone.

"Yes." I looked at his name tag over his breast pocket: Muntz. That was it. No "Sergeant," no "Captain," just Muntz.

"Where is it?"

I pointed. "It?" My tone questioned his poor choice of words.

"She is over there. She is behind the boxes." I think my point was made; or else I was being annoying. The light from the open garage door offered limited light but was still adequate.

The police officer removed his flashlight and added much-needed light to the grisly scene. He carefully walked over to where the body lay, paying special attention to avoid contaminating the scene any more than I had already done.

"Shit!" Pause. The officer looked up at the shotgun scatter in the roof. "She really did a good job on herself!"

"What is up with her face?" he mumbled. I couldn't see his face well, but I knew he would be forcing his eyes to focus and reveal more details.

"Jesus!" You could hear Muntz swallow. "The blast blew her

freaking face off!"

Catherine lay on her stomach. The back of her head was visible, her hair still pulled back in a ponytail. The shotgun blast had shot through her chin like a knife slicing up inside her skull. The skin on the right side of her face had acted like a hinge and had allowed her face to swing out. After falling to the floor, Catherine's face was looking back at us.

Skin, hair, brain matter, and bone had been blown away from Catherine's skull and were now splattered across the boxes and strewn along the floor, where the force of the blast gave way to gravity.

Catherine's arms were both down by her side. She was not holding onto the gun and her hands were nowhere near the triggers. The gun had fallen away, leaving an imprint in the dirt when the triggers were pulled.

"What makes you think it was suicide?" I was immediately defensive.

"From the initial look of the place," Muntz paused again, waving the flashlight from side to side and up and down, speaking with the light instead of his hands. "It must have been suicide."

Muntz kept the light moving over the boxes, into the corners, and around the body.

"Wait!" I yelled. Officer Muntz paused. "Go back, ah, move your flashlight back toward the wall!" I directed.

Muntz obeyed. He slowly retraced his steps. The light was a bit low.

"Higher!" I commanded.

"Where the hell do you want me?"

"Just give me the fucking light!"

He tossed me the large black metal light. In the dim light, the beam floated and moved like Luke Skywalker's light sabre from *Star Wars*. I didn't know which end was the handle. I let the "Force" guide me. The butt end of the light hit me flat in the chest and fell to the floor. So much for the "Force" being with me!

I picked up the light and tried to remember where I saw it. I stared at the top of the wall where it meets the roof and moved back and forth, methodically, attempting not to miss any square inch of the wall.

"There!" I yelled as the light found its target. I realized I was not in control of my emotions.

"There!" I said again with emphasis. This time I was in control of my voice and I was not so panicked. I adjusted the end of the light from spot to flood. The entire image was revealed.

"A big, red plus sign. A plus sign? Big freaking whoop!" Muntz said with attitude in his voice.

"It's not a plus sign. It's an inverted cross written in blood!" I replied with a touch more attitude, to even the playing field.

He walked past me, snatched the flashlight from my hand, and stepped in closer for a better look. Muntz adjusted the lens back to a spot and pointed the light directly at the wall.

"You're right. It *is* blood," Muntz said. His fingers hovered millimetres over the bloody inverted cross as if he could magically obtain more information through osmosis. Why do we feel the need to touch? Some ancestral coding in our DNA that equates touch with truth, I suspect.

"Kind of hard to scribble on the wall in your own blood after you blow your face off, isn't it? I think you'd better call the Ottawa PD in on this one," I said to him.

Muntz turned and looked at me, puzzled.

"I have the number, if you need it."

14

GALEN PICKED UP THE PHONE after quite a few rings. You could tell his mouth was full.

"Can't you pull the doughnut out of your mouth long enough to answer the phone, buddy?" I was trying to keep the mood from getting too serious.

"I knew it was you," he mumbled as he swallowed. "Call display, remember? Why are you calling me from your cell?" A few more chews and his voice cleared. "And," he paused, his voice rose a bit, "it was a carrot, smartass."

"Care for a drive?" I quipped back. "Brockville has a case you might be interested in."

I heard him crunch on more of the carrot.

"What the fuck is in Brockville?" You could visualize the orange, chewed-up shards of carrot flying out of his mouth.

"I found a body!" I was more than a little cocky, like I had found some long, lost treasure.

"And . . . ?" Galen did not sound amused.

"There was a cross on the wall."

"Lots of people have crosses on their walls, dipshit." Galen was getting more colourful with his metaphors.

"Upside-down ones?" I quipped back. "And," I purposely paused for effect, "drawn in blood?"

There was silence . . . stunned silence broken only by the sound of snapping carrots being bitten and chewed. The silence went on longer than I thought it would.

"I'm on my way. Can you give me the address?"

I gave Galen the address and the names of the officers in charge of the scene. I knew he would be frantically writing all the details down in his usual scribble. Later, driving down to Brockville, Galen would curse his penmanship in his attempt to read the directions.

I hung up and turned my attention back to the crime scene. The rain had slowed to a drizzle. The street was filled with cruisers, and the Brockville Police Forensics Crew had already arrived and the staff were milling about. A local Leeds and Grenville gold and blue-striped EMS rig had already arrived on scene and confirmed the death. The EMS crew was coordinating details with the police, swapping notes and call numbers and chatting away about anything other than the dead body in the garage.

I walked up the driveway and went to lift the crime scene tape to walk underneath it. A police constable stopped me. I glanced around him and looked at Muntz. With a nod of his head, Muntz granted me permission to enter. Suddenly, I was one of them.

"Thanks for letting me back in." I wasn't being sarcastic.

I really wanted back in. With all that had happened, I was more than involved. I was part of the investigation whether I liked it or not. And I really wanted this.

I re-entered the garage, noting that what was once a dimly lit old garage was now an intensive crime scene awash in light. Every detail lay before me. I don't think I had ever seen a room that brightly lit before. There was not a crevice, not a corner, not even a crack in the ceiling that was not lit by the strong lights installed by the forensics team.

I walked to the back of the garage and squeezed in between two white Tyvek-clad men. Without looking, they parted and granted me access to the crime scene. I looked at the body, looked up at the holes in the roof of the garage and the bloody cross on the wall facing us.

By now, the forensics team had begun their investigation. It reminded me of the scene at the Ottawa apartment. Same concept, same format. It was as if the police had a team that roamed the province, going from crime scene to crime scene. Each forensic investigator went about his or her work without speaking or looking at each other. It was a well-orchestrated scenario. These people were well trained.

I kneeled down, looked over Catherine's injury and the placement of the shotgun and how it laid. I envisioned the way the killer placed the victim over the gun and pulled the trigger. Was Catherine awake and aware of what was about to happen or was she already dead at the time? I tilted my head one way, imagined the killing, tilted my head the other way, and imagined again. I felt a little like the toy dog in the rear window of the car with the bobble head. I took in every possible detail.

I still felt like an intruder at this scene. In Ottawa, where I knew most of the cops, I could possibly get away with more than I could here. The Brockville PD were extending me every possible courtesy, and I took advantage of their hospitality.

Just then, a loud repeating thumping sound just outside the garage took the police and me by surprise. Everyone got up and went outside to investigate the noise. Standing to the side of the garage, one arm outstretched to brace himself against the garage, a lone uniformed officer was repeatedly stomping his foot against the ground. He kept looking down in frustration. With each stomp, he would turn his foot so he could examine the sole of his boot. Everyone stood around watching the panicked officer repeat the same moves over and over again.

One of the lead investigators walked up to the officer, "Would you mind telling me what the fuck you are doing?"

"I accidentally stepped in something on the floor of the garage. I am pretty sure it was a big chunk of her brain. It's stuck in the treads of my boot. It won't come out!" the determined officer replied while he kept trying to clean the treads of his boots.

"Stop!" the commanding officer demanded.

The officer had no intention of stopping until all the brain matter was freed from his boot. It was as if a parasite had attached itself and would consume his leg if he didn't cleanse himself of the mass on his foot.

"Stop!" the officer looked at his commanding officer. He continued stomping.

"Now!" The commanding officer was standing close to the rookie, screaming, his spittle spraying the officer's face. "Stop! You're destroying evidence."

I snatched a pair of nitrile gloves from Muntz, donned them, and went over to the young cop. I placed my hand on his knee and forced his leg to the ground. I held the officer's leg tight. I asked for an evidence bag. Someone tapped my shoulder from behind. A clear bag appeared before me. Opening the bag, I placed it under the officer's boot. Whoever handed me the bag knew what I needed next and offered me a plastic scraper. The matter stuck in between the treads of the boots was indeed Catherine's brain. I began to scrape everything I could find stuck to the sole of the boot—dirt, gravel, brain matter—into the bag. The brain matter was still, well, gushy and rubbery. I added it all to the contents already in the bag.

I looked behind me for approval from the white clad officer who handed me the bag. A gentle nod indicated he was happy with my job of cleaning the boot and collecting what I could from the ground.

I handed the bag to him. He uncapped a marker, and started to write something on the tag that hung from the bag. He turned and walked away without a word.

Muntz had come over to comfort the distraught man. He was pulled over to a cruiser and taken away from the scene.

I stood up, looked around. No one was paying any attention to me. I went back to the crime scene. As I walked back, a voice behind me simply said, "Thanks for stepping in." I nodded. I thought it best to simply keep walking without saying any more.

My phone rang. I reached into my pocket. The LCD screen did not reveal who the caller was. My phone never did display the Caller ID. Something didn't feel right, but I clicked the green answer button anyway.

15

HE SAT IN THE VEHICLE. He was cold, dark, and alone. The car was parked a fair distance away from the crime scene to avoid attention from passing police cruisers. His passenger window was cracked just enough so that the car windows would not fog up. The sky still let loose with the occasional raindrop, but he dared not use the wipers. He could make out the scenario up the street well enough.

He knew why the police were focusing today's effort on Catherine Johnston's house. He had done well. He was actually pleased. A smile appeared thinly on his lips. He was beginning to enjoy this. Murder was enjoyable. Enjoyable? Could he actually enjoy the taking of a life? *Of course,* he thought to himself. It was easy. It was . . . what word fit best? he thought to himself. *Fun!* The voice inside his head said out loud.

Yes, *fun* was exactly the word that best described this feeling. Fun! He not only enjoyed it. It was fun! He noticed a large bulge in his pants. This was the first time he had become sexually aroused by killing someone.

He rubbed the outside of his black jeans over the bulge. The woman had fought hard. He rubbed harder. She'd fought very hard. He put his head back and pressed against the seat. Her brains had sprayed all over the garage, all over him. He rubbed harder. She'd fallen down and her face had been almost completely torn away. He rubbed faster. He'd loved seeing the blood, the brain matter, the taking of life. He pressed his head against the seat, his feet pushed against the floor of the car. He exploded hard. His underwear was wet with his sperm. He felt the warmth, and it made him feel good.

He came harder than he ever had when he had sex with a woman. Killing was no longer just fun. Killing had become

surrogate sex. He liked it better. He no longer had regrets. Regrets were no longer part of his life. Killing was now his life.

The warmth inside his pants made him feel alive. He smiled, not a thin smile, but a wide, toothy grin. He had graduated to where he wanted to be. He liked what he had become.

He picked up his cell that lay on the passenger seat, flipped the lid, dialed a number, and waited.

Ethan's phone rang. He looked at the monochrome LCD screen. Nothing! Ethan knew it was time for a new phone.

"Hello?" the voice answered.

"Mr. Tennant?"

"Yes?"

"A little out of your element, don't you think?" The caller smiled to himself.

"An ambulance driver playing the part of a cop is a bit of a stretch. Did you have fun finding our lady in the garage?" He sensed Ethan's hesitation on the other end of the phone.

"Who the fuck is this?" Ethan yelled.

Several police officers stopped what they were doing and turned to Ethan. Ethan started to wave his free arm frantically to get their attention.

"I did a great job of posing her just before I pulled the trigger. You should have seen the blood and shit splatter all over. I still have her all over my shirt. Of course, she fought better than you run. You run like a little faggot. I could have outrun you at half speed. Maybe you should get in shape before our next meeting."

"How did you get my number?" Ethan questioned. He was stalling. He tilted the phone so Officer Muntz could listen in.

"Ethan," he paused. "I killed, oh gee, I'm losing count of how many people are dead, and the police didn't link them until you got involved. How hard do you think it would be for me to get your precious cell number? Please, don't insult me!"

Muntz and Tennant had their heads pressed together to hear every detail the caller gave. Muntz turned and whispered directions to another cop who ran back to his cruiser. Ethan was too preoccupied to wonder why the uniformed officer had run off.

"I just thought I would call and introduce myself. I think we should get together soon. Don't you? I will let you know when the next one bites the dust. I am beginning to enjoy our little cat and mouse game." The caller's voice was jubilant. He enjoyed the game, the killing, the taunting. "I would like to chat more, but I really have to get back to work before they miss me. Keep in touch, Ethan. Oh, right, you don't have my number. Well, I will call you when I get the urge." There was a short pause. "Until then, have fun trying to track me down."

There was silence, an awkward silence, but the line was still connected. Tennant and Muntz looked at each other, not wanting to say anything for fear they would interrupt the caller.

"Ethan?"

"Yes."

" 'Bye."

"Wait. I need to know something. Will you answer a question for me?"

"Depends."

"Why the inverted cross?" Ethan tried to keep the caller on the phone as long as possible. "I need to know what the meaning is."

All Ethan heard was breathing, deep wheezy breathing. His mouth must be close to the phone. Could he discover anything from this, a medical history, a physical ailment? Was he thinking of an answer?

"Cross? Oh, the plus sign!"

"What?" Ethan screamed back. "Fuck that! You know perfectly well it's a cross!"

"Actually, Ethan, it IS a plus sign!" Ethan was floored. They had never considered it to be anything other than an inverted cross with some religious meaning.

"I guess I have bad penmanship when it comes to writing in blood. It was meant to let you know there would be more." Ethan felt like an idiot. "And, there will be more."

"How many more?" Ethan quipped.

"Nice fall on the wet grass! Take care of yourself, Ethan. I enjoy the game and I really don't want anything to happen to you!"

The line went dead.

Ethan realized the caller, the killer, was close by or had been close by. He ran to the street. Ethan looked one way, then the other. Nothing looked out of place. Like he would know, anyway?

He was in a strange city, on a strange street, looking for something that was out of place.

That was fun, too! He closed his phone, placing it on the seat beside him. He was pleased with himself. It had been a productive day. It was a good day.

He turned the key in the ignition to power up the radio. He felt like something loud with lots of rhythm. He found a station and watched the police fumble about up the street.

He watched. He waited. The rain stopped, and his view of the police show was coming to a close; cars began to leave and pack up their gear. He saw the body being taken away. He got hard again at the sight of the body. It was far away, but the sight of the body was very recognizable. He could visualize and replay the entire scene in his mind.

He turned the key and revved up the engine. Just then a cat walked along the street curb in front of him. He waited, his eyes never leaving the tabby that walked along the road side. Like the larger predator he was, he pulled the gear lever to D and gripped the steering wheel with both hands, loosening then tightening his fingers. He powered down the radio, not wanting to scare the tabby. Like his father taught him as a child, don't speak, it might scare the fish. Be patient. He hoped the tabby was a female.

The cat casually stepped off the curb. He gunned the accelerator. He looked back in the rear-view mirror. The cat was in full death roll. It jumped and withered in pain, then lay motionless. He smiled and noticed the new bulge in his pants again. He was happy. He smiled. More fun!

16

I LOOKED DOWN AT THE PHONE. Muntz knew something was up. He'd come over with a puzzled look on his face as I was talking on the cell. He'd heard most of the conversation I'd had with the caller. I tossed him my phone. His right hand sprang up with the speed of an NHL goalie. He caught the mobile, examined it and looked back at me.

"I want it back, you know!" I yelled to Muntz.

"You'll have this antique back in a day or two."

I wasn't sure if Muntz knew what era the phone was from. My cell phone was not exactly state of the art or current technology. Muntz handed the cell phone over to a female officer and whispered some orders. She walked to a cruiser, got in, and drove off.

I stood motionless, blank, not wanting to believe that a murderer had decided I was his plaything, somebody to be toyed with. I could feel the rage welling up inside, slowly, like a watched pot, just waiting for the exact moment when the water reaches the boiling point.

Death had been a part of my life for so long, it was beginning to feel natural. It wasn't comfortable. It wasn't a warm blanket on a cold winter's night. It was simply death. It was unwelcomed, unwanted. Death was now very familiar; I had seen it as part of my job and my personal life, and now it had taken control of any remnant of my free time.

I am tired of death. Paramedics don't save lives; paramedics delay the inevitable. Now I am part of death and I don't like it one bit. I was brought into this scenario and I want to make sure it comes to an end—the sooner, the better.

I turned back to the task at hand. A few of the police cruisers had already left by the time Galen met me inside the police barrier tape at Catherine Johnston's residence. I was kneeling down, looking over the biological evidence, providing what little assistance I could.

A gentle tap on my shoulder from Galen was enough to pull me away from my unassigned task. I removed my gloves, bundled them, and handed them to a technician, who bagged them. I extended my hand to Galen.

"Sorry, I don't know where the hell that thing has been!" he said, backing away slightly.

"I always wear gloves," I sniped back.

"I don't give a shit. I hate dead bodies and sticky, warm crap." His shoulders went up, his body gave a quick shiver, and he handed me a Tim's coffee, all in one motion. I was impressed with his ability to handle more than one sarcastic task at once. The coffee would be a double-double, no doubt. The warm summer day had turned into a muggy, wet day, and the coffee would fill a void. Strange how, even with the smell and sight of the remains of Catherine's body lying only a few metres away, I could feel my stomach asking me when I would eat. The life of a paramedic: food and coffee first, bathroom second, patients in there somewhere, based on the sliding priorities of the first two.

"Did you just say that the guy you were on the phone with was the killer?" Galen asked with just a note of skepticism.

I introduced Galen to Officer Muntz. As soon as the obligatory introduction was over, Muntz pulled Galen from me, and off they went to do their "police thing." A group of police, suits and uniforms, gathered in a circle. Gestures were made, heads turned all at once toward the garage, then turned and looked down the street. It looked like a well-orchestrated football huddle. Muntz played the quarterback, everyone listened to the instructions, everyone knew the play, and everyone knew the game plan. All that was missing was the obligatory hand clap, and everyone broke. Galen walked toward me. I sipped my coffee.

"Apparently you made quite an impression," Galen commented as he walked toward me.

"Good?" I replied. "Or bad?"

"Good, all good." He looked down. "But you gotta go, Nash."

"What?" My surprise and astonishment was not well hidden. Galen seldom called me Nash. My mouth went instantly dry. I took another sip of coffee.

"You did good. This is still a crime scene. Last I checked, you were not a cop and we have to follow protocol. Muntz, or Mincemeat, or whatever the hell his name is, asked me to let you down." Galen still wouldn't look up. He truly was upset.

"Muntz was going to call your boss and get you a commendation or a varsity letter, or some insane stupid thing. I'm sure you will get a huge increase in pay." Sarcasm coming from a cop! I never would have imagined. They must instil that in "Cops 101."

"Some guy wants to get a debriefing on your call, Ethan." Galen paused for effect no doubt to show his sincerity. "I really do appreciate your work on this, even if these guys have no idea what you've gone through."

I had never known Galen to show emotion before except when there was food involved. I finished my coffee, looked around to find a place to recycle the cup. Nothing! Fuck it! I tossed it to the ground.

"I am staying here for a while. Your car is safe until you get back. I think this is your ride." Galen nodded his head toward an unmarked car that had pulled up to the curb.

I walked over to the police officer who looked to be in charge, shook his hand, made sure he had all my contact information, and followed a uniformed officer who led me away to the suit getting out of the unmarked cruiser.

This man stood alone, as if he enjoyed the anonymity. He threw his cigarette away in the wet gutter as I approached. Again, the police head bob was given between my escort and the man at the car, acknowledging some hidden code. The uniformed officer turned and walked back to the crime scene.

"You want anything?" I was asked by the stranger leaning against the car.

"An explanation would be nice." I tried to use my stern, administration voice.

"Get in." He opened the passenger door, indicating where I was to sit. He walked around to the driver's side, got in, adjusted his seat belt, and started the car. I looked in the back seat. There sat another guy sitting in the back seat. A hand was extended between the bucket seats. I twisted to the right and returned the greeting. We shook.

"Don Mueller, OPP." He was thin, with a thick neck that made his bald head seem like a ping pong ball sitting atop a pedestal. He stood out and my immediate impression was not what I would have expected from an Ontario Provincial Police officer.

"Hungry?" The driver asked, looking straight ahead. "Let's go get a bite." He was either psychic or he'd heard my stomach growl.

He put the car in gear and drove away from the scene without looking at me. He stared straight ahead. I was just invited to lunch with someone I don't even know, someone who won't look at me. This was starting to feel uncomfortable.

Mueller did not introduce me to the driver. No exchange of names. I sat, looking forward. This was extremely uncomfortable. My new chauffeur sat motionless, knowing exactly where he was going.

A mass of jumbled brown and white fur covered with bloody soft tissue and bones lay in the middle of the opposite lane. It was a fresh kill. I had become hardened to seeing people in death and in distress but I still have a soft spot for animals. The poor cat hadn't stood a chance.

I wasn't sure where we were going. I had blind faith in a stranger who was driving and assumed he knew where he was going. As long as he was buying, I was okay with it.

17

I WAS DRIVEN TO THE DOWNTOWN main street of Brockville. King Street, in its day, must have been grand and the mainstay of the community. Many of the buildings had ornate stonework at the roofline, with the year of construction proudly displayed in the centre. Now, there were empty shops with bare windows and few shoppers on the sidewalks.

My chauffeur pulled into an empty parking spot down from a pizza restaurant on the corner of King and Perth Streets. As I stepped out of the car, I looked up to see a faded yellow and red sign that once was colourful and bold. Milos Pizza is a small restaurant with a delicate wood façade and large window looking out onto the main street. The owner was Greek selling Italian food with a Greek flair. They served arguably the best pizza in Brockville. Inside, pictures of local people in cheap wooden frames were screwed to the wall—locals who felt like celebrities posing with the restaurant's food proudly displayed before them. The food was the real celebrity; the customers were the icing on the cupcake. But it made everyone in the pictures feel special. I was about to find out just how good the food was.

We were seated in one of the few booths and handed a laminated menu. I was definitely hungry, but my mind was elsewhere. I wasn't disgusted by what I had just witnessed, touched, or anything like that; it was a combination of mental fatigue, lack of sleep, lack of food, lack of . . . well, a lot of things.

"Tennant?" I heard my name being shouted.

I was in a daze. I lowered the menu just enough to peer over it and look over at the stranger across the table. Mueller sat staring at his menu, not looking up.

"It speaks!" Sarcasm! I should be more careful. I suspect he was paying for my meal. "What?" I was completely lost in thought.

"Are you going to order? The poor girl has been standing here for two minutes watching your bald spot get bigger while you ignored her. We've already ordered. Pick something."

I closed the menu, looked up at her and handed the laminated menu back. "Whatever he is having will be fine. Thank you!" I gestured toward my silent chauffeur.

She wrote something down as she walked away. She didn't look amused. Yup, I would have to double her tip.

"So who the hell are you, anyway?" I asked my strange date with a voice that showed my fatigue and disdain.

"Zachariasz Kostyantyn." He extended his hand.

We shook. He could tell I was puzzled. Mueller was silent.

"I go by Zach Constantine. Part Ukrainian, part Bulgarian. My parents immigrated after the Second World War. They wanted to give me a little piece of the old country. I would have preferred something less obvious, like a coffee table or a rug. Instead, I get saddled with this." He sipped the coffee that he'd ordered when my mind was elsewhere.

His thick black hair, square jaw and forehead, massive fingers, and large stature gave away his heritage.

Shit, if Zach ordered coffee, the waitress would bring me coffee, too. And I was all coffeed out.

On cue, our server placed a cup in front of me, poured the coffee, and left a dish of creamers in the middle of the table. I smiled at her and she turned toward Zach without repaying my gesture. She refreshed his black coffee and smiled at him. He smiled back. She placed a Coke with ice in front of Mueller. Oh, she was so going to do something to my food.

Zach held the coffee cup with two hands as if he were trying to warm them against the cold of winter. He stared into the black liquid of his cup.

He didn't look up when he spoke. "We need a complete breakdown of everything—and I mean everything—you have on this guy."

He sipped.

"Don't leave out a single detail. What may seem trivial to you may be an important detail to us," Mueller said. I looked at the ping-pong head and smiled inside. If only that bald head were a little more white. He looked up. His expression changed. Zach was serious, too.

"And who exactly are you, Mr. Constantine? And you too, Don?" I quipped back. "No introduction, no name exchange until now, nothing! I don't even know who you work for." Mueller and Constantine looked at each other.

Without saying a word, Constantine placed a business card before me on the table. "Ottawa Police" blazed across the top of the card. Z. Constantine was printed perfectly in the centre, but no title was beneath it, no telephone number or email address.

"I didn't realize the Ottawa Police had a secret division." I placed a single finger on the card and slid it back to his side of the table. "I would give you my card, but I left them in my other pants," I quipped. Nothing! Not a smirk, a smile, the perfect poker face from my lunch partners.

"No secret. I just prefer not to broadcast things. I'm Galen's boss. Everything you told him, he told me. I am here because shit like this doesn't happen all that often in Ottawa. And, I want it stopped now!"

Okay, I was impressed. I slid the card back to my side of table, flipped it over and over again, looking for more information, then pocketed it. Who knows, it might come in handy.

"The OPP are in charge. I report to Mueller." Constantine sipped his coffee. "And you . . . you report to me." There was no mistaking the tone in his voice. His eyes were solid, face stern, back straight, shoulders square.

Our server returned with Zach's order and placed it before him. It looked like a medium pizza with mushrooms, bacon, and pineapple. Great, I would have killed for a Reuben. The pizza looked good. Something I probably would have ordered if I actually took time to read the menu. Again, a large toothy grin from our server to Zach. Our server placed a Reuben in front of Mueller. I should have asked for what Mueller was having. She walked away without as much as a word to me.

Zach placed the napkin on his lap and dug in. She returned, placed the silver elevated platter heavily before me and smiled. Not a polite smile, more of a grin. I lifted a slice, expecting to find something out of place. I turned it over and repeated the move.

Nothing obvious.

The pizza was hot, filling, and pretty damn good.

"So, where do you want me to start?" I asked.

"The beginning is always best. My beginning starts before you even realized there was a beginning, so start before where you think you should start. Understand?" Zach Constantine was serious. Mueller wiped a little sauce off his chin. I was feeling like I was being interrogated by a good cop, bad cop team.

Answer a question with another question. Typical cop!

The conversation went back and forth as Galen's boss took notes with one hand and ate with the other. Any holes I left in the story were immediately questioned and my story altered to meet his strict doctrine of details and facts. Details I inadvertently omitted were met with doubt, reasons for my conduct became suspect, and why I became the centre of attraction for the person committing the crimes was dealt with skepticism. I felt as if I was a potential suspect. Realistically, I was. If I were in their shoes, I could justify putting me under suspicion.

Zach Constantine was well prepared. He knew the case; he knew it better than I realized I knew it. Zach took pages and pages of notes. The tiny pages in his notebook flipped fast as he wrote in his form of shorthand.

I continually asked questions, and then was reminded that he was the one asking and I was telling. Not the other way around. Point taken! Mueller was silent. He finished his Reuben, then worked on what was left of his fries.

The plates were finished, coffee refreshed over and over again, and the storytelling went on. Three dessert plates with some sort of pastry were placed before us, consumed with little thought to taste or enjoyment. I pushed the plate forward, grabbed the coffee cup and tilted back. The coffee was done, as was my energy. I had been hungrier than I thought and now I was tired.

"I have to take a leak."

Constantine nodded as if I needed his approval to leave the table. It was a good excuse to stretch my legs. I stood up, looked around, lost in my new surroundings, found the logo for "Men" on the door, and headed in that direction.

I stood before the urinal, unzipped, and felt instant relief. I moved back and forth in an attempt to melt the ice cubes in the bottom of the urinal, a game I am sure played by almost every man. I was doing pretty good. I had plenty of ammunition and felt I could easily melt my opponents. After failing to overcome the entire army at the bottom of the ceramic battlefield, I washed and returned to the table.

The plates and cups were gone, the table clean, with no one sitting there. I looked around. No one was at the cash register. My new friends were gone. I walked outside and decided to try the parking spot. My worst fear at this time was having to take a cab back to pick up my car. I really didn't know where I was.

Zach was leaning against the car having a smoke. Don was speaking on his cell phone.

"Sorry, you were taking too long and I really needed a butt." Zach finished his smoke, crushed the butt under his sole and positioned himself behind the wheel. I got in on the passenger side and buckled up. Mueller opened the back door and adjusted his seat belt. Without looking in my direction again, Zach drove back to the crime scene. Not another word was said, no mention of the crime, nothing.

Zach pulled up to the opposite curb, turned the key and the engine went silent. He got out of the car and walked toward the police officers who remained on scene. Mueller stayed in the back seat, cell phone in hand. Like a well-orchestrated dance, the circular line opened a spot and Zach fit right into the police melee.

I got out of Constantine's car and walked over to join the group. Galen Hoese noticed me and pulled away from the group. He met me before I had a chance to get too close to the group.

"How was lunch with Conny?" Galen asked.

"Conny?"

Pause. "Zach Constantine!"

My eyebrows rose.

"Dry, isn't he?" Galen offered.

"Sahara. And just about as much fun to be with. He part of your group?"

"He is all on his own. Answers to no one! No one! Does what he wants, when he wants. For him to be here, he must be interested. No one knows exactly what his job title is. How often do we have a murder in Ottawa, let alone a serial killer? I never thought Ottawa PD would have a Cloak and Dagger Department when I joined, but weird shit goes on that some of us old shits don't ever question."

"Complete opposite from Mueller," I replied.

"Mueller?" Galen looked honestly surprised. He turned one way then the other to find Mueller.

"Inside the car," I said softly.

He looked over toward the car and noticed the figure sitting in the back seat.

I got Galen talking. Galen never talks unless he has a point to make. I decided to press further to see what more I could get out of him. This police stuff was starting to wear off on me. I liked it but as a hobby, a new hobby that I sort of fell into unwillingly.

"How would this case interest a guy like that?" I pressed the issue.

"How? Are you fuckin' nuts? Okay, let's do a little review, here! Let's see if your little ambulance driver brain can follow this." Galen paused to assemble his thoughts.

"We have multiple murders supposedly committed by the same guy. The victims are related by a photo. A fuckin' newspaper photo! A photo that sheds no light, no clues, no, well, nothing on the case! Some fuckin' nutcase is killing these people because he picked the picture from the newspaper. That's it, out of a newspaper. Now we have, what, four, five dead people. All because some fuckin' nut case decided that killing was fun. And this asshole wants to play games with you by making you the central focus of his obsession. Jesus Christ, Ethan, I want this guy stopped. I want him dead. This is the last thing you need right now, and frankly, I don't want you dead."

A warm thought from Galen Hoese. I was beginning to believe in Santa Claus again. He was genuinely concerned for my well-being. Maybe I should be worried, too.

Galen pulled my cell phone from his jacket pocket, flipped it over, looked at it and tossed it at me.

"Get into the '90s, will ya!" I caught the phone and looked at it curiously.

"Piece of shit is so old, we couldn't get anything off it."

18

THE DRIVE HOME WAS QUIET. The rain had stopped completely, but dark clouds remained. The sunroof was closed, radio off, windows all the way up. I wasn't in the mood for much of anything at this point. I needed someone to talk to.

I flipped the phone open. The screen did not light up. I pressed and held the power button. Nothing! Great! They either killed the battery or broke my phone. I reached over, opened the glovebox and rummaged blind until I found a curly cable. I yanked hard to free it from the tangled mess of junk that is usually found in the glovebox of most cars.

I plugged it into the cigarette lighter port in the dash and inserted the adapter in the bottom of the phone. I waited a few minutes, held the power button, and watched the scene brighten, declaring the police innocent of any wrongdoing to my phone.

Without looking, from sheer repetition, I dialed Tom's home number. The phone rang for five rings. I knew his voice mail picked up after six. I hit the red button to cancel the call. No answer. I was about to try his cell when my phone rang in my hand.

I accepted the call.

"Ethan?" I recognized the voice from a few hours earlier.

"Ethan, please don't hang up. I just want to talk." It was him.

I didn't want to talk. I wanted to hang up. It took everything in me to hold my tongue. I set the cruise at 120, took my foot off the accelerator, pulled my right foot back until my heel touched the front of my seat. I needed to be comfortable if I was going to be believable.

"Ethan, are you there?" There was almost a sombre tone to his voice. As if he were disappointed that I wasn't speaking with him.

"I'm here." The fewer things said the better on my part.

"I just wanted to thank you for being a good sport. You're

playing the game really well, I have to admit. I didn't think you would even get the itch to play along." His voice was coy, almost whimsical in its tone. He had me, the police, everyone completely baffled. If he were to stop today, no more killings, no more mysterious phone calls, he would never be caught.

"This is a game to you? You're killing innocent people who haven't done a thing to you, and you have the fucking nerve to call this a game, you sick piece of shit!" It was strong, but I knew he almost expected this tone from me.

"No one is innocent. No one! Not you, not Tom, not Maddy, not ev—"

I hung up the phone. I was furious. He knew me. That was fine. He knew Tom. I could live with that. But Maddy didn't need to be brought into this. Not now. I slammed the phone down on the warm, black leather passenger seat next to me with such force, the charger ripped out of the dash, recoiled back, and hit the back of my hand.

The stress came over me in waves. My stomach first. The nausea hit hard. I could taste the vomit at the back of my throat. My chest tightened. The weight seemed immense as I gasped for air. My throat closed. I fought against the taste of vomit and the constriction of my lungs. My grip on the steering wheel got tight, so tight that I could see the tips of my fingers under the wheel turn white. Tiny beads of sweat formed on the backs of my hands. My fingers loosened. I knew my blood pressure was high; my pulse pounded in my temples. The stiffness grew in my neck, but the headache came on faster. I turned my neck hard; the snap of my cervical spine was evidence of the stress.

I needed to calm down.

I rolled down the driver's window to let some air in. The humid, cool wind whipped around the car. I took a deep breath. I could feel my pulse slow, the tension in my neck ease. I felt calmer. The day had been so long already. I would definitely be ready for bed by the time I got home. I leaned my head against the headrest, my arms pushed hard against the steering wheel, and I let the tension go.

Knowing the phone was almost dead, I plugged the charger back into the dashboard's lighter socket. I pushed the adapter in hard, gave it a twist in some vain attempt to keep it secure in case I yanked it out again.

Highway 416 had dry pavement. Any evidence it had rained earlier had evaporated. The trees were fuller; the leaves were greener. The air had a new crisp smell.

I was beginning to feel normal again.

The electronic ring on my cell cut the silence. I looked at the display. No call display. I really, really needed to upgrade.

I didn't want to answer the phone, but I needed to know. Was it Tom? Was it work? Galen? Only one way to find out.

I held the phone in front of me, high on the steering wheel so I could see the road ahead and pressed the green button. The tension was back.

"Hello?" The tone in my voice announced my apprehension.

"Ethan?" His words broke the silence. I batted my eyes to shake the sleep from them. "Ethan, it's Dave Green."

The voice was unfamiliar.

"Yes?" I replied, my tone making it obvious that I was unaware of who my caller was.

"Christ, Ethan. Dave Green from Ottawa EMS," his voice had definite ominous tones.

"Yes!" I repeated for the second time.

"I spoke to you after the shooting, a while ago. Remember?"

"Riiiight!" I extended the "i" by at least three syllables. Okay, so now I remembered. I could sense Dave's apprehension.

"Do you know about Tom Lister's accident?"

Silence!

"Of course I don't know anything about an accident!" My tone changed. "What the *hell* are you talking about?"

"Tom was involved in an MVC earlier today."

My mouth went dry. "Where?" Single-word question.

"General." Single-word answer.

19

THE ROOM WAS BLACK. Not dark, black. The kind of black that only happens by design. Black that nature would envy. Dark walls, windows completely covered with opaque cloth or no windows at all. No light whatsoever. Silence! Not a sound. No electric hum, no birds singing in the distance, no radio or TV to disrupt the silence. Thick carpet covered the floor, damping the sound coming from the apartment below. Total sensory deprivation for anyone in the room.

In that room, the lone chair was occupied. He sat naked in the chair, staring into the abyss. Clothing would cause him to feel more than he wanted. Eyes open, seeing nothing. He sat unmoving, enjoying his anonymity. The heat made him feel a bit uncomfortable against the leather.

He felt at one with his emotions; no sound, no sight, no light. He reached beside the chair and retrieved his pack of cigarettes and ashtray. He placed them on the left armrest and lit one.

The glow from the lighter lit the room momentarily, and then the room went black again. With each drag on the cigarette, a tiny orange glow at the end of the cigarette before him beamed brighter. He inhaled deeply each time, held it in and exhaled. He enjoyed smoking, it was a relief. When the first cigarette was finished, he started a second then a third. He had nowhere to be, nothing to do.

He could feel the heat rise in the room. Tiny beads of sweat formed on his brow. Occasionally, the sweat would drip off his nose and land on his bare chest. He couldn't see this happening but he could feel it. He curled his toes on the carpet making tiny fists. He tightened his leg muscles until his calves hurt, then relaxed. He sat upright, straightening his back, then relaxed again.

The lack of light and sound heightened his senses. He could think better, hear better, remember better.

He thought back. His life had been different the past few months. He was happier, more fulfilled. Everything that lacked in his life had suddenly been replaced with contentment. He no longer wanted for anything. He had found his purpose.

He took another drag of the smoke and filled his lungs. He held his breath, then slowly exhaled through his nose. He blindly flicked the ashes into the ashtray. He held the cigarette firmly between his index and middle finger in his left hand. The nicotine stain that he knew was there was evidence of his ongoing habit. Once the cigarette was finished, he pushed the butt into the ashtray until all that was left was a broken filter stem.

He tilted his head back against the top of the chair, closing his eyes out of instinct. He rotated his head from shoulder to shoulder and felt his neck snap several times.

The funeral had been quick after she died. If memory served him, it was the next day. Her father had wanted the cremation immediately after she was pronounced dead, a quick service, then move on. The past few months had been hard on her parents. The cancer had metastasised to her brain faster than any of the specialists had predicted. She was supposed to have six months to a year. But it was less than three months from the initial diagnosis until the funeral. He'd felt cheated, so did her parents. In the end, she didn't recognize anyone, not him, not her parents, no one. What the cancer had left behind was not the person he loved, not the person he married, not the daughter they'd raised. The cancer had done its job well. It destroyed the healthy cells and the lives of those who loved the host.

Cancer is a terrible thing. Healthy cells mutate, turn on themselves, and destroy the being it calls home. Doctors bombard the host with radiation and caustic drugs to rid the body of those mutated cells in the vain attempt to restore life. Sometimes it works; other times, the host is left as an emaciated shell that does not resemble what it once was. Those who love the host pray for a miracle. Sometimes they are rewarded by God and medicine. Sometimes they are not. This time, they were denied more time with the one they loved.

It had been a long time since he'd felt emotion. Tears came freely and rolled down past his ears as he kept his head back. No sound was made, but inside he hurt.

This was his excuse. Although he'd known what he was before she died, her death had given him a reason to hate even more. To him, it was a valid path to follow. He didn't need the excuse. Her death provided him with the push that he could use to justify his actions.

He stood up, cracked his neck again and felt what little tension remained in his body melt away. He used the towel he kept beside his chair to wipe the sweat from his body.

His eyes took time to adjust to the light when he opened the door. As he walked down the hall to the bathroom, the hardwood floors were cool on his feet. He reached in through the glass shower doors to turn the single faucet handle to the preset temperature. The shower quickly began to fill the room with hot steam.

He stepped in the tub, cupped his hands and massaged the hot water over his face. He repeated this action over and over again. It was a cathartic action to cleanse himself of the deeds he had committed earlier in the day. He turned his back to the water. Eyes closed, his head hung. The water continued to run off his body and form a tiny vortex before disappearing down the drain.

20

I STOOD OVER THE BED at the Ottawa General Hospital ICU where Tom Lister lay unconscious, motionless, his eyes closed. The room was quiet except for the constant beeping of the overhead colour Vital Signs Monitor, which displayed his pulse in one colour, blood pressure in another, blood oxygen saturation level in another, and his ECG in yet another. Everything looked normal for someone who should be awake and not lying in bed with an ET tube held in place.

Visibly, there was nothing to indicate why he should be unconscious, other than a few contusions, one around his left eye, the other a small bruise on his chin that added a splash of vibrant orange, green, and blue colours to his pale complexion.

Completely supine in bed, attached to a monitor, with two IVs running fluids, my friend and partner, Tom Lister, was now on the other side of the job, patient instead of caregiver.

Lost in thought, I failed to hear someone enter the room behind me. Brought back to reality by a woman's gentle cough, I turned around slowly.

"Mr. Tennant? Friend? Family?" she asked quietly.

"Neither," I replied softly trying not to wake Tom. "Partner." I turned back toward Tom. "Do you need me to leave?"

"No, actually, I came to talk to you. Mr. Lister's family has already left."

I turned back toward her on my heels.

"Me?" I was confused. Who would know me here? I had not introduced myself to the staff when I came in.

"Why me?" I repeated.

"How well do you know Mr. Lister?" She paused, looked down at the transparent acrylic clipboard she carried, turned a sheet over, then looked back up at me.

"How well?" I realized I was now habitually repeating myself.

"Yes," she lowered her voice and slowed her speech. "How well do you know Mr. Lister and his wishes?"

I suddenly felt exactly how some of my patients feel when I speak with them when they are overwhelmed and have difficulty processing even the simplest of tasks. Seeing Tom lying there and not being his usual sarcastic self, with no witty comeback, was difficult to process at best.

"Pretty well."

"Mr. Lister put you down as his Power of Attorney should anything happen to him. Perhaps we should take a few minutes to talk." She tilted her head, silently indicating our conversation should continue elsewhere. Without saying another word, she turned and walked away, fully expecting me to follow. I decided it was best to follow. She walked out of the ICU, down the hall, and to the door of the Quiet Room. Several Ottawa medics stood silently outside the ICU. A brief nod acknowledged my presence as we walked past. I nodded in return.

She opened the door, peeking inside to ensure that no one was there. Once she was confident the room was free, she entered. Not once did she look back to make sure I that I was following her.

She took a seat and extended her hand, granting me permission to sit close beside her. The clear plastic clipboard was placed firmly on her lap, hands folded tightly upon it. The silent pause suggested the severity of the conversation to come.

"Are you aware of the concerns we have regarding Mr. Lister at this time?"

"None, why? And who are you, anyway?"

"Dr. Ingrid Weitz." Again, she looked at the clipboard. "When Mr. Lister was admitted, his family said you have Power of Attorney over his medical matters."

"Is Tom that bad?" I was almost a little afraid to actually ask the question.

"His condition is critical, but we need to know whom to speak with just in case."

In case! In case, what? I already knew what the "in case" meant. I just didn't want to admit it. Or believe it.

"I can speak with you regarding Tom's medical condition, but we will have someone from the hospital speak with you regarding the responsibility of the Power of Attorney."

Dr. Weitz went into detail regarding Tom's condition. From the police report, Tom's motorcycle had been broadsided by a carload of teenagers who'd blown through a red light and hit him. The motorcycle had spun around and thrown Tom across the oncoming lane where he'd landed on the sidewalk. Tom's full face helmet had taken the majority of impact when he hit the concrete.

I could only imagine how hard it was on the medics who had to pick up Tom from the scene. Ottawa is a big city. Ottawa EMS is a big service. Tom has a big personality. Almost everyone knew Tom or knew of Tom. News would spread fast.

"The CT and EEG were good. But—" that long difficult pause that they teach in "How to Be a Doctor 101" or "Bad Medical Show Dialogue Screenwriter" followed—"he hasn't responded the way we would like."

Dr. Weitz flipped through Tom's chart, paused, scanned a report, turned the sheets back, and looked up at me. Again, the cliché pause and look written into all the daily soaps and most of the medical TV dramas. Dr. Weitz looked concerned.

"His labs are okay. Pretty much everything looks okay, but I think he just needs to recover on his own. His ICP (inter-cranial pressure), BP, all his vitals are within normal limits. Time is what he needs, I hope. In case time is not what he needs, you need to be ready to help us decide our course of action."

I needed to talk to Maddy. I needed to relax and vent.

21

SURPRISINGLY, I drove through gates that were still unlocked this late at night. The gates were tall, hinged at either end, open in the middle, and swung effortlessly. No power motors were needed to open or close the gates, just old-fashioned manpower. The ornate ironwork was reminiscent of a time when things like that meant something. That "something" has been lost for a long time. Now things are mass-produced with little thought of design or longevity. Today, iron gates have been replaced with yellow fibreglass barriers with reflective tape. No originality.

I drove through the grounds with its manicured lawns, groomed trees, and paving stone pathways, until I found our spot. The sun had gone down. The sky had been replaced with shades of red and yellow against a dark blue hue that were so vibrant, so rare, almost impossible to recreate in words or in thought unless you saw them in person.

Off to my left, pushing a wheelbarrow, was someone I had come to know, like, and respect very much. Ike Patterson, the groundskeeper, was always here. It didn't matter what day or what time, Ike was here. He, like some of the trees, had been here longer than anyone cared to mention. I waved, and Ike tipped his head, not wanting to put the wheelbarrow down to return the gesture. I understood.

I killed the engine, set the parking brake, and retrieved the box from the passenger seat. I walked a few feet, set the box down, and started to pull out the contents and lay them before me. First, I placed a small cloth on the ground. Then I pulled out a Corona Light and a Diet Coke. I twisted the cap off the Corona, scratching my palm, only to remember that I needed a bottle opener. You'd think that years of continuously scraping my palm and fingers on the ridges of the cap would remind me not to do that anymore!

I used the edge of a toonie instead to open the bottle. The lime wedges were in a zip-lock baggie. I forced one into the bottle.

I pulled back the tab on the Diet Coke and took a mouthful, paused, took another, then rested it beside the bottle of Corona.

I popped open a can of Pringles, tilted it, and a handful too large for my mouth was forced into it anyway. Old habits are hard to break.

I turned on the iTouch and scrolled through the menu until I found the video I wanted. I selected the Ottawa Senators playoff run from 2007, when they'd made it to the finals of the Stanley Cup against the Anaheim Ducks. I pushed "play" and the game started.

I pulled out my cell phone. It was dark now. The glow from the game and my cell lit the area with a timid LCD white light. I speed-dialed Maddy's cell and waited for her voice mail to pick up. While I waited for her pre-recorded greeting on the other end, I leaned back against her headstone for support.

I looked up into the night sky through the trees, hoping to get a last glimpse of the colours I had seen as I drove in, but they were gone. So many things had disappeared. Maddy's voice came on the phone to greet me. She answered, but she wanted me to leave a message so she could call me back. I am still waiting for her to call me back.

Paying her cell phone bill every month is worth every penny to keep some small part of our past alive. It became a habit for two busy people who lived on their cell phones to leave messages for one another. I still call her with things that happened during the day, just to keep memories alive. Her voice keeps me going.

With my head against her headstone, I closed my eyes and listened. The voice was crisp, clear, and musical.

"Hi, there! You have reached the cell phone of Maddy Tennant. I am obviously not here or I would have answered my phone. I am really sorry I missed your call, but I will call you back. I promise. Have a great day. I will. 'Bye-bye."

Her voice was as clear as I remembered. Each time I listened to Maddy's message, it was as if she were right there beside me. It was as if she would be there when I got home.

The play-by-play continued on the iTouch, my mouth was still full of Pringles, and the sky was dark. I didn't leave a message, but called back to hear her message once again.

Without speaking, I thought of all the things I wanted to tell her, a psychic one-way conversation. The way I had done for so long before she died. The things that made me feel better and more at ease. I told her about Tom, whom she loved like a brother, the killings, my recent stint playing detective, everything.

"Mr. Tennant?" I jumped in my skin, shaken from my trance, and I looked upward.

"Ike, you scared the crap out of me!" I closed my phone and sat up.

"Sorry, Mr. Tennant. I just wanted you to say hi to Mrs. Tennant for me." Ike is large. Everything about him is large, and his hands are huge, with thick, calloused palms, broad, football-pad shoulders, and long, muscular legs; he had a soft, gentle voice that confuses everyone.

"Say hi, yourself, Ike. Join me. Maddy won't mind. You can have her beer."

"No, Mr. Tennant!" He shook his head side to side with vigour, as if I didn't understand his verbal refusal.

"Ike, she never drinks it, and I know she would want you to sit and chat once in a while." I extended the Corona to him. Ike reached for the beer, and his hand dwarfed the clear bottle. He sat down, looked at the game playing.

"The Sens really blew that series, didn't they."

"Yup, that they did!"

For the next few hours, Ike and I talked about Maddy, the Sens, his work at the cemetery, pretty much anything. The Pringles disappeared, the Corona bottles were emptied, and the Diet Coke cans followed suit. The Sens game played on until the batteries died. They lost.

Instead of Ike's being merely an acquaintance, Ike had become a friend.

WITH ALL THE CHANGES in my life in the past few weeks, the last thing I needed was a change at work. I had a new partner! Not the kid's fault. I just hate new partners. Tom and I could complete a call without even saying a word. Now, everyone has to talk, reveal their innermost thoughts and emotions, and let everyone know exactly how they feel. Psychiatrists need to teach people how to shut the fuck up. There is a time to talk and a time to keep quiet. Or at least know when to express themselves to someone who actually gives a shit.

I didn't shave today, and the kid didn't say a word. I think I purposely didn't shave just so Tom would have something to complain about when he got better. I may not shave until Tom comes back.

The kid sat there, eager, in the passenger seat of the rig, willing and wanting to please. All that came to my mind was a black lab. Young, long hair, pulled back into a ponytail that went through the hole in the ball cap, tiny by comparison to a lot of other medics, a ring on her "I'm married" finger, and, dare I say it again, young. Everyone looks younger to me with each passing year. Funny thing is, now all I want is a partner who can lift. Not much else.

I sat beside her, not wanting to be impressed. The single stripe on her shoulder indicated she was a PCP, a primary care paramedic. The PCP program is a two-year, full-time college paramedic program in Ontario. A PCP performs most of the skills required for most of the average calls we do: twelve-lead, defibrillation, advanced airway management, IVs, and medications. You had to be a PCP before going back to school to take the ACP program. As an ACP, we have more skills. Some of those skills are questionable. We rarely use any skills outside the realm of a PCP—except on the rare occasions when they are really needed.

Between Tom and me, we were lucky to each pull a good ACP call every month or so. I had thought about going back down to being a PCP again; the wage difference paid for my satellite bill every month, but that was it. It wasn't worth the cost of the course or the responsibility, and it would be nice not to be in charge of the new kids when they come out of school. I truly came to believe that ACPs were, well, overrated, unjustified, and glory seekers. Well, maybe not all of them. But I really am a bitter old man—old by EMS standards, anyway.

I had never seen my new partner around. Not surprising. Ottawa EMS had done another huge contract hire lately and we would be working with more and more of them to cover vacation time, sick time, and time when your partner was in the hospital following a motorcycle accident. Another newbie with no experience as my partner. More stress. Great! I needed a coffee, bad!

We booked on and I drove into the city. The ride was silent. The radio chatter was normal, and our vehicle number didn't come up at all. Unlike Bingo, in this business, you don't want your numbers called. I continued to drive until I found a Tim Hortons that didn't look too busy.

"Anything?" The question was simple. The intent was self-explanatory. She knew what I meant. She shook her head with a negative reply, ponytail wagging from side to side. I grabbed the portable and headed inside. The lineup was short, and I waited patiently. I finally got a chance to order my double-double, paid my $1.72, and walked to the end of the counter to wait for the coffee.

Suddenly, the radio blared: "4132!"

"Go for 4132."

"Code 4. Possible VSA. Prepare to copy."

"Stand by." This was a common reply to "Prepare to copy."

I looked behind the counter. No one made any rush move to get my coffee. Great, I was without my paid-for coffee and going to a possible VSA. I started walking out of Tim's. I looked through the windshield directly at my new partner for the day. She still had her head buried in some EMS manual or school book, no doubt.

I hopped into the driver's seat. My partner seemed unaware that we had a call or aware the call was meant for us. Newbies!

I grabbed the mike. My partner looked over at me with

wide-eyed wonderment. She'd missed her opportunity to speak on the radio.

"Go for 4132."

"Proceed Code 4, 1014 St. Martin Street, possible VSA. Details to follow."

"10–4. 10–8." Short, sweet, to the point. No verbal diarrhea.

I slowly accelerated and went to reach for the switches to activate the emergency lights, but my partner beat me to the punch. I looked over at her, eyes once again wide open, pupils dilated beyond reason, like a fat kid locked in a Baskin-Robbins overnight. I was going to punch her if she didn't calm down. God! Was this her first day?

"First Code 4?" I asked.

"First shift off orientation. First call. First Code 4. First vital signs absent patient." She couldn't have said that any faster. The words flowed together without a break, without time to breathe.

"Not surprised," I said softly, lips barely moving.

"What?"

Great, a new partner with hearing like a dog. She could probably hear tones that only dogs and whales can distinguish.

"Nothing! Just bitchin' about the traffic."

"'K."

I could have said anything at this point. She was the deer caught in the headlights, completely oblivious to anything except the sounds of the yelping siren, the speeding through traffic and dodging drivers who didn't know the difference between pulling over and slamming on their brakes right in front of you. I always said: "We need a high-calibre turret gun instead of a siren." It would thin out the stupid people and only take a few months before the word got out to "Get the hell out of my way!"

I really think I need a vacation.

Ottawa city traffic was an anomaly. On the days you would expect traffic to be at a congested standstill, you fly through the streets. Then, on days that normally had little or no traffic, it was bumper-to-bumper, with little chance to weave through the cars. No one could pull over as I approached. The option was driving in the oncoming lane, the choice I preferred. You knew that the oncoming drivers could see you and had no choice but to pull over.

I waited for a break in the oncoming traffic and made my move. No signal, no indication to the other drivers on the road of my intentions. I swerved to the left. The heavy diesel vehicle rocked under the hard turn. The rig dipped to the left, then back up to the right. Looking over at my partner, I figured I would probably have to clean her seat when the run was over. She had a firm grasp on the handle on the passenger door and was holding the seat belt buckle with her left hand. I think she wanted to make sure that the seat belt didn't come loose.

I always wanted to hear my tires squeal on the ambulance but the slow speed and the inability to make hard turns made it impossible. Well, not impossible, just not recommended. These huge Ford E–350 rear-wheel drive rigs are not meant for the racetrack.

The onslaught of cars facing me pulled over faster than I had ever seen. Of course, the sight of a large white cube van with flashing LED lights and a blaring siren coming at you head-on would make most drivers suddenly recall the traffic laws and get the fuck out of the way. I drove straight at them. Cars from both oncoming lanes pulled to the curb as I sped past. I have so little fun in my life right now that this brought me more joy than I could remember. The siren bounced off the buildings and echoed the sound back several times. It was like driving in a tunnel. Tom would be laughing his ass off right about now. Instead, I had a newbie dropping a load in her pants and mentally preparing to write me up to the boss at the end of the shift. What the hell! This was too much fun. This was something an amusement park just can't duplicate, even on the roller coaster.

Looking ahead, I saw a break in the lane I was supposed to be in. When traffic permitted, I pulled back into my lane. The newbie relaxed her shoulders and fell back into her seat.

Welcome to Ottawa EMS!

Dispatch called back with details of the call. A gentleman in his late fifties had fallen face first into his breakfast oatmeal in mid-sentence while talking to his wife. A second crew had been dispatched, and fire also had been tiered. Great, I had a newbie and water fairies for help on this call. A year ago, thoughts like this would never have entered my head. Now, they seemed to be a daily occurrence.

Unfortunately, the rest of the drive was uneventful. The newbie, what's her name . . . I think she told me, maybe not, or maybe I just don't really care . . . finally took a breath. I turned off the parkway and pulled down a beautiful tree-lined street of two-storey brick homes with large front yards. The grass was green. It was the type of green that only comes with illegal pesticides designed to kill everything except the grass. There were multiple cars in every driveway: BMW, Mercedes, Audi. I think you had to be a doctor, lawyer, or a politician to move to this neighbourhood. Probably way out of my price range, but something Maddy and I would have looked at in a few years.

I pulled in up front of the house, backed into the driveway, and booked "10–7 scene." Neighbours had gathered, and a very panicky woman in a business suit was standing with friends who were holding her while she cried.

First scene impression: husband and wife woke up, showered, made breakfast, had some light banter over scrambled eggs and toast and the *Ottawa Sun*—correction, *Ottawa Citizen* or *Globe and Mail*, too high-class for the *Sun*—husband keeled over, wife called 911, called the neighbours for help, everyone came over, and who was tending to the dead guy in the house? Probably a freaking orthodontist or a chiropractor, if my guess was right.

"You ready . . . ?" I was going to say her name but I realized I still don't know it.

"Yup. Let's see how much I screw up on this call. Don't worry about hurting my feelings. If I do or don't do something, tell me."

Son of bitch! I liked this kid.

We calmly exited the cab of the rig. Eyes from the people who had gathered followed us as we walked around to the back doors. Everyone thinks it's like TV and we are supposed to run from the rig to the scene. My partner and I pulled the cot out with the Zoll defibrillator and all our bags already strapped to the stretcher. We lowered the stretcher carriage and we pulled/pushed it to the house.

Under normal circumstances, this would cause performance anxiety: having a dozen people or more watching your every move, analyzing how you do things, with preconceived notions of how you should act or behave, and expecting you to save every life, like they do on TV.

This isn't TV. We don't save every life, things don't always work out, and we never run to a call. There was probably some lawyer in the group with a stopwatch clocking us to see if our pace was worth investigating.

We were able to pull the cot right into the main foyer. The off-coloured pink ceramic tile formed a circular design that met in the middle. A large, ceramic, tan sunburst indicated the centre of the foyer. Directly above the sunburst hung a chandelier, the style that is usually reserved for museums or hotel lobbies, which caught the morning light through the skylight. A spiral oak staircase separated the foyer and led to the upstairs. This house was too fancy for my style and way out of my price range. *Experience or indifference?* I wondered to myself. I seemed to have lost all compassion. Someone was dying in the next room and I was doing a walk-through for a real estate appraisal.

"This way! Please!" a panicky voice pleaded.

A man was motioning to us to follow him as he disappeared down the hall to the left. His voice was filled with panic and concern. As I pulled on the foot handle of the cot to guide it down the hall, I could see two men performing CPR on the body on the floor. "This way!" he said again.

I pulled the cot close, turned to grab the foot handle, and looked at what's-her-name.

"You ready?"

"As I will ever be." Suddenly her eager eyes focused and experience replaced wonderment.

We lowered the cot to chair height. I grabbed my two bags, she pulled the Zoll defib off the stand and prepped for her first VSA.

The two men in suits were actually doing a damn fine job of CPR. The majority of time when we have the public doing CPR before our arrival, CPR resembles a poor version of pump and blow. These guys seemed to know their stuff, probably had some medical background.

"Dr. Jack Arnold. I'm a cardiologist at the Ottawa Heart. Him, too." Dr. Arnold's head pointed across the body to the man doing the rescue breathing.

I was right; doctors. He got the words out between his rapid 100-plus compressions per minute. He knew what he was doing.

Sweat rolled off his brow, from the tip of his nose directly onto the patient's chest. I looked at the man across from him. He looked more concerned. He had been doing artificial respirations for some time. His lips looked a little swollen and red. He would grimace with each breath given to the patient after thirty compressions.

As my partner was getting the defib ready, I positioned myself at the patient's head and reached over for a right carotid pulse. Dr. Arnold continued CPR just like he should. The pulse was weak, thready, but regular and in perfect sync with the compressions. The patient's skin was pale; cyanosis had been kept to a minimum with good strong CPR and good perfusion.

As I was checking the patient's pulse, Dr. Arnold continued his report.

"Brenda, Ian's wife," his head pointed to the patient, indicating his name was Ian, "rushed next door to get me before she called 911. We've been doing CPR for less than ten minutes."

He paused. The sweat was flowing freely now.

"I don't think he has a cardiac history. I came over and he was VSA." He paused again to catch his breath and two ventilations were given.

"We started CPR probably within one to two minutes of arrest."

While the two neighbours were performing CPR, my partner applied the defib pads: one was right mid-clavicular, the other, left axillary area. The plug end of the pads were plugged into the Zoll defib cable. Our protocol stipulates two minutes of CPR for an unwitnessed cardiac arrest, but the quality of CPR was good, was being administered by medical professionals, and was ongoing prior to our arrival. Once the defib was ready, I looked at my partner. She knew what I wanted.

"Clear! Analyzing!" she spoke calmly, not so much as a hint of excitement in her voice. Both men pulled themselves away from the patient laying supine on the floor before them. Tom and I usually analyze the ECG manually. Today, I decided to let my PCP partner run the arrest using the auto-analyze on the defib.

Not surprisingly, the patient was flatline, asystole. Shocking the patient without a cardiac rhythm doesn't do any good. My partner asked the two rescuers to continue doing CPR. She had already opened the IV and intubation kits and placed them in close proximity to me. Without asking, she pulled an eighteen-gauge catheter to start an IV. I pulled the intubation kit across the kitchen floor and placed it close to my right side. As I dragged the kit closer to me, I looked up to see that a crowd had gathered at the kitchen entrance. The wife of the patient was standing in the doorway being comforted by a female friend, probably a neighbour. She was crying, arms crossed against her chest as if to hug herself in comfort, eyes red, nose running.

Working a VSA was stressful enough, but having an audience added more stress, especially having the wife watch as we worked on her husband. If this had been the ER, she would have been gently escorted out while the team worked on the patient. In the home, it was a hard scene to control.

I grabbed my ET tube, fed the plastic-coated metal stylet down the length of the tube and formed my favourite hockey blade curve at the end. I rolled the end of the tube in the clear, gelatinous lube and replaced the tube in the package. Pulling the handle from the nylon case, I flipped the handle like a switchblade, with the Mac3 blade locking in place for quick insertion. I always pre-attached the Mac3. It was my favourite blade and could clear passage straight through to the vocal cords. The wrist flip motion and locking click must have impressed the doc. Even with the sweat dripping from Dr. Arnold's nose, he tilted, looked up, raised his eyebrows, relaxed and then went back to CPR. I would have offered to do CPR, but every medic knows that this is payback. Watching a doctor doing CPR, sweating, tie swaying to the cadence of the compressions, makes you feel that there is a God. When we bring in a VSA to the ER, the medical staff pull us into the ER Resuscitation Room to perform CPR while they run the call. This kitchen is now my ER room, under my control, and I am getting my sick perversion satisfied. It was hard not to smile, just a little, watching the beads of sweat form a puddle on the patient's chest.

I got down on my stomach and elbows, tilted the patient's head back, inserted the Mac3 blade with my left hand, and lifted. The white vocal cords came into view illuminated from the Rusch fibre optic light at the end of the blade. I slid the tube through the cord on my first attempt, righted myself and pulled the stylet out from the centre of the ET tube. I tossed the stylet behind me; Tom said it was my way of keeping my work area clean at the expense of the rest of the scene.

By the time I looked up, the IV was in, line primed, and a bystander, probably a neighbour, was holding the bag as if it contained some magical potion. This guy would definitely tell friends and family of his role this morning. I was down for thirty to forty-five seconds, tops, and my new partner had managed to get the IV going already. Impressive!

I secured the tube in place, fitted the BVM, and took over ventilation from the red-lipped doctor. He stood up and wiped his mouth with his left sleeve. His tie was still tucked inside the front of his shirt. Pit stains were evident under both his arms. He would be late for work today. He looked at me, secretly and silently asking me if the patient was dead, waiting for me to confirm his suspicions. My eyes responded; the patient was indeed dead. If this call had been in his hospital, he would have been in control, with no evidence of concern, no sweat stains under his arms. Someone else would have been doing the dirty work and he would have made the decision, calling out the orders. He would have called it already.

Dr. Arnold pumped away at the fast pace of 100 compressions per minute. His face was wet, not just sweaty, but dripping wet. He looked at me, then past me. I turned to see what he was looking at and it appeared that the woman consoling the patient's wife was Mrs. Dr. Arnold. The patient's wife was pulled away out of sight.

"Are you going to call it?" Dr. Arnold was asking if I was going to declare our patient dead.

"Not yet. I wanna go for the full three No Shocks before calling it." Protocol demands that we get three consecutive No Shocks on the defib before we get to call it. This was going to be a practice VSA for my new partner.

The rest of the call went as expected. Despite the IV, drugs, defib, chest compressions, and oxygenated ventilations, our patient died. The two doctors on scene who later showed me their IDs to prove their credentials agreed with me. In one way, the old days of transporting every patient was better. Instead, we can now leave a patient on the kitchen floor, for the family to see and remember where dear Dad died. The patient would lie there while the police conducted an investigation to rule out foul play.

I spoke briefly with the two doctors who helped out. When family is around, you automatically go into "silent mode." Your tone is subdued; your head is down as if staring at the floor, no quick body movements. Notes, names, and run numbers were exchanged with the police. Our bags were collected and reorganized and packed up on the cot. As we pushed our cot through the house, we were stopped at the door by the patient's wife. These encounters can be difficult, and I never know what to say or how to say the right thing.

"I just wanted to thank you for your efforts. We," she paused, then continued, "*I*," she emphasized the "I," "saw how hard you worked, and Dr. Arnold spoke very highly of the two of you just now."

She turned her head to indicate where he stood. Dr. Arnold, a bottle of water in hand and still looking exhausted from his morning workout, gave me a look of approval. I felt as if I should put my hand on her shoulder, say something that would make her pain go away, let her know that we shared her sorrow.

Who was I kidding? I had all the typical comments made to me when Maddy died:

"We understand what you are going through."

"If there is anything we can do?"

"Call me if I can help."

"I am so sorry for your loss." It wasn't a loss; she'd died. It's not like I misplaced her and would find her again in the hall closet when I did spring cleaning!

I was about to say something that would have been viewed as insensitive, something that would have shattered her life and got me fired when my partner stepped in and took control. She gently touched her elbow and guided her back to her group of neighbours and friends. Gentle voices could be heard, gestures to one another and a Kleenex box passed around to wipe away the tears.

My partner returned, saw my look of disbelief, and without hesitation stated, "Girl talk!" She grabbed the foot of the cot and pulled.

AN EXIT OFF OF WELLINGTON STREET at the foot of the Booth Street Bridge leads to a tiny bit of land that juts into the Ottawa River. There is an old building that sits on this parcel of land just south of the Quebec border and has been vacant for decades. The stonework is still strong, and there are holes in the walls where windows that once kept the weather out now let the rain, snow, and sun pass through unobstructed. The Willson Carbide Mill looks more like a 200-year-old jail for the criminally insane than anything else. And that's somehow prophetic, considering the cat and mouse game I am playing now.

The building sits on this island in the middle of the Ottawa River, and someone, I assume someone from the government, keeps the grounds immaculate. Almost always devoid of visitors, it was the perfect meeting spot. Looking east, the grey stone building that houses the Supreme Court of Canada backs on the river from the edge of Ontario, as if it were mooning Quebec. The Parliament Buildings are perched on a hilltop just east of the Supreme Court building.

Canadians, for the most part, are more familiar with the White House and such American symbols than our own because of TV and movies. We should be proud of our buildings, our heritage, and our way of life. We may not have the grand, overstated buildings and pompous ceremonies of the United States, but what we have is unique and grand in our understated Canadian way.

Maddy and I would meet there to share burgers, pizza, Diet Coke, and talk, but mostly just spend time together. This was the best part. I hadn't been here in a long time. Too long, in fact! I hadn't been here since Maddy died.

Today, I have my double-double, which should have been an Iced Capp. I'm sitting in the cab of my bus, window open, breeze flowing through, parked with the mill over my left shoulder. It was a nice day. Well, for me, anyway. I had one patient who'd died, but like most medics, you deal with it and move on. Paramedics develop a sense of detachment, but we are not thick-skinned or callous, like many people think when they see us after a call where someone died. For us, for me, it's part of the job. If you do your job well, do all you can, then to my mind, you've done your best and nothing you could have said or done would have changed the outcome. We never yell "Come on! Fight!" or "Don't go to the light!" to the patient as we straddle his or her chest and perform CPR.

"Fuck it" pretty much sums it up.

Funny how the death of one stranger who died while I was working on him barely affects me, but the grief lives inside me for someone who died long ago.

My current partner was slouched down in her seat, cap over her eyes, sleeping. Tom would be doing the same. I would have to go check on him today.

Ottawa dispatch was hopping, calls everywhere but not here, not now. They left us alone to finish lunch.

My partner for the day tilted her head back, readjusted her ball cap, stretched, and sat upright in the seat.

"Ready?"

"I was the one waiting for you to wake up. I'm just sitting here enjoying the view."

She grabbed the mike, booked back into service, and we headed east on Wellington. Traffic was hell. It was afternoon in downtown Ottawa, after all. We passed the Supreme Court of Canada building and continued east toward Parliament, just a short distance away. The afternoon sun was high and just starting to tilt to the west. Each of the facing windshields or back windows of the vehicles ahead reflected the sunlight back toward us like hundreds of mini-spotlights aimed at us.

Approaching crowded Elgin Street, the dispatcher called our rig number.

"Go." My temporary partner was getting the hang of quick, short responses.

"Ethan, can you go over to the Ottawa General? It's Tom."

24

HOSPITAL MONITORS are the eyes and ears of the nursing staff, permitting them to oversee multiple patients in the ICU. Most multi-parameter units will monitor the essential vital signs: pulse, oxygen saturation levels, ECG (electrocardiogram), diagnostic twelve-lead, end tidal CO_2 (carbon dioxide) . . . and will alert the staff when any of the many vital signs go outside the parameters with alarms and flashing icons. Every patient is hooked up to a monitor sending vitals to a central monitoring station.

Patients are kept in solitary glass rooms with oxygen, suction, monitors, and rails on the ceiling suspending IV poles. Each room faces a central nursing station where notes are recorded and nurses maintain an eye on the status of the patients in their charge. The ratio is one to one: one nurse to one critical patient. Intubated patients or severely critical patients will quite often have nurses stationed at their bedside.

I had been in the ICU a few times to visit Tom, so my presence in my paramedic uniform drew little attention. I walked over to Tom's cubicle and peered in through the glass door. Tom lay in the bed, supine, motionless. I glanced up to see the overhead monitor displaying his vitals. Heart rate, oxygen saturation levels, blood pressure, ECG—all looked normal. Normal for a stable patient who should not even be in the hospital.

I looked over at the nursing station and was summoned closer by a look from one of the male nurses sitting behind the desk. A quick glance back at Tom and I walked slowly over to the desk. The nurse rose and walked toward the lounge behind the desk. I followed.

The lounge was sparse, with few chairs, a table. It was not a living room, but a room to simply sit and shut down for a few moments to recharge. I closed the door behind me and sat across from the nurse, who had already taken a seat. What followed were several moments of silence, a silence that I recognized usually had ominous undertones.

"Are you going to say anything or do I have to guess?" My voice was unmistakable. You don't get invited into a private hospital room in the ICU to discuss good news.

"We already spoke to Tom's parents, so I can tell you what happened this morning." He paused. "His parents wanted to tell you themselves, but I suggested they go home."

I knew where the conversation was heading. Tom was brain dead or going to die. The reasons didn't matter. I stood up and looked through the glass panel in the door. Tom's room was directly across from the desk before me. Tom's ECG rhythm was constant, the pulse rate steady, and his oxygen saturation levels unwavering. I heard someone mutter: "fat embolism in the brain," "massive stroke," "unlikely to recover." It all meant the same. Tom was gone or most likely not going to recover fully. Physically, he was still here, but Tom was gone. The nurse was still discussing Tom's prognosis as I opened the door, walked around the nursing station and across the hall, opened the door to Tom's room, grabbed a chair and sat.

It was only then I realized that just a few years ago I was sitting in this very ICU watching over Maddy. A sour taste formed in the back of my throat, one of recognition, a taste of death, vile and putrid. We live to defeat death, delay death, but it always wins, regardless of the fight we put up.

There was still constant radio chatter emanating from the speaker attached to my leather mike clip. I reached down and turned the radio off.

25

A GENTLE TAP ON THE GLASS woke me from my silent trance.

I wasn't sleeping; my mind was just someplace else. "Somewhen else", was more like it. I was in the past, before Maddy's death, before Tom's accident, feeling more than just a little pity, more like cursed. If things truly happen in threes, I had better keep friends and family far away from me.

I turned to see who was tapping on the glass. I expected to see one of the ICU nurses or one of the hospital staff. Instead it was . . . what the hell was her name? It was my new partner, the girl who had been assigned to me since the start of shift. I hadn't even asked her name. She was just someone to replace Tom until he came back to work.

Slowly turning back toward Tom, I looked to see that he hadn't moved. His vitals were pretty much the same as when I arrived. Tom didn't even know I was there. I stood by his bed, leaned in close. "I'll stop by again soon," I whispered into his ear. I desperately wanted to see the cardiac rhythm on the vital signs monitor beep a few more times indicating that Tom understood, that he would squeeze my hand telling me, "Don't give up, I'm still here."

Instead, Tom lay motionless, unmoving, not knowing that I was even in the room. It's hard to see a friend lying in bed, knowing that, in all likelihood, he will never regain himself. It was hard to imagine that all of Tom was gone. I would hold out for the impossible.

As I turned, my partner slid the glass door open for me.

"Dispatch called and wanted to know if we were going to book off for the day or what." Her tone was almost apologetic. I speculated that she would have preferred to just leave me there until I was ready to leave.

"Let's go."

My tone was silent, funeral home silent. No emotion, just a matter-of-fact, monotone, boring, "Let's go." I really needed to get drunk.

I followed what's-her-name out of the ICU and down the hall, to the elevators. The walk down the hospital corridor was silent. I looked around as we walked, remembering when hospital corridors used to be white, sterile, and unimaginative. Now, colour themes and modern décor mix with the cleanliness of the institution. I felt more like the hospitals of old: bland, vacant, and devoid of all emotion.

My partner pressed the lower of the two circular buttons, and the pale background with the black arrow pointing down illuminated white. We stood in silence and waited. A faint ping echoed from the elevator shaft.

"Ethan," I said. The elevator doors opened.

"I know. Becky," she stared straight ahead at the elevator doors.

"Hi, Becky."

We stepped in and pushed the button for the ER.

The sun was still high when I turned on the gas barbeque to get the grill ready for the steaks. Becky sat at the patio table in the shade of the umbrella. She watched Molly and Snickers run around the fenced-in backyard and sipped her beer directly from the bottle. Her hair was not restrained by the pony tail now and it appeared longer than earlier today and rested comfortably on her shoulders. Instead of unflattering uniform pants, she wore denim cut-offs and sandals. She looked different now, relaxed, and comfortably at ease. Now she sat with her legs crossed, arm resting on the table, beer bottle in hand, the other hand tapping in rhythm to the docked iPod belting out '80s tunes.

She kept the cats busy as I went back into the kitchen to get the steaks ready. Looking out the window, Becky had her back to me as she tossed cut grass in the air for Molly, who practised her acrobatics in a vain attempt to catch whatever was airborne.

"Molly and Snickers, huh?"

"Yah!"

"Molly I can understand. But Snickers?"

"Maddy's fave chocolate bar, chocolate brown cat, hence Snickers."

I scrubbed the potatoes free of dirt, kept the skin on, and cubed them. I coated two sheets of foil with olive oil, added the minced garlic, chopped onions, and butter, then tossed in the cubed potatoes, wrapping them all tightly. It was only after the two foil packages were ready that I realized I had prepared Maddy's favourite barbeque potatoes.

My wedding band was still part of my left ring finger. I turned it over and over again. This was the first time another woman had ever been in our house. My house, now! I hadn't removed the ring since the day I'd put it on. A massive wave of guilt churned my stomach and I tasted that sour partial regurgitation that never quite makes its way all the way up and out. Becky looked like she was having fun playing with the cats. I felt guilty.

"Dinner will be ready shortly." I had the steaks, foil-wrapped potatoes, and mushroom caps all neatly assembled on a cutting board and brought it outside, placing it on the side shelf of the barbeque.

"Can I get another?" Becky asked as she stood, holding up the beer bottle.

"I'll get it."

"Don't bother. I can find it. Besides, you look really cute playing housewife. Fridge, right?"

"Big silver thing in the kitchen. Keeps the stuff cold. That's where you'll find them."

"You want one?"

"Nope, never drink and cook." God, that was bad. I was nervous and my stomach reminded me.

She returned, opening the bottle and tossing the cap on the patio table. Becky had also brought out the cutlery, napkins, dinner rolls, and ketchup. She better not put ketchup on my steaks. That alone is a deal-breaker!

"I didn't know if you wanted ketchup for your potatoes, but brought it out just in case. I can't stand the stuff." Saved!

"How are you holding up?"

I put the foil packs of potatoes on the lower grill and shut the lid.

"Right now, I don't want to even think about it. I bitched at Tom every freaking spring about that bike. Not an 'I told you so!'

type of thing, but the bastard knew the risks. Christ, I can't count the number of times we picked up riders killed on bikes. Most times it's not the rider's fault, but the drivers who can't see the other guy or they can't see the rider." The pitch of my voice was getting high and I was speaking fast. I was pissed and it showed.

"Sorry. I should have known better."

"Hey, shit happens."

The night air was starting to roll in. The sun was low in the sky. Steak bones, a few bits of potatoes and some bread were all that remained of the dinner. Becky had secretly fed the steak fat to Molly and Snickers. The bottle of ketchup remained untouched. Dinner conversation was mellow, friendly, and felt a lot like a first date. The talk stayed clear of anything relating to Tom, Maddy, or the murders. I had actually forgotten all about them. It was nice to have a normal evening for a change. It was a feeling that wouldn't last long.

When the mosquitoes started to gather in the cooler night breeze, the cats went in the house, and we followed their lead. We scooped up the dishes and placed them on the counter. Becky closed the patio door.

"Another beer?" I opened the fridge.

"Two's my limit. Besides, we both have to work in the morning, and you don't want a hungover partner, do you?" I nodded in agreement.

"Question?" I was trying to sound casual.

She looked over as she organized the dishes in the dishwasher.

"Don't bother with those," I instructed.

I raised my left hand and spun my wedding band around with my thumb. A poor attempt to pose a silent question without really asking.

"Yah, I know you were married. Your point?" she quipped.

"Funny!" I gave her the look. I glanced to her left hand. "Yours? And how do you know so much about me?"

Becky took her ring off, opened the cabinet beneath the sink and tossed it in the garbage.

"Dollar store crap. It keeps the unwanted guys and the occasional girls away. I don't need it anymore. I checked you out when we were in the ICU."

My eyebrows went up. I cocked my head to the right. I felt, well, something I hadn't felt in a long time.

"On that note, I gotta go." She gathered her backpack and pulled her car keys from the front pouch. "I left my cell number, home number, and email address by your phone in the living room."

Becky led the way to the front door. I followed. It was after nine, and the western sky was ablaze with a reddish-orange hue, and directly above me, blackness with spots of white light. The stars were in full force. Not a cloud in the sky to cover them. Tomorrow should be beautiful.

She walked casually to her car, pointed her remote and it made that familiar dual beep as it unlocked. She tossed her backpack past the driver's seat onto the passenger seat.

Look back! I thought to myself. It's always a good sign when they look back. It shows interest, or at least that's what I always thought. Then again, Becky threw her "ring" in the garbage and left me her contact information. How much more interest do I want? *Look back, please!* I screamed in my head.

Becky was about to step into the car when she paused, looked back, and smiled.

Got it!

THE DAY STARTED OUT just a little sunnier, coffee tasted just a little better, and my outlook was just a little brighter. I'd had a great time the night before with my new work partner. As much as I liked Becky, I wanted Tom back—but in the short term, Becky was about as good as it was going to get, for work, anyway. In my personal life, only time will tell.

It was a day like any other day working EMS in a large city: calls coming in, switching from one channel to the next as the rigs got deployed or got cleared, off-load delays in the ER, socializing with other medics from surrounding services. Becky and I had our fair share of calls; nothing stood out, no lives were saved.

As we cleared the Civic ER, we got a call for another possible VSA, vital signs absent, patient just north of the hospital. Possibly the same type of call as yesterday.

It was a low-rent building—brownstone, two storeys high, with wooden window frames that should have been repainted in the '70s, cracked concrete front stoop from too much salt over too many winters, clean—or cleaner than I expected. In this job, emergencies are not limited to a social class or neighbourhood.

A middle-aged woman stood inside the doorway, awaiting our arrival. Greek, perhaps, Middle Eastern, it was hard to tell. The sun hit the glass and caused a reflection, making it appear as if I were looking at her face at the bottom of a pool of water. It had to be at least twenty degrees Celsius out, and she wore the cliché slum landlord worn-out, oversized sweater. She opened the door as we exited the vehicle.

"It's about time. I call because man no answer his door and I smell something funny." Her accent was thick, undistinguishable. But she didn't sound like Mrs. Dorcas, who runs my favourite Greek restaurant. So Greek was off the table. Contrary to what

I would have expected for her ethnicity, behind her oversized glasses, she had plucked her eyebrows free of hair and redrawn them on. I've never really quite understood why women do that.

"You smelled something funny?" I asked as we pulled the stretcher out of the rig. Becky smirked.

"Yes, I smell funny." She looked upset with me. "Almost a week, his radio plays. His radio always plays but off at night. No this time."

We entered the small apartment building with bags in hand, the stretcher left at the front steps. Usually, the smell of ethnic cooking is distinct, as new arrivals work to make their lives better and this is all they can afford. It's still better than what they left behind. As Becky and I followed our caller farther down the hall, we both recognized the distinct aroma of death that permeated the hall. It definitely wasn't the cooking.

How this stench could have gone unnoticed by the other tenants until now would remain a mystery. Perhaps they thought that this was just really bad foreign cooking. The landlady continued to lead us, oblivious to the aroma. Perhaps she, too, thought it was just the cooking and had become accustomed to ethnic diversity.

"10–2s?" Becky asked; 10–200 is the code for police assistance required at the scene.

I nodded in agreement.

Becky kept back a few feet, keyed the mike, and spoke softly, requesting police presence.

The landlord turned the key in the knob to the apartment door. As she pushed it slightly inward, the aroma became more pungent, drifting its way hard out the door into the hall. The smell, almost acidic, burned my nose and made my eyes tear up. The landlord turned, put her hands to her mouth, gagged and began to throw up whatever she'd had for breakfast. Her vain attempt to keep the contents in by holding her hands to her mouth, made the vomit spray off in multiple directions between her fingers. She leaned forward, pumping herself up and down as more and more vomit hit the adjacent wall and bare floor.

Odd things to think when something like this happens: first, as the vomit hit the wall, I realized that it needed new paint anyway; second, good thing there wasn't any carpet in the hall; third, the smell of decay overrode the smell of her vomit on the wall, floor and her hands; fourth, you can always tell what a person's last meal was.

As I watched the poor lady lose it, Becky pinched her nose and closed her mouth. I knew better. I always carry a few small packs of Odour Screen. No larger than a flat ketchup pack, I pulled one from my glove holder, tore it open, removed my glove, and swiped a little clear gel under my nose. I put the balance on another finger and walked over to Becky and did the same. The smell of decomposing body and fresh vomit vanished almost immediately. The gel doesn't produce a smell, but it tricks the mind into thinking that everything smells like vanilla. Cool stuff! Becky's eyes widened, amazed at my magic as the smell disappeared.

"For my next magic trick . . . !"

"You're gonna disappear? 10–2s will be here shortly. You want to go and confirm or do you want me to?"

Back to work. The bags were left in the hall. I pushed the door open. The room was dark except for a sliver of light that cut through the darkness from the break in the curtains. I reached down, grabbed my light, and thumbed the switch, adding more light to the room. This was all too familiar. I was reminded of the shooting incident that took place only a few weeks ago. Without looking back, I gave the universal signal to "wait" by putting my left hand down, palm back toward Becky, requesting that she wait in the hall.

"Understood!" I am glad she got the message.

A faint sound of "popping" could be heard in the darkness. The room was small, maybe twelve by twelve. Directly in front of me was a table with framed pictures. Above the table hung worn curtains on a rod that sagged in the middle, thick and opaque, keeping most of the light out except for the gap between the two panels. Music was coming from a radio to my right. I didn't recognize the station or the music. To my left, the popping continued every few seconds or so. I turned my attention to where the sound originated and illuminated the body.

It lay on the sofa, supine, bloated to nearly twice its original size, discoloured, almost black, with miniature volcanoes erupting as gas produced by the body as it decomposed made its way to the surface. My guess was male, from the size of the corpse, facial features, and obvious facial hair (but these days, who knows?). His head rested on the sofa arm, his feet were elevated on the opposing arm. His right arm was hanging down with his hand on the floor. Unless it was suicide or homicide, it looked like he just fell asleep and died.

A decomposing body will produce ammonia in the lungs shortly after death, which diffuses out the nose and mouth. Other gases are produced more slowly, and, as the skin and tissue break down, they take the path of least resistance and "pop" free. The nose and lips were bulbous, fake-looking, cyanotic, skin ripping free as the tissue died. His fingers, now swollen to the point where there were no definitive fingers or thumbs, making his hands look like mittens. If he had rings on, they were long buried under the rotting, swollen flesh.

On the coffee table in front of the sofa, a bowl with what I could only guess had been his last meal of Kraft Dinner, was now growing a lime-green fuzzy mould. By the look of things, if this had been his last meal, he had been dead for a while. Not much to be done for this poor guy.

Outside in the hall, a crowd had begun to gather. Neighbours who earlier had put up with the stench emanating from the apartment wanted to get a peek at the corpse and gossip with the latest news. I found the wallet of Mr. Krzyzowski in the kitchen and was making notes when the police arrived on scene. Two uniformed officers walked down the hall, bowing their heads and pinching their noses.

"A fiver says at least one of them slips on the puke," Becky said without looking up from her notes.

"You're on."

The words were no sooner out of my mouth when the officer on the right slipped and caught himself before tumbling backwards.

"Pay up," she cast a thin smile.

"Hi, guys."

"Hey," a polite, not too sincere greeting from the cops. "So what's the story?"

The other officer was cleaning his shoes.

"We got the call as a possible VSA. Arrived on scene and smelled the patient long before we found him. Landlady unlocked the door. She never went in. Found him on the sofa."

The landlady returned with fresh clothing, the same glasses and her painted-on eyebrows to provide the police with whatever details she could.

"I no like this. This no good. Poor Mr. Krzyzowski. Can I go soon?" she asked one of the cops. Crying makes her accent even thicker.

"Soon, we just need to get more information from you."

The cop who slipped was still wiping vomit from his shoe looked up. "Are you Ethan Tennant?"

"Yeah," I turned toward him.

"Detective Hoese wants to see you now."

"Why?"

"He says they found another body!"

27

THE YELLOW POLICE BARRIER tape was already wrapped from the car in the driveway to the large maple tree in the front yard. The house was located in the corner lot of Arc en Ciel Street, backing onto Gardenway Park, just north of Innes and west of Orchardview Avenue in the east end of Ottawa. Cumberland has grown fast in the past decade, harbouring quaint detached homes on postage-stamp-sized lots with green lawns and few trees. Unlike older sections of most cities, where the streets are straight, either vertically or horizontally, new subdivisions have twisty, rounded streets to prevent traffic from speeding, making it difficult to find any house because the same street name is used multiple times, but end in Street, Avenue, Lane, or Crescent. This neighbourhood was typical of urban planning.

There were at least a half-dozen marked police cruisers and more unmarked cars parked in all different directions, blocking traffic to the scene. Lights were flashing, rotating, and blinking. No other ambulances were on scene. A good indicator that our services were not needed. Neighbours had already milled out onto their manicured lawns, coffee cups or water bottles in hand, taking in the show. Becky pulled the rig over three houses back from the crime scene looking south at the scene.

"Do you mind staying here?" I asked her.

"This is your scene. If you need me, call. Don't let this get to you, okay? I'm just gonna sit here, relax, and watch the men in blue."

"I'll be on portable," meaning I would have the portable radio in case we were needed. Two days and I already I felt comfortable with my new partner. Becky was young but had the soul and maturity of someone much older.

Galen must have pulled some strings to get a Medic Rig removed from service when a patient isn't involved. As soon as the

officer investigating the bloated body call told me that Galen wanted me, dispatch radioed to say we were out of service, and we were
directed here.

Taking it all in, I realized this was a carbon copy of the Brockville crime scene. Uniformed officers on the radio, others taking
notes, people walking in and out of the house, pictures being tak-
en of possible evidence. It was just another page out of the police
handbook on how to run a crime scene. A group of men in suits
stood in a circle at the end of the driveway. As I approached, Galen
broke off and walked toward me. He was wearing his suit jacket.
They must be expecting media soon. Sweat had formed on his
brow. He did not look happy.

"Hey, bud! Sorry to pull you away from work."

"Don't sweat it. I'm not on commission. What's up?" I already
knew the answer.

"Pretty sure we have another one." Galen paused, turned toward the house and started walking.

"*Pretty* sure?" My voice made it clear that I wanted certainty.

"The cross is there!"

We now knew it was a plus sign, but I was not going to argue.

"The house backs onto a park, easy access, easy egress. The
backyard has enough tree coverage to let someone hide while he
waits. The park has a ball field, three tennis courts, and multiple
soccer fields. Someone walking or running through here wouldn't
attract any attention whatsoever. He would look like someone just
enjoying the park."

Galen wiped the sweat from his forehead.

"He had time. The vic's family is out of town. He either got
lucky or he knew."

Galen and I stood at the back of the house overlooking the
park. He wasn't kidding—Gardenway Park is huge. To the south,
soccer nets laid out the boundaries for the two fields. North of the
soccer fields, a baseball diamond; and farther west, three tennis
courts and the Jeanne-Sauvé French elementary school bordered
the field. Galen was right: Anyone walking around the back of the
house wouldn't be given a second look.

"So," I paused, looked at my friend. "You wanted me here because . . . ?" I trailed off.

"You want to see the body?"

"Yours? No!"

A rare smile came to the detective's face. Without a word, he turned and walked back toward the house.

"We have seventeen homicide detectives for the entire city of Ottawa. Maybe ten homicides a year, if that! We have about a dozen cold cases going back twenty years. We can go weeks, sometimes a month or more between homicides. Then you come along. You know what makes this hard?"

Galen stopped dead in his tracks, turned, and looked at me. "Well, do you?"

"I thought it was a rhetorical question."

Galen took a drink from his bottle of water. He was sweating even more now. "Random attacks, no relation to the victims, no motives. The savagery of the attacks escalates with each vic. He's refining his methods, becoming bolder, cares less about getting caught." He finished the water. "No fucking connection to one another. Every lead we've had turns into shit! No connection except you!"

"Me?" My voice rose to show my displeasure. "How the fuck do you figure?"

"He likes you."

"Why?"

"Come with me."

Christ! After all these years in EMS, I thought I'd seen almost everything, but this was more than I would ever have expected. The body was gutted. Not the way a fish gets gutted. Autopsy gutted. Galen and I stood before a male victim who lay on a bed with his arms and legs spread out and tied with cheap yellow plastic rope to the four bed posts. It smelled of feces—strong, pungent, and recent.

The man was naked. Deep grooves were cut into his wrists and ankles as he pulled against the ropes to free himself or squirmed in agony from the torture. His eyes were open, seeing everything that was happening and who stood before him, eyes with a look of sheer terror and pain still visible deep inside. Even more disturbing was the way the killer had gagged the victim.

Seven stitches held the victim's mouth closed. The man had

probably tried to scream and pulled several stitches through his lips. The killer had not used standard sutures but what appeared to be regular heavy sewing thread and tied in a shoelace knot instead of medical suture ties. Whoever did this had had no medical training. Any first-year med student, RNs, and even most paramedics know how to suture properly.

Blood had trickled out where the lips had torn through the sutures as if he had bitten his tongue or blood had come back up and had nowhere to go but out.

From the sternal notch, the semi-circular spot at the top of the sternum, to his crotch, the skin was ripped open. It wasn't a smooth cut like one made with a scalpel, but jagged as if ripped by hand or with a dull knife. The skin lay against itself at the sides torn from the ribs, blood and soft tissue still moist. The abdominal fat looked like tapioca pudding stained red in clumps beside the body and affixed to the skin.

The ribs hadn't been cut like in an autopsy, but snapped out. The assailant had grabbed the sternum and twisted to pull the ribs apart from one another. I could make out faint shoe prints in the blood below his arm pits, where the killer had stood over him and pulled the ribs out.

There were no organs: no heart, no lungs, no liver, no bowels; nothing remained in the chest and abdominal cavity. A small pool of blood was all that remained inside the shell.

The bedspread was stained dark red with blood. The victim had bled quite a bit before he died. The victim had been tortured and possibly gutted while he had still been alive.

"Look here!" A man with thick, dark blue nitrile gloves and protective glasses said. He pulled himself away from a group of men speaking by the bedroom door. A laminated ID card hung from a cord around his neck. All I could make out was the name "Dr. Fielding" beneath his photo. He had disposable Tyvek sleeves that went up above his elbows and Tyvek boot covers. Dr. Fielding lifted a small flap of skin that had covered the victim's crotch. His genitals were missing.

"This is what I suspect was the first cut. The amount of bleeding is heaviest here. He removed his scrotum and penis. The cuts were fast and not with a sharp instrument. There were no hesitation marks, he just grabbed, lifted and severed, and removed. No hesitation marks. He thought about this, planned it all in advance, wanted to do it, and executed it. Dull knife or tool, it will take some time to determine what was used."

Dr. Fielding pointed to several locations inside the cavity.

"He knew where to cut, how to hold the skin, how to make cuts to remove the skin from the ribs, how to remove the organs. He had some knowledge, like a butcher, not a doctor. Maybe he was schooled or maybe he watched too many YouTube videos. Either way, he took his time and knew what he was doing. It would have taken time, at least an hour or more, possibly two."

"We are checking the whereabouts of his family, neighbours, who saw him last. The uniforms should have something by the end of the day." Galen didn't look as hopeful as he sounded.

"Where are his organs?" I looked at the doctor.

"Bathtub! Follow the blood trail from the other side of the bed to the bathroom."

From the left side of the bed to the bathroom, several trails of blood could be seen on the dark brown carpet. Little numbered yellow cones plotted the blood path. A lighter carpet colour would have revealed the true horror of the trail going back and forth from the bed to the tub. Hiding bloodstains was probably never a factor when the victim was choosing dark brown carpeting.

Galen followed me to the en suite bathroom. The scent of feces was strongest here. Techs were inside the room, taking photos and notes. One look from Galen and the two techs simply walked out. Dr. Fielding was behind Galen, describing what he thought was the timeline for the death.

". . . and if you noticed on the way to the bathroom, multiple trips were made. All the organs are in the tub."

The tub was the depository for the removed organs: heart, lungs, liver, bowels, all were easily distinguishable. I now knew what an animal slaughterhouse floor must look like.

I turned to Galen. "You said he likes me. You still haven't shown me why."

Slowly, methodically, purposely done for effect, he closed the bathroom door. Dr. Fielding, Galen, and I were forced to step deeper into the bathroom. As the door closed, revealing the message drawn on the back of the bathroom door, in dark red blood, my name was written in large, bold letters. Capital "E," all others were in lower case. The tool, whatever it was, that had been used to write my name was saturated with blood. Each letter had prominent drip marks down the wall. The blood in the letters had dried to a crusty hard shell. At the end of each drip a tiny dried bubble of blood had formed. Beneath my name was what we had thought was an inverted cross but had come to realize was actually a plus sign. The plus sign was identical to the ones seen at the other murders.

"This guy is unique. No two murders are the same, not the method used, not the way he displays the bodies, what he does with them. Nothing! If it wasn't for you linking the victims to the newspaper picture and the murderer letting you tag along for the ride, we would be up the proverbial creek." Galen paced, knowing full well that if something weren't done soon, the shit storm of all time would be coming down on him. Galen had tremendous pressure being placed upon him and it showed in the way he looked and his stance. Galen was not used to failure.

The doc broke the silence. We were all feeling the tension.

"We think he may have used one of the organs to write your name on the door."

I looked closer. The contour of the letters did not show any striations or pattern to indicate a glove or piece of material being used. The texture was smooth, not a brush, a single plane across the entire letter.

"Which organ did he use to write with?"

I looked over at Dr. Fielding, thinking there would be a science or "ology" of blood-writing.

"It could be anything in the tub. If you grab the organ, hold it tight and use it like a rag soaked in paint, you would get the same effect except for the texture of the blood."

Dr. Fielding walked over to the tub and peered in. He may have been looking for the writing instrument in question to see if there were visible signs to indicate which was used.

"Once we get everything back to the lab, we may have to send it all to Toronto for a proper autopsy. This is way above my pay grade."

Galen and I joined Dr. Fielding looking into the tub. It didn't take long for me to notice.

"Do you guys notice anything missing?" I turned and looked at each of them.

"Missing?"

"Reconstruct the anatomy."

"I don't know the first thing about this stuff. The only thing I know is what liver and onions are supposed to look like." Galen walked out of the bathroom.

"Doc, complete the puzzle! Part of the trachea and the oesophagus is attached to the left lung. The right lung is partially seen there under the section of bowel." I pointed. "The stomach, heart, liver . . . some have lacerations but are whole and intact."

Dr. Fielding took over. "The small bowel coming off the stomach, duodenum, jujenum, ilium; there must be, what, sixteen feet there, in total. We will know more once we clean out the tub. The bowels must be cut and feces leaked out. That accounts for the smell."

"What's missing?"

"What? I don't think any . . ." The doctor's words trailed off.

"His genitals!" he exclaimed.

"Doc, would you be able to bite your tongue with a rag stuffed in your mouth?"

We looked at each other and walked quickly over to the man lying exposed on the bed.

Galen had been eavesdropping.

"You don't think?"

The doctor carefully placed himself over the victim's head and began carefully cutting each suture. The man's lips remained tightly shut. The dried blood between his lips now acted as a bonding agent to keep his mouth closed. Gradually, with the precision of a surgeon, the sutures were convinced to give way. The thread was pulled out from the upper lip and as he withdrew the thread, it disappeared from the lower lip then hid inside his mouth and reappeared as the long black thread finally gave way through the upper lip. Once all the sutures were removed and bagged as evidence, the doctor pried the lips open enough to visualize his entire mouth. You could see the white strip of rag that had been inserted into his mouth. Using forceps and skill, the rag was pulled out and placed into another evidence bag. Dr. Fielding placed his head over the mouth and looked in. One of the techs who had been following the procedure handed the doctor a small flashlight without being asked to.

"Look inside!"

No one was surprised. The testicles and scrotum were visible. How much had been pushed further down would be revealed in the autopsy. The man had had his genitals cut off, stuffed in his mouth and had been gutted like a salmon at the fish market.

"Name?" I asked Galen quietly.

"You already know, don't you? Terrence Russell, one of the guys from the crash photo. Surprised?"

"Not in the least."

28

ETHAN WALKED AWAY from the ambulance toward a group of men standing on the front lawn. All the men wore suits and ties, shirts open at the collar, ties pulled loose. *Typical!* Becky thought. *No women in that little group yet!*

She watched Ethan as he joined the group and then he and a larger man broke off and walked around to the back of the house. A sense of pride, joy, and a whole lot of "like" formed inside her as she thought of Ethan being held in such high regard by the Ottawa Police.

Becky pulled her cell from her shirt pocket. Finally she had time to text Allison Beckett.

OMG he is so hot
 ?
 ethan
 him? Nash? Last night fun? Did u go home? details
 yes him he hates Nash & I went home
 so?
 who knows? time will tell
 like?
 Ya! big time
 what about your "ring"?
 trashed
 no more man bashing?
 just no Ethan bashing
 call me after shift. I want all the details

It was nice having a new male "friend." Until yesterday, that dollar store ring had been on her finger for a reason. That reason was nothing more than a distant memory now. Becky couldn't remember the last time she had fallen so hard or so fast after just meeting a guy. She pocketed the phone, stepped out of the truck, and leaned on the hood. The radio was turned up, Ethan had the portable, and the bus was out of service until further notice. Now Becky had nothing to do but wait, enjoy the light-blue sky, the warm weather, and the comings and goings of the police. The neighbours who had gathered were now sitting comfortably in lawn chairs, talking among themselves or with cell phones pressed hard to their ears.

Becky loosened one button on her shirt, tugged on the collar to force the shirt open just a little more, closed her eyes, tilted her head back, and felt the warm sun on her face. She pulled her sunglasses down from her ball cap and adjusted them to cover her eyes.

A really cold beer, sand, palm trees, a tropical breeze, guys in Speedos, and this would be perfect! she thought to herself.

The sun was hot—not just hot, but intense. Standing beside the ambulance, Becky looked skyward; the heat from the midday sun was welcome. Becky was twenty-seven years old, divorced, just starting a new career, and had met a really nice guy in the first month on the job. Becky had stayed away from dating in her two years of college. It wasn't that she hadn't been asked out several times. Each time, she'd given a polite "Thank you, but . . . !" The guys asking her out had seen the tacky band on the left fourth finger, but they'd asked anyway. To Becky, that said a lot about the ones asking. The constant refusals had given her a reputation as a bitch. At first, Becky had despised the small talk, the quiet looks from classmates, but later she came to realize being ostracized meant more alone time to study, work, and be accountable for her choices in life. She had responsibilities, a mortgage she couldn't afford, parents helping with the bills, and a part-time job as a server at Swiss Chalet. Her ex had requested full custody of their son, and she'd conceded. Marriage had been and still remained her biggest regret in life. For two years, that dime-store ring had been on her finger, turning her finger green, forcing her to spend another two dollars for a new one every few months.

All that was behind her now; a new chapter had begun. One date and only two shifts with Ethan Tennant, and she was hooked! Two days! Becky had known nothing about Ethan prior to these two shifts and now she wanted to know more. She was happy. She smiled: the sun was hot on her skin, and the day was good. No plan had been formulated, no scheming, it had been just circumstance that had brought them together, and she was going to take it slow.

Eyes closed, she heard the buzzing of chatter, neighbours talking about the crime scene, police radio volumes up a bit too high, EMS dispatch coming from the rig. Becky paid no attention to the chatter. It was nothing but background noise.

"Excuse me!" Becky didn't hear the woman speaking until she felt the tap on her shoulder.

Becky turned, startled, returning to reality! She gave a weak smile, trying to hide her embarrassment for being so lost in thought. The older lady before her looked a little scared, panic on her face, and fear in her eyes. Calmly, Becky laid a hand on the lady's shoulder.

"What's the matter?" she asked gently.

"Are you with the other medic?" She glanced beyond Becky over to where the police stood in front of the house.

"Yes, but he is busy right now. Can I help you?"

"My daughter fell, and it really doesn't require an ambulance. It's a small cut, but since you're here . . ." her words trailed off.

"Sure, let me get my bag." Becky hopped into the back of the rig, grabbed the small trauma bag, and followed the woman. Becky had the second portable radio and knew if she called it in, she would have to complete paperwork on the call. Besides, a quick cleanup, apply a Band-Aid, and her Good Samaritan work was done. The panicked lady said nothing, walked quickly, and did not look back. Her actions took Becky by surprise, but everyone reacts differently, she thought.

"This way, please!" the woman directed, turning to make sure Becky was behind her.

"I'm right behind you!"

Just three houses north of the police investigation, the lady turned, walked around the garage, and went to the back of the house. Becky followed. The lady turned again and entered through the back door of the garage. She took a few steps into the darkness and turned. Sunlight poured into the darkness from behind

Becky's back and lit the woman inside the garage as she stood in front of the car. She stood, chest heaving, head bowed, tears on her cheek.

"I'm so sorry!"

"Sorry?"

Becky didn't feel the blow, falling to the ground unconscious.

He placed Becky in the trunk of the car, retrieving her cell phone from her shirt pocket. He removed the battery and placed the phone under the rear wheel of the car. He taped her hands behind her back, wrapped duct tape several times around her mouth, making sure her nose was free of any obstruction. He wanted her alive, not dead—yet! He had plans for her.

"I will call you in fifteen minutes to tell you where your daughter is. She is safe. She means nothing to me. Don't call the police. Don't say anything to anyone. The police will know soon enough," he instructed the distraught woman.

"You promised you wouldn't hurt her if I helped you. You'll keep that promise?" The older woman was crying so hard, she was panting as she spoke. She could feel herself shaking.

"I promise."

He got in the car, positioned his seat, pulled the seat belt across and pressed the remote to the garage door opener. *Attract as little attention as possible*, he thought to himself. Looking through the back window making sure the driveway was clear, he put the car in reverse and rolled out to the street.

Before him stood the woman, crying and shaking, staring down at the crushed remains of Becky's cell phone on the floor of the garage. The garage door closed, with his reluctant accomplice staring at him, wiping tears away with the back of her hand as he pulled away with the police in his rear-view mirror.

GALEN AND I WALKED from the house. You could tell he was taking heat over the murders. Two familiar faces turned and watched Galen and me walk down the driveway. Mueller and Constantine, my two lunch dates from Brockville, stared silently. Pressure was surely being applied to Galen. If I could help a friend, I would in any way possible.

Serial killers in the city of Ottawa are as rare as an honest politician in this town. Who knows whether these actions were random, a sick reason to kill simply because people stood around to watch someone die, or for some unknown cause that meant something to someone in a world all his own? A world apart from ours!

Galen led me to his car. A simple nod indicated that he wanted me to join him inside it. The air inside the car was suffocating. The sun had heated the interior to well over forty degrees Celsius. He turned the key, and immediately the air conditioning started blasting through the vents. Heat must be hard on people of Galen's size. Galen pulled hard on his tie, the one end sliding free and around his neck, then tossed it into the back seat. If that tie had had any weight to it, it would have gone through the back window.

"You okay?" Galen was concerned for me.

"Me? You're asking me if I'm okay?"

"You've had a lot of personal shit going on. Mine is all work. I can live with it." Galen put his head back on the headrest, took in a deep breath, and blew it out with pursed lips.

"What's your gut telling you on this? Does he have any medical background or is he self-taught?" he asked.

"If I was doing this, and I had the time, I would have done a better job. Maybe he is smarter than we are, maybe he really does know what he is doing and botched the job to make it look like it was an amateur. Maybe he doesn't know what he is doing and that was the best he could do. Who the fuck knows, Galen? He has killed so many people and each one was different. Based on that alone, I don't think he has any experience slicing people up."

I was rambling and I knew it, but like Galen, I was feeling the pressure, too.

"You know, if I don't close this fast, the RCMP will be taking over. I was already hauled in and raked over the coals for not getting any results. I have until week's end to find the guy, get a solid lead, or hand it over. I have two Mounties already reviewing my case documents. It's like college all over. Everything I did, do, call, staple, copy, file, or interview is being looked at to see if I screwed up. They expect suspects to be categorized, analyzed, organized into neat piles; and everyone is supposed to have a reason for what they do. Sometimes, people just do it. No reason. Just, well, because! They are making me feel like I screwed up. Me, screw up a case?"

How do you console a friend? If it was a woman, you would lay your hand on her shoulder, change your tone, remain calm, and give reassurance. A guy, you say nothing; silence is the preferred option. If we'd been having this conversation at my house, I would have grabbed another beer for the both of us. If Galen could get off the case, I would suggest it.

Two uniformed officers were holding back an obviously distraught woman. Galen and I were in the car, engine running, A/C blowing hard, but we could still hear her shouting. Even restrained, she continued to shout and kept pointing at me, yelling my name.

One of the uniformed officers turned, looked at Galen for direction. Galen killed the engine, and we exited the vehicle simultaneously. Galen walked over; I stayed behind the open door for protection. I really should start wearing a vest and carrying protection. Galen met with the woman and waved me over frantically.

"You have to pick her up now!" The woman was yelling, out of breath, but finally calming down.

I walked slowly over. Looking around, gauging my options. What was she talking about? Pick her up? Pick who up?

"He released my daughter, but he has your partner. I'm so sorry. I had to help him! He had my daughter!"

I turned, looked at the rig. Becky wasn't in the passenger seat. I ran. I broke the yellow barrier tape and felt a burst of more adrenaline than I had ever felt before. Even in this heat, the hot wave of adrenaline pulsed through me, down my legs, up my spine and into my brain. I ran faster than I ever had run before. I pushed through the crowd that had gathered. Some of the crowd fell backward, some were caught by others who were standing close by, and others gave way.

As I approached the rig, I noticed that no one was in the cab, so I darted to the side door. The door was still open; no one inside.

"I tried to tell you. He has your partner! He took her from my house!" The woman had followed me as best she could. She was yelling from several yards away. Galen couldn't keep up, let alone breathe in this weather.

"Which house?" The question was obvious. She pointed. I ran to the house with the open garage door.

Too much TV and not enough practical training directed my moves. I ran up to the house, stopped with my back against the brick facing the street. The garage door was to my left. A quick look inside the garage revealed no car, just silence.

"I told you, he left my house about fifteen minutes ago." She was out of breath, panting, hands to her knees. "He put her in the trunk." She paused to catch her breath. "He called to tell me where my daughter was, told me to come and get you and gave my daughter the cell phone and drove away." She started crying again. "I am so sorry!"

Galen finally arrived with several uniformed officers in tow. Galen looked like he was going to be my next patient.

"I already called 911 and told the dispatcher what happened and gave my daughter's location. They are sending someone to pick her up." She looked at me, guilt filling her eyes, knowing that her actions may have saved her daughter but put Becky at risk. "I had no choice."

Galen pulled his cell phone, flipped it open, and pushed the autodial for his office. "Did you see him drive away?"

"I was in the garage when he put that girl medic in my trunk!"

Galen and I looked at each other in amazement.

"Your trunk?" Galen spoke first.

"Yes, he hit her so hard, she fell. He taped her up and threw her in the trunk of my car."

"I need your plate number, colour, make and model of your car." Galen turned toward me. "Can you call Becky's cell and see if we can lock on to her GPS signal?"

"On it!" I hadn't even put my hand in my pocket when the woman interrupted.

"He took her cell phone, removed the battery, and drove over her cell." She pointed. "See, it's there."

Galen stood over the remains of the crushed mobile. He scanned the parts. "You said he took out the battery?" She nodded in agreement. "I don't see it."

"He tossed it to the side." She pointed again. "See, it's there." She bent over to pick it up.

"No, no, no, no, no!"

The woman stopped mid-reach. Galen was definitely getting his point across. "Don't touch anything, please." He nodded to the uniforms. They understood and turned to get forensics involved.

"Was he wearing gloves when he abducted the medic or took the battery out?"

"No, I don't think so," she said, paused, closing her eyes. "Definitely not!"

Galen and I looked at each other again.

"He also had trouble with the duct tape and flung a piece that stuck to his fingers." She pointed to the other side of the garage. This time she pointed and didn't move.

With the patience of a saint, Galen visually inspected where he was about to step, took the step then repeated. Once he found the tape, he got down on all fours, looked closely and smiled. On his hands and knees, he looked at me. "I guess the Mounties will have to wait to take over my case. I think I see a print."

The woman's daughter, Ashley, was returned safely home by a cruiser shortly afterward. Galen had phoned in the information on the car that held Becky hostage in the trunk. Galen assured me that with the high profile of this case, every cruiser on the street would be looking for that car.

My hands were tied. I couldn't go after Becky—I didn't know where to look, what my first move would be. It was best if I stayed with Galen.

Ashley seemed fine. Her mother, on the other hand, seemed a wreck. The three of us sat in the living room with Diet Cokes while the mother sat in the kitchen and had a good cry.

"Ashley, I need to ask you a few questions. Is that okay?" Galen was full of fresh energy. Finally there was a break in the investigation. You could see it in his attitude.

Ashley sipped from the can. "Sure, anything to help." Kids! Ashley didn't appear fazed at all by her recent abduction.

"Can you tell me what happened?"

"I stopped by the store to pick up a pack of smokes." Ashley looked all of twelve, with too much makeup and too much attitude. "You won't tell my mom, right?" Another sip. "Anyway, I bought a pack, went around to the back of the store to light one up when this guy walked around the back toward me. I got a little nervous at first, but then he walked right past. Then, like he just changed his mind, he stopped, turned around, and asked to bum a smoke. I gave him one; he lit it, and started to walk away again. I didn't even feel it. He turned and hit me really fucking hard on the side of the head."

Ashley paused to rub her head behind her left ear. "I didn't black out or anything, but it felt like when I drink too much beer. I fell down, he picked me up, and threw me in the back of his van and used some tape to tie me up. Next thing I know, he unties me and drops me off at some corner downtown."

"Did he put the cigarette in his mouth?"

"Duh? How else do you light up?"

"DNA!" Galen was even more enthusiastic. "Can you take me to the store to see if we can find his butt?"

"Sure, as long as you don't tell my mom I smoke."

"At this point, I don't think she would care," I broke in.

Galen's mobile rang. He flipped it open, stood, and walked about the room.

"They found the car abandoned. The guys in white suits are towing it in to go over it and see if they can pull anything off it."

Galen knew what I wanted to hear.

"No sign of Becky?"

He shook his head and snapped his phone shut. It rang again almost immediately. Galen opened the phone and before he could say anything, his eyes lit up, concern took control of his expression. He put a single index finger across his lips. I understood; Ashley was lost in her own little world.

Galen listened intensely, saying nothing. He paced around the room and as quickly as the call started, it was over.

"What?"

"It was him!" Galen sat down. "He took Becky to prove his point. He took her because she was your partner today. It's his way of controlling you, showing you who's in charge."

"What did he do to her?"

"He said she is alive and gave me the address where she is."

I stood up, kicking the chair back a few inches.

"Let's go."

"Ethan, he said he did it because he can get to you anytime, anywhere. He told me to tell you." Galen looked right at me. "You're next!"

30

BECKY WAS SLEEPING, sedated, attached to a monitor to check her vitals, with an IV running. The police were adamant that she be placed in the ICU until she was released. The ICU was secure, a card key required to gain access or have someone buzz you in. There is a secure wing for prisoners, but Galen knew I wouldn't allow it. In the room next to Becky, Tom was still hooked up and monitored.

Tom had shown some positive signs. He had opened his eyes this morning and blinked to indicate he knew where he was. The neurologist was hopeful. That was the neurologist's way of saying that he was keeping his fingers crossed.

There was little I could do. In one bed lay my best friend, in the other my newest friend. I felt helpless and angry. More angry than anything. I needed to do something now. Galen was at the nurses' desk taking up a chair and a phone. Two uniformed officers stood guard, one outside Becky's room, one at the main door, each facing the other. I'm sure this was not their perception of their ideal posting.

Despite all the events that have taken place in the past few weeks, I wasn't that upset. It's as if I had reached a new plateau of tolerance. You build up immunities to one level, then the next, until there comes a time when you can handle anything or are simply numbed by the things happening in your life, and nothing matters.

My thoughts were broken by the sound of a phone being slammed down hard and Galen shouting out obscenities. The two cops on sentry duty looked over but remained at their posts. The ICU is analogous to a library: You go about your business, but remain quiet for the benefit of others.

"We have a mole!" Despite the air conditioned temperature in the ICU, beads of sweat formed on Galen's brow and nose.

"A mole?"

"I have to find a God damned computer. We made the front page."

"That was to be expected, right? We had a dozen cruisers, a coroner's van, EMS, forensics, and God knows what else you guys had at the scene today. Of course reporters are going to write about it."

"That's not what I'm talking about." Galen clicked away at the keyboard. "They figured out the pattern to the murders. They know we have a serial killer." It didn't take long to pull up the newspaper website with the abridged article from the front page.

Serial Killer in Our City?

A recent homicide in the city this morning has been linked to several unsolved murders.

The city of Ottawa has experienced more homicides in the past few weeks than all of last year combined. A source who wishes to remain nameless, but with close ties to the team tasked to solve these horrendous crimes, says that another killing this morning is most likely by the same person responsible for up to five currently unsolved murders.

Without providing details, the serial killer uses the same MO for each victim. Our source would not reveal the patterns noticed by police, but says it was easy to link this killing to the others.

The Ottawa Police Department has so far refused to confirm or deny any reports of a serial killer in the city. Calls to several departments within the force say that all questions must be handled through the public relations department. The PR department, meanwhile, has not returned any calls.

For full details, please pick up a copy of the Ottawa Sun at your local stands now on sale.

The newspaper website had chosen a particularly large font for the title, bright colours, and given it status on the front page of the site.

Galen was beside himself with rage. Someone on his team was talking to the press, and that just compounded his problems.

"They left your name out. That's good, I guess. Either our leak has enough common sense not to say too much or he's a fucking moron. He's dead when I find him."

"Did you have a chance to talk to Becky before they sedated her?" a quick change of topic.

"She was still tied and gagged when we got to her. Didn't see a thing. Poor girl is scared shitless. First thing she asked for was you! She wanted to make sure you were okay. Gutsy kid! You know how to pick them. Maddy was just as strong-willed, wasn't she?"

I chose not to respond. There were a few moments of silence.

"Has EMS brass called you in yet?"

"Funny you should ask. Does someone from your office know how to pull strings really well?"

"Why?"

"Apparently, without speaking to me, I have EMS bosses telling me I have their full and complete co-operation and understanding. I am on paid leave to assist with the investigation. Officially, they are calling it," I fingered the quote signs, " 'Stress Leave.'

"I was pulled aside in the ER on my way up here, and they whispered it to me, told me not to tell anyone, and walked away. Very Mulder and Scully, don't you think?"

"It didn't come from me. What does come from me is your tail. Whatever you decide your next move is, you have a shadow, so try not to lose him."

"Me?" I was shocked. "Why me?"

"The killer said, and I quote: 'You're next!' In my book, 'You're next!' pretty much tells me your ass is being watched. And if we can catch him watching you and put an end to this, so much the better."

"Who's my tail?"

"Not telling. If you don't know who he or she is, you won't give them away."

"Great!" I commented with eyebrows raised. I wasn't happy, and Galen knew it.

I snuck into Tom's room to see if there had been any positive changes. His ICU nurse followed me in and told me that the doctor had been in earlier, and they would be doing more tests later. I really wished Tom knew that I was there to see him. Medics had been in constantly to see him since the accident. Their visits would slowly diminish until no one came—unless, of course, he got better. At least they were still stopping by.

Becky was another story. She was in a sedated sleep, traumatized by my ruthless "fan." I looked at her and realized that Maddy and Becky were polar opposites in appearance: Maddy had short, blonde hair and was tall. Becky has long, brown hair and is quite a bit shorter. Maddy wine, Becky beer. I realized that I knew almost nothing about this girl but I felt genuine concern and anger at what he did to her.

I stepped out of the ICU cubicle. Galen was still at the desk.

"Galen, I need a few things."

* * *

The drive home on the Queensway was slow, as is usual for an afternoon. Drivers were blinded by the sun as it hung high in the west. I had pulled the car's visor down, but even with my sunglasses on, I had to squint. The radio was silent. I was not in the mood for music of any kind. I tapped the steering wheel, not out of frustration due to traffic, but because my mind was going through details. Did I miss something; did we overlook a tiny little clue? Galen's team of investigators had been thorough. The forensics team had gone through every inch of that house. Galen was going to let me know if a positive match came back on the latent print on Becky's cell phone battery and discarded duct tape.

A separate team had gone down to the convenience store and picked up hundreds of cigarette butts to match the brand and see if DNA was possible. Once they narrowed it down to the right cigarette, it could still take weeks or even months to get a DNA profile. Unless someone pulled strings again?

I kept looking in my rear-view mirror for a black sedan with tinted windows with a guy in a black suit, short haircut, and an earpiece, tailing me. Regardless of what I did, what lane I chose, how I varied my speed, I couldn't make out my tail. Not unless Galen was bullshitting me to keep me in tow.

I stopped off at the grocery store, picked up some much-needed essentials for my fridge, which had been neglected in the past few weeks, along with some litter and cat food. I also picked up a can of tuna and a can of salmon, Maddy's special treats for Snickers and Molly when she felt they needed a little extra attention. I can't even remember the last time I scooped the litter box. Thank God for the cat door in the patio door. Even in the grocery store parking lot, I failed to spot my tail. Galen was definitely bullshitting me.

Pulling into the driveway, I killed the engine, only to have the smell of barbeques in the neighbourhood overwhelm my senses. What a great idea! Bending over to retrieve the bags from the passenger seat, I realized that wasn't a barbeque that I smelled. That was wood burning! I dropped the bags and looked up at my house. Nothing! I looked around the neighbourhood. Nothing! Leaving the car door open, I ran up to the front door, unlocked it, and ran inside. The smell was stronger now, and thin, white smoke was visible upstairs.

Maddy had me put in a wireless phone extension inside the front foyer. I picked it up to call 911. The phone had power, but no dial tone. I let the phone fall to the floor. My cell was in my car. My police tail or one of my neighbours would smell and see the fire and call 911 for me. At least I hoped they would.

"Molly!" I looked around. "Snickers!" I called out. Again, I expected a verbal reply. No sight of them anywhere. I ran to the patio door off the kitchen. If the glass patio door was open as it usually is, the cats would use the cat door in the screen. The patio door was shut and locked. My mind raced with events of this morning's routine; did I close it? Did I? Instinctively, I always leave it open in the summer. Maybe today I changed my habit. I grabbed the handle of the glass patio door and pulled hard. It wouldn't budge. I fumbled, fingers getting in the way of other fingers trying to get the lock open. It was broken or jammed. The dining room chair was solid wood and heavy and made a thunderous crash as glass shattered outward onto the stone patio. The screen was shredded by the glass and the door fell off its track. I felt the rush of fresh air force its way into the room. I pushed the dining room set away from the door to give the cats a free run outside.

"Ethan?" Someone was yelling for me. I didn't recognize the voice. My surveillance?

"In the kitchen! I can't find the fire, can you?" I yelled back in a panic.

"Just get the hell out of the house. I already called it in."

I ignored his command.

I kept the fire extinguisher inside the kitchen cabinet. I can't remember the last time I checked to make sure it was still charged. Maddy was the one who hated fire and put extinguishers and smoke detectors everywhere in the house. It hit me just then that none of the smoke detectors had gone off.

There were only a few things that really mattered to me, the cats and our wedding album. I'd given the cats their chance. I just hope they'd take the hint. In a panic, it would be next to impossible to find them both.

With the five-pound extinguisher in hand, I took the stairs two at a time. The smoke got only slightly thicker and darker as I got closer to it. Option one: get the wedding album and leave. Option two: find the source and see what I could do. Visibility was still good, take option two. I know a little about backdrafts or flashovers. So with what knowledge I had from speaking to firefighters and watching movies, I looked to see which door presented with the most smoke emanating from the room. The second bedroom had more than wisps of smoke coming from the end of the hall. Its door, like that of the third bedroom, was supposed to be closed. Today the door was open.

I bent low, gulped as much fresh air as possible and stepped in. Like a child walking into the dentist for the first time not knowing what to expect, I was greeted with my metal garbage can billowing smoke that was spiralling upward resembling a white contained cyclone. Oddly, there was little heat.

I pulled the safety pin, stood back and swept the white powder from the extinguisher. Not wanting to put too much pressure on the can for fear it would fall over, I gauged my movements on the diminishing smoke. Within seconds, the extinguisher sputtered, spit out its last bit of powder and died. I have been living in this house for years and I can't remember where we keep the upstairs fire extinguisher.

I ran out into the hall and almost pulled the linen closet door from its hinges. Blindly reaching in to the left corner, my mind told me that's where it should be. Sheets and pillow cases fell from the upper shelves blocking my view. Hard, find something hard!

My hand scraped along the handle, I felt the skin pull and open against the metal. Pulling on it, sheets sprang up into my face as I turned and headed back into the bedroom.

I repeated my slow, methodical sweeps, layering the garbage can with white powder. Slowly, the smoke faded until the can was just an out-of-place receptacle in my bedroom.

Sirens could be heard in the distance, getting closer. I really needed to thank my shadow. I opened windows, every window upstairs I could find, then sat on the top step and waited for the fire department to arrive. My heart raced, sweat flowed freely. I was nauseated and tired. I put my arms back and looked up. The smoke detector at the top of the steps was open, the cover hung down from the hinge. After years of marriage, one thing I did learn was to change the batteries in the detectors twice a year. Someone had tampered with the smoke detectors, no doubt the same person who had lit a smoke bomb in my garbage can.

Sirens could be heard outside the house. The air brakes were applied, the siren turned off, and footsteps and voices could be heard downstairs. I stood and went to greet my visitors.

31

THE FIREFIGHTERS had done their job, inspecting the whole house, ensuring it was liveable, despite the broken patio door. All the smoke detectors had had their batteries removed and the batteries had been stacked neatly on the vanity in the downstairs bathroom. Whoever had set off the smoke bomb had followed some crude instructions and the technique indicated a homemade device. Homemade or not, it was effective at scaring me.

Galen sat across from me in the living room. Silence followed for several minutes as he waited for the fire guys to leave. The situation was going from bad to worse, the timeline was escalating, events were unfolding in unpredictable ways, and the police could not guarantee my safety. My surveillance guy had found Molly and Snickers outside and they were now running about the house, sniffing the new scents of the visitors who had been there. Fortunately, the smoke bomb wouldn't leave any lasting burnt smells in the house. All the damage to the house was what I had done when I walked in.

"You are undoubtedly the luckiest son-of-a-bitch I have ever met."

"Lucky?" I pointed at my chest. "Me?"

"How many people get to run into a burning building and play hero as they try to put the fire out, only to have no damage. Mind you, of course, your house wasn't actually on fire!" Pale attempt at humour.

"I should play my lucky numbers tonight," I returned.

A uniformed officer walked in with a pizza box, laid it on the coffee table and left. I looked up at Galen, puzzled. I couldn't possibly eat right now. An hour ago, I was buying groceries to make dinner and now the thought of food nauseated me. Galen reached down, flipped open the pizza box, and pulled a slice. The smell was too intoxicating. Nauseated or not, I was hungry and grabbed a slice and dug in.

"So," he swallowed, "prints came back already with a prelim report. Nothing so far." Another bite. "If we don't get a hit, we are running it cross country and asking the U.S. for help to see if they have anything. DNA is another story. That will take a while, and we already know that, so don't hold your breath."

Three bites and the slice was done. Galen tossed the crust into the pizza box and took another slice.

"You throw away the best part."

"Take it if you want." Galen barely chewed his food. Inefficient use of time for a police officer, he always said.

"I got that favour you asked for. I'll bring it in before I leave." Second slice done and crust tossed in the box. Galen started to inhale his third slice. I was still on my first slice.

"Any report back on the autopsy of Russell?"

"Not much they could do. The poor bastard was already gutted and COD would be next to impossible to determine. They didn't find anything yet in toxicology, but they will keep looking."

"Becky?"

"There really isn't anything wrong medically. She is staying in the hospital overnight, then heading out of town to stay with a relative, one that will be hard to track down. We hope! And, you are not permitted to communicate with her until this is over. Becky did ask me to tell you that she will call you when she is ready. Be patient, okay, buddy?" Galen knew I was going to ask that.

"Our next step is . . . ?"

"Follow our leads. Do some digging? We've got one report of someone seeing a stranger walking a dog in the park behind the house around three in the morning. The guy didn't come forward until he saw the paper because he doesn't live there."

I tossed a puzzled look.

"The guy is banging his boss's wife. He knows the guy's schedule, so he goes over for a few hours late at night when the boss is out of town, lays one on the wife, and makes it to work for nine. The house is only four or five down from Russell's, and when he parked his car and walked around the back, he saw this guy walking the dog. It's a corgi. Not many corgis out there."

"What's so unusual about walking your dog at night?"

"This guy knows the dog. He said he sees a guy walking that same dog quite a bit. So seeing the same dog being walked by another guy got his attention. He is being co-operative as long as we keep silent as to why he was there. I'll keep you posted."

"Galen," I drew a deep breath, "I don't get this at all." I tried to formulate the sequence of questions in my mind.

"The victims have no connection to one another?" Galen shook his head side to side.

"There is no personal relationship to the victims?" Same side to side motions again.

"There is no timeline to follow before or after an event that lead to the killings?" He repeated the same movement.

"Random attacks on random people with no connection to one another?" Galen's head moved up and down instead of side to side.

"You honestly have no clue what your next step is?" Up and down.

"So bait me!"

Galen sat upright and put his elbows to his knees.

"Bait me! I've got an idea."

Later that night, the police had called a press conference to inform the public that they had a solid lead and asked for the public's assistance in finding the suspect.

Before eleven that night, Galen, his team, and I sat around the police station looking over photos of various crime scenes trying to find a common thread, a common reason, a common method to the killings. It was the randomness of the killings, no two alike, no two ways of killing the same, that made for a difficult profile.

"Do you play poker?" The question was out of place and caught me off guard.

I looked at Galen, puzzled.

"Why do you ask?"

"Well, do you?"

"Very, very badly."

"You have to join us when this is all over and lose money."

"Who is 'us'?"

"You have to wait and see. Besides, there's no guarantee you'll make it out alive if your plan fails."

The eleven o'clock news started. That was all it took for everyone to stop what they were doing and pay attention to the flat screen on the wall. The news anchor did her usual world reports of war, unrest, and political turmoil before the local news.

"On the local front, police have confirmed that several murders in Ottawa and possibly one in Brockville may be related and may have been committed by a single individual. The uniqueness of each of these crimes is making it unusually difficult for the police to narrow down their list of suspects. Detective Galen Hoese of the Ottawa Police Service states that they are closing in on the suspect, but need the public to come forward with more information. With more on this story, we are joined by Elly Potts."

The camera panned left to another reporter sitting at the desk. Her name appeared in large, bold, white letters on a contrasting blue banner at the bottom of the screen, along with her email address.

"I had a chance to speak with the lead detective in this case after the gruesome find of a body in the west end of Ottawa early this morning," she stated.

They cut away to scenes of Arc en Ciel Street, with concerned neighbours standing along the east side of the street, watching as the police conducted their investigation. The camera panned right and zoomed out to show the house with the yellow barrier tape stressing the enormity of the investigation. The voice-over continued:

"Detective Hoese indicated that several leads at the scene should direct police to the identity of the killer or killers responsible for the rash of random attacks. Detective Hoese refused to speculate on the reasons for the killings or why certain people were targeted."

The scene cut away to another with Galen being interviewed.

"Actually, we have several confirmed leads as to the identity of the person or persons responsible. One of the medics on scene from Ottawa Paramedic Service noticed a 'nanny cam' in the room where the killing took place. The camera is currently in police custody and the recording is being analyzed."

"And how do you know if the camera was working at the time?" the reporter asked.

"The camera is motion activated, so any direct movement in front of the nanny cam teddy bear would have been recorded. We just don't know what or how much is on the SD card or if it was even working.

"If the camera was working, we may have the actual homicide recorded with the identity of the person or persons responsible. This does not happen very often, but it certainly is a lead that could close this case sooner than expected. We have Ethan Tennant of the Ottawa Paramedic Service to thank for noticing the recording nanny cam teddy bear."

The camera panned back to the reporter who turned to her right. There I stood in my uniform, looking professional, ready to lie.

"Mr. Tennant, what made you look for the nanny cam? And why are you involved in the investigation?"

I looked directly at the reporter, not the camera: "I was asked to join the investigation because of my medical background. They assumed I might be able to help. As it turns out I did, just not in the way they thought. When I was going over the scene, I noticed a teddy bear exactly like the one my sister has to watch over the kids when she isn't at home. I brought it to Detective Hoese's attention, and we got lucky, I guess."

"Do you have any idea who might have done this?"

"In my experience, these types of crimes are typically committed by individuals with extremely low self-esteem, unable to hold a job or maintain a relationship. He will be between twenty and forty years of age, most likely white, make excuses for his inability to perform in bed, of low to moderate intelligence, and socially awkward. He should stand out in a crowd."

The reporter came back on scene.

"Police confirmed that Ottawa has not had a serial killer in decades and they are doing everything to find the person or persons responsible to put an end to our summer of terror."

Suddenly a round of applause came from the squad room. It was meant in jest at Galen's ability to lie on camera with a straight face and my rigid performance. The whole interview had been scripted specifically to invite the person responsible and make him reactive instead of proactive. We wanted him to go after me, sooner rather than later.

"You want me to play poker with you? You lie very well."

Galen looked at me, "Don't expect to win big."

"So now what?"

"Now we wait. We've put you in harm's way and we'll just have to see if he takes the bait. You're sure you want to go through with this?"

"You're the one who said I was next. This is the only way to know when and where he will strike, because he will have to find me."

I secluded myself in a quiet, unoccupied section of the room and called Maddy's cell for comfort and reassurance. Being scared only began to scratch the surface of my apprehension.

32

HE SAT ALONE IN THE DARK. This had become his favourite way to enjoy his free time. No clocks, no television, no radio in this room. It was his and his alone. He enjoyed the feel of the leather on his naked skin, slouched in the chair, head back. His senses deprived of light or sound, eyes closed, he could be anywhere, doing anything, feeling heat or cold. Tonight, sweat formed between the leather and his skin, bonding him to the chair.

He was up late last night, had spent hours alone amazed at how even today, with security systems so cheap, so many choose not to have that extra protection. It was easy to gain access to a house when the owner lay sleeping in bed, unaware of what was about to happen. Surveillance had been meticulous. The man's daily schedule, his comings and goings, his wife and children were so predictable. Every day the same, every weekend the same, people leading boring, scheduled lives with no sense of adventure or excitement. He could only imagine, in the last few minutes of the man's life, he experienced more terror and pain than anyone has a right to. He imagined that his victim experienced more emotions before dying than he had his entire life.

The more he thought about what he had done last night, the more excited he became. He felt his pulse quicken, his respiratory rate accelerate, and he became engorged at the thought of reliving the events of last night. His tongue moved slowly over his lips, his right hand moved down from the arm rest. His palm slid over his abdomen, becoming wet from the perspiration, and he wrapped it slowly, softly around himself. He stroked up, held it, then down. His imagination heightened his emotions: blood and bodily fluids flowing, skin ripping, fear and panic; the victim had remained alive, in fear hoping that he would die fast or be killed to end the pain. He had reached inside his victim's body and felt blood flowing through his arteries, felt and saw his lung fill, then empty of air, had his hand around his still pumping heart and squeezed. The bound man's eyes had widened, he'd made muffled sounds through the gag. He'd had an orgasm at that very moment he held and squeezed the heart, and fought to pump within the jail that was his hand. That same hand was now squeezing himself; he pushed up, skin pulling away from the leather. He moaned slightly and exploded. He felt the hot semen spray his chest, neck, and right cheek. He kept stroking and squeezing and the semen flowed again, softer this time, but still satisfying.

He relaxed, sitting back onto the leather and rubbed the semen into his skin. These orgasms have been better than he ever had with a woman. His only joy was when he could cause his lover pain. When his lovers no longer permitted the type of pain that excited him, he moved on to paying for sex. Now the ultimate joy was not just pain, but the ultimate pain, ending a life that felt the epitome of agony become the kindness of death.

He licked whatever remained on his fingers. It was a salty mixture of sweat and semen. Even though his pupils were dilated to admit as much light as possible, no light could be found in this darkness. His breathing slowed, his pulse returned to normal. He would relive those events as often as possible, maybe again tonight.

Soft sounds emanated from further down the hall. How long the phone had been ringing he didn't know nor did he care. This was his time, his moment to celebrate. The ringing continued. Ignoring the phone, his thoughts returned to the fantasy he'd brought to life.

The ringing continued, forcing him back to reality.

It was late, he thought. Surely it must be him. No one else had his number. Like a blind man keenly aware of his surroundings, he did not require lights to navigate about his apartment. The illuminated keys of the handset were bright on his eyes.

"Yes?" No need for social, polite introductions. He knew who it was.

"Is your TV on?"

"No."

"Turn it on to the local news. You're famous again."

He quickly walked to the television in the bedroom, pointed the remote by feel and powered the set. He thumbed the remote to find the correct channel. The reporter was interviewing the large, red-headed, freckled-faced detective. The television was muted. He adjusted it.

He stood in darkness with the light radiating over his sweat-covered body, phone in right hand, remote in left, both arms down by his side. He listened attentively, paying close attention. His exploits were being described for the world to see. When Galen Hoese made mention of the nanny cam, his chest fell. He heard the voice on the handset calling him and brought the phone to his ear.

"What did you do?"

"Wait."

Once the reporter was finished with the detective, Ethan Tennant stood discussing the psychological makeup of the suspect. His hero was calling him a coward, unable to perform. His hand still sticky with semen clutched the phone. Not able to perform? It was the best orgasm of his life. He'd just had the best orgasm of his life. The report finished and moved on to another story.

He put the phone back to his ear. "So what will you do now?" questioned the caller.

He didn't know what to think. Was there a teddy bear in the room? Were they lying? Had they seen his face? He hadn't been wearing a mask. Even if they had seen him, no one in Ottawa knew who he was. But it could complicate the chain of events they had planned. However, plans were meant to be broken.

He had come to admire the man who chased him and then followed his victories over those he had killed. If he had truly found a camera and if that camera was working and contained a video that showed the murder, he had truly made a grievous error.

"I told the detective that Ethan would be next," the voice on the phone said loudly to get his attention. This surprised him. The caller knew of his affection for the medic.

"What?" Only moments ago, he was in ecstasy; now he was furious with rage. "You had no right to tell him that. The paramedic is mine! I've got him playing my game. *I* decide when he dies."

The voice on the phone became angry, too. "I tell you who to kill. I tell you when to kill. I tell you how to kill. I am still your commander and you listen to me. Without me, you would have been caught long ago. If I say your boy dies, he dies."

There was no discussion. It had been a symbiotic relationship for years. The killing used to be sporadic, maybe one every year or two, the frequency and the victim determined by his mentor. He set the pace, the method, did some of the surveillance and made sure no one got caught as long as his plan was followed. And if he said Ethan had to die, he died; there was no argument.

"When and where?" his voice submissive.

"I put a scare into the paramedic tonight. I set off a little smoke bomb in his house to let him know how easily we could get to him. He was fun to watch as he fumbled around thinking he was saving his precious house. Then the fat cop came and the hose brigade showed up. I am sure the interview was staged, but it served its purpose. Kill the medic first, then the cop!"

"You were in town tonight? You didn't tell me! And if we kill a cop, won't that make things hotter for us?"

"I've been in and out of town for a while. Surveillance on the subjects required it. You knew when I wanted you to know. Things will only get hot for you, maybe—they don't even know about me. We will do the same thing we do every time the cops get close, we move. Is that a problem?"

"No, sir, not at all. It's just that I was beginning to enjoy watching this guy playing cop chasing me down. Come to think of it, you are right. It is time to end it. Thank you for making me see things as they should be."

"I would like this to be a fitting end to our stay in this city. I will call you tomorrow. Get some rest."

With that, the line went dead. He was excited again. He had grown fond of the medic, but now that had to end as well. He felt the excitement grow again.

He kept his personal belongings packed. Being prepared had been drilled into him. It made for a quick getaway.

Once he had cleaned the apartment, he went to bed and dreamt a peaceful sleep. He was happy to move: That meant a new city, a new life, and new assignments.

33

I DIDN'T SLEEP AT ALL. I tossed and turned all night, and both cats were annoyed by my constant moving, which made their sleep impossible. First I shivered, then I tossed the sheet away trying to cool off, then I became nauseated. I went to the bathroom every few hours either to pee or throw up. When the clock chimed six a.m., I put on my sweat shorts and T and went downstairs.

Galen slept in his clothes on the sofa. He had taken several pillows and jacked his head up for comfort or to ease his breathing. By the way he snored, I suspected he had a CPAP machine at home that he should have brought along.

I fed the cats and pried open a section of the wood covering the screen door to let them have the run of the backyard. Who would care for the cats if anything happened to me? Molly and Snickers were our kids. Maddy and I had raised them from kittens. They felt her loss and now I was worried for them. Once the wood gave way, they both ran outside, all fear and trepidation of the prior day's events gone, replaced with the joy of running free in the fenced-in yard.

I thought about breakfast, but my sour stomach spoke for me. With a glass of water in hand, I sat at the dining room table that the firefighters had righted the night before. Thoughts popped in and out of my head. Would Tom get better? Would I see Becky again? Missing Maddy went without saying. I valued Galen's friendship and dedication to his job, and questioned my profession and whether I want to go back to my job or not. All of these thoughts swept in and out of my mind rapidly and ferociously.

I called Maddy's cell just to hear her voice again and to give me a little strength to make it through the day. But the phone rang several times and failed to go to voice mail. I dialed again, same response. Again and again, the phone rang continuously without Maddy's voice greeting. Wave after wave of nausea crashed through my stomach. I stood up, bumping the table, toppling the glass of water. Maddy would have cursed me for letting water pool on the table.

Grabbing my cell, I keyed the numbers to get direct assistance from the cell phone provider. The line rang several times, and an overly pleasant automated voice greeted me, listing several options. Once offered, I pressed the correct extension.

"How may I help you today?" Her voice was so perky I already wanted to strangle her, but managed to maintain my composure.

"I have a problem with my wife's voice mail. Her greeting is gone from her line. Can you see what the problem is, please?"

"What is your wife's cell phone number, please?" Again, too perky.

I gave her the number and waited several minutes.

"Sir, I found the problem. It seems we texted all of our customers several times over the last two months indicating that an upgrade in the system would erase all stored voice mail messages and greetings. Your wife should have received these texts. Our records show that her plan does support text and voice mail. Did she not receive those texts?"

"I have no idea. It's my wife's phone. Can you just put her message back on, please?" It would be too difficult to explain that I was unable to let go of my wife and that her voice mail greeting was all that kept me grounded.

Galen walked into the kitchen. My voice must have woken him.

"I'm sorry, sir. Once the greeting is erased, there is nothing we can do. I would suggest you ask your wife to record a new one."

If reaching through the line and strangling the operator at the other end had been an option, I would have exercised it. Her perky, calm voice only infuriated me more.

"Thank you for your help," I said slowly and quietly with the tone of a priest taking confession. I pushed the disconnect button, turned on my heels and threw my cell, venting all my frustrations into one fastball pitch. The phone flew in slow motion, rotating, floating as I watched it hit the fridge. Small pieces of plastic broke off into new shapes and took flight in new directions. The kitchen was now scattered with fractured pieces of black and clear plastic.

The stainless steel fridge door now showcased a new dent where the phone had made impact.

"Telemarketers?"

"Bad day, that's all," I said, shrugging my shoulders.

"You wanna talk about it?"

"Later? Got a phone I can borrow?"

Galen tossed me his phone. "That phone is department issue. You break it, the city pays for it."

I righted the toppled glass from the dining room table, used my shirt to clean the spilled water and went to the sink to refresh my water. I stepped on a few pieces of cell phone on the floor, picked a large piece of the case from the sink, tossing it on the counter.

"Get out!" Galen is normally pretty laid-back, likes to drink beer, eats too much pizza, and is seldom serious. Today, he sounded serious.

"Get out. Leave. Take a fucking vacation, go to some spot in Mexico, get completely shit-faced, get laid! Get out, now! With all the shit going on in your life, you are ready to blow a gasket and it ain't gonna be pretty when it happens."

"Why?" I turned to look at him. "Why should I? We are closer now than we ever have been to find out who this guy is. Now is not the time to back down."

"Closer? Who the fuck are you kidding? Let's be serious. We are so far behind the fucking eight ball right now, I don't know which way is up, down, or straight ahead. Now is exactly the time to back down, walk away, leave it all behind, take a breather, whatever cliché you want to use. Honestly, I think you may be suicidal. You have been totally depressed since Maddy died. You haven't taken any time for yourself. Christ, you still call her. That's what the call was about, wasn't it? If you ever meet this guy face to face, I think you will want him to kill you, won't you? What happened on the phone?"

"They deleted Maddy's message from her cell account."

"That's it."

I stepped in closer. We were now only inches apart. Voices had gotten louder and tenser.

"Yah, that's it! I lost another little bit of her. So sue me if I can't let her go just yet."

He placed a hand on my shoulder. His voice was calming, soothing.

"You stupid fuck. Everybody takes their own time to let go. Maddy was great. You have every right to feel like you lost big time. You can unload on me anytime. That's what friends are for, to help you get fucking drunk and forget. I just don't want you doing anything stupid."

"Can't you ever say anything nice without swearing?"

"No fucking way. Now clean up this mess. I've been standing on a broken piece of plastic for the last few minutes. It would have broken the mood if I had tried to dig it out from my heel while we argued."

After a quick shower, I got ready to make myself the bait for the bad guy, a ghost of a man that no one has really seen. We didn't know what he looked like: Caucasian, Black or Asian, tall, short, fat, or thin? I thought I was calmer than I actually was. Hands trembling, I could barely button my shirt. Hands together, I looked at myself in the mirror. I could barely recognize the face looking back at me: dark circles under my eyes, lines on my forehead that seemed to have appeared overnight, and grey hair infiltrating my sideburns. I had aged ten years in the past few months.

I steadied myself, finished buttoning my shirt, and tucked it into my jeans.

"So this is what I look like with an extra ten pounds!"

I expected Galen to say something, but realized I was talking to myself again. This had become a regular thing for me since Maddy died. I would start talking aloud, start entire conversations, forgetting Maddy wasn't in the room or close by. Then, whenever she failed to respond, a pulse would shoot up my spine reminding me that I was alone. That feeling had haunted me since Maddy's death, and the sensation had not diminished at all. The thought of being alone for the rest of my life scared me as much as this crazy stunt I had suggested.

Standing in front of the mirror, with no one behind me, made me realize how alone I really was. A feeling I hated.

"Did you say something?" I didn't hear Galen walk up the stairs.

"Just admiring how I look in the mirror."

I steadied myself and followed Galen downstairs.

A tray of fresh Tim Hortons coffee sat on the table in the living room. The plywood in the dining room didn't fit the mood this morning.

"Ethan, this is Dan Elliott. He defines undercover, he's fucking invisible. Dan will be in an Ottawa City Works truck, delivery truck, whatever. That truck will follow, disappear, reappear, change colour, change style, but Dan will always be close by. Don't look for him. Don't try to find him. He knows you, your car. You just go about your business. I just wanted you to meet Dan so you know his face in case you happen to bump into him or see his face in your rear-view mirror one time too many. If you do see him too often, he's doing a shitty job."

Handshakes were exchanged.

"You're going to keep me safe?" my voice cracking.

"Gonna do my best unless you give me the slip or screw up."

"Your best! Your best! Losers always try their best!" I was shaking, scared, and my voice was two octaves higher.

Galen and Dan smiled at each other enjoying themselves at my expense.

"Time to play," Dan slapped me on the back as he passed me on his way out the door.

"Ethan, it's really important that you look the part." Galen's voice was deadly serious. "I want you to go about your business today as if it was a normal day, shopping, gym, whatever you would normally do. If this guy knows you like we think he does, he may know your routine."

"I don't have a routine, Galen. I seldom do the same thing on the same day. So what do I do?"

"Then act as if it was a nothing day. I don't give a shit what you do—just don't do something you wouldn't normally do."

Galen was trying his best to give me his serious voice with as little profanity as possible.

"As long as you don't screw up, lose your shadow, and do what you were told, you'll live through it. No biggie!"

I walked out the door, sat in my car, and felt the tiny beads of sweat rolling down my back. Leaning forward, my head resting on the steering wheel, I blindly reached up and turned the ignition key. The familiar sound of the engine roared to life. I flipped the switch and the sun roof lifted up, permitting warm, fresh air to enter into the car. As I backed out of the driveway, I looked both ways to spot my new best friend. Dan had left only moments earlier and was nowhere to be found.

Go about my normal business, he says, I thought to myself. I can't think what I would normally do on my day off. Voices sound louder in your head when you're scared. I swear the voices echoed in the vast hollows of my cranium. Every thought was magnified tenfold, and my mind wandered as I came to when I heard the car horn blaring. I slammed on the brakes and turned hard to the left as I noticed the car to my right. We came to stop only inches from each other's bumpers. I had driven through a stop sign and had almost hit a car that had the right of way. We both exited our vehicles, not sure who was more scared. The young female driver walked calmly over to me.

"Are you okay?" she asked.

"Me?" I was confused. Everyone has been asking me that a lot lately.

"You look like hell warmed over." A hand reached up to touch my forehead. Obviously a young mother. "Are you sick or something?"

"Something like that. I feel horrible today and was heading over to get checked out at the Riverside ER." *Good lie*, I thought to myself. I was close to the hospital, and I looked the part. I glanced around to see if Dan Elliott would make an appearance. He was nowhere to be found.

"You shouldn't be driving. Can I call an ambulance for you?"

I smiled and looked at her.

"Thank you so much for your help. Is everyone okay in your car?"

"I am alone and I'm fine. You go get yourself checked over."

She stayed to make sure I got into my car and was able to drive off without further incident. Not everyone is a bad person, I thought to myself as I left the intersection.

I collected my thoughts, paid attention, and drove around Ottawa. I let my car dictate my direction, wherever the flow of traffic went, I followed.

Seven hours later, my back was aching, my butt numb, and my neck tense. I had forgotten about my shadow all day and had enjoyed the drive around Ottawa. The radio was on but barely audible; my mind was a little more aware as I ran through the events of the past few months. Perhaps Galen was right; a change was needed.

The gas gauge read only a quarter full. I filled up the car, picked up a quarter-chicken dinner, and headed home.

Galen met me at my house. We split the chicken dinner, discussed the case, and made plans to repeat the events the next day.

Three days later, two tanks of gas, 1,200 kilometres, and more fast food than I have eaten in the past five years, Galen and I were no further ahead than we were the first day. Dan Elliott was true to his job title; I failed to spot him even once.

34

I SAT AT THE BACK of the squad room in the Ottawa Police Department. The room was filled with cops, criminal psychologists, CSIS profilers, coroners, and mental health professionals. I was alone in the field of EMS, way out of my comfort zone.

The head of each group gave their opinion of who the killer might be, along with his motives. They speculated on his childhood, where he would hide, his connection with the victims, and what drives a man to kill for pleasure. A guest from the FBI gave a detailed analysis of the killer based on extensive study in the United States.

For the most part, I was fascinated by the ability to form conclusions on such little evidence, but based mostly on past history of similar offenders. Short of a high-definition photograph, the group had a complete picture of the suspect.

After a few hours, I began to walk around the station, learning my way around. I was studying plaques proudly hung behind glass of officers who had stood out from the rest. A large figure appeared in the glass behind me. I continued to read the plaques.

"Bored?"

"You deal with the 'what if's.' I deal in absolutes. My patients have a problem, I try to keep them alive until we get to the hospital—and I never see them again. I see my patients for a few minutes. You guys can study criminals for years in an attempt learn more about them."

I turned and stood before my friend.

"Galen, what am I doing here? Really? Am I really making a difference?"

"Believe it or not, you are helping. Staying here keeps you alive."

"I took your advice today. I called a travel agent and got information for a trip. It's almost as expensive to go single, but I need it. Thank you, my friend."

"Any word on Tom or Becky?"

"Tom is doing better, but Dan said I shouldn't visit until you catch the guy because I could put the hospital at risk. And no, Becky hasn't called. Of course, I still don't have a cell, but she hasn't called the house, so . . ." I shrugged my shoulder and trailed off. "Hey, it's July first, Canada Day. I am going to go home, wave a flag, crash, fire up the barbeque, have a steak, and spend some time with the cats. Maddy would be pissed as hell if she knew I was ignoring our kids."

I turned on my heel to go. "There is a T-bone and beer with your name on it. You gonna join me or stay here?"

Galen thought long and hard about the offer. A simple negative shake of his head side to side was his nonverbal response. As I turned my back to Galen, he yelled out, "You still have your tail. Don't lose him. Or you can give him my steak."

I returned his suggestion with a silent finger salute of my own as I walked away.

Driving west on the Queensway with the sun in my eyes, windows down, and sunroof open, I began to realize just how tired I was. I rested my left elbow on the window ledge, my head tilted back on the headrest; my sunglasses kept the strong rays of the late evening sun at bay. The radio was silent. Air rushed in and the familiar sound of passing cars whizzing past me at high speed was the only thing keeping me awake. I kept my speed at just over 100 kilometres per hour and drove in the old men's lane, letting everyone pass me on my left. I also didn't want to lose Dan. Of course, he or a combination of officers had managed to keep me in their sights for days without letting me know they were close by. I kept a close eye on my rear-view mirror for Dan, a familiar truck, or any vehicle I could remember following me the past few days.

Cars flowed by, the traffic jams of late-night commuters long since over. Now the traffic belonged to those getting off after a twelve-hour day shift or those heading west to the suburbs away from the city hub. As cars passed, I would glance to my left to see people chatting to themselves into their Bluetooth earpiece or singing out loud to the tunes on the radio. Most cars had only a single occupant.

I had another twenty minutes or so before getting home and was enjoying my drive. A small black car slowly caught up to me on my left, inching its way past me. I looked to my left and caught a beautiful woman staring forward. She must have felt my stare and looked to her right at me, smiled, and turned her attention back to the road. Even though it was still hot outside, and the setting sun splashed colours of yellow and orange across the sky, a smile made me feel just a bit warmer, in a good way.

I turned the CD player on, adjusted my sunglasses, and squared my shoulders to relax. I looked back to see if the smiling lady was still looking over. Instead, her car had been replaced by a green Volvo station wagon with tinted windows.

The car pulled alongside me and matched my speed as travel ahead slowed with congestion from the on-ramps. We both slowed just a little, and something caught my eye and I turned to look left. The passenger window had been opened and I could see into the cab. I glimpsed the male driver. He wore sunglasses and stared forward. I turned my focus back to the road ahead as traffic slowed before me. A sparkle of sunlight caught my eye to the left. Turning, the driver held a silver gun pointed in my direction.

In a split second, I calculated my options: the car before me was too close, and there were too many cars behind me. I slammed on the brakes and depressed the clutch. I lurched forward. Above the sound of tires braking on the asphalt behind me, a loud "pop" was audible and a burst of light emanated from the car window beside me. The seat belt caught me as I flung forward from the sudden deceleration. The sound of imploding glass followed as I was pushed back into my seat. The car behind me slammed into the rear of my stopped car.

The green Volvo braked hard and stopped about one hundred metres ahead. I looked behind me. My large glass hatch had shattered and sprayed the entire cab and trunk of the car with tiny, square shards of glass. The woman who had rear-ended me had both hands to her head. A quick survey of the scene, I turned the steering wheel hard to the right, let off of the clutch and floored the gas. The rear-wheel-drive Porsche spun hard on its back wheels, the back end shot to the left, and I hit the car in front of me. Finally, the tires caught traction and propelled the car forward. I guided the car left and fishtailed, hitting the concrete wall with the right back quarter panel. I rode the narrow shoulder on the north side of the Queensway, scraping the side barrier rails on the passenger side of the car. Sparks flew past me as I accelerated along the shoulder.

Looking back, cars had stopped, and people were exiting their vehicles to survey the damage. The driver of the green Volvo had driven forward into parked cars, pushing and smashing vehicles aside to make a clear lane. I couldn't continue to look back. I had to see where I was going. The noise from the open side windows and the shattered glass hatch only added to the confusion. I prayed Dan Elliott was still shadowing me and had started his pursuit.

Traffic was clear as I drove along the north shoulder. Without signalling, I darted across three lanes of traffic, almost causing more collisions. I wanted the south concrete divider to be on my left, making any further attempts on my life to come from the right, furthest away from me. I was still accelerating. Looking down, I noticed that I had already hit 130 kilometres per hour.

"Oh why not!"

I dropped from fifth to fourth gear and the vehicle kicked back; the engine over-revved, and my speed increased fast. I was pushed back into the seat and dropped it back into fifth before redlining at 140 kilometres per hour. Cars in front came up and disappeared behind me like spindles on a fence. In my rear-view mirror, the green Volvo had broken away from the pack and was making pursuit.

I laid on the horn, warning the drivers in front to move to the right. If they didn't move, I swerved in and out of lanes, not bothering to signal to indicate lane changes. The green Volvo appeared larger each time I checked the rear-view mirror. I didn't notice any other vehicles speeding in an attempt to catch up with us. I figured either Dan was caught in the initial traffic jam I'd caused or he'd decided to give up shadowing me days ago.

I pressed down harder on the accelerator and watched my speed increase. At 160 kilometres per hour, I had put more distance between myself and the green Volvo. Exits and off-ramps approached fast and disappeared even faster. The sound of air rushing over the roof of the car and buffeting into the shattered hatchback drowned out any chance of hearing the driver of the green Volvo approach. Travelling at sixty kilometres over the posted speed limit, I expected the city police or Ontario Provincial Police to receive several 911 cell phone calls of two cars racing on the Queensway.

The Queensway, normally bumper to bumper during rush hour, snakes its way east to west through Ottawa. At certain times, the drive across town seems to take hours. Today, however, the Queensway disappeared beneath my tires in minutes.

To the right of the Queensway, the Bayshore Shopping Centre, which sits on the north shoulder of the 417, appeared and became larger fast. Bayshore is one of Ottawa's largest shopping centres, situated just a few kilometres east of Highway 416 and heading south, with the 417 continuing west.

The Volvo was no longer a dot in my rear-view mirror; it had grown larger with each glance back. Unless I was willing to push the car a little harder, the Volvo would close the distance fast.

At Greenbank Road, I pulled to the far right and slowed my speed to accept the upcoming off-ramp to Richmond Road. The Volvo followed suit. The distance between us closed. Gauging my speed and the other cars, I took the off-ramp 120 kilometres per hour, then hit the brakes hard. The tires froze in place, remnants of black rubber traced my path, and white smoke trailed behind me. Before the final split of pavement between the off-ramp and the road, I dropped the stick shift into second. The Porsche engine revved high, and the car lurched forward. I floored the accelerator and turned the wheel hard left. The car tires hit the low curb, jumped, and the tires squealed when they hit dry pavement. I pulled back into westbound traffic on the 417. Drivers slammed on their brakes or swerved to avoid a collision.

Behind me, the Volvo hit the brakes hard, too. The sound of bending metal and smashing glass could be heard as I drove off. I turned to look behind me as the Volvo went into reverse and rammed the car behind it in an attempt to merge back into traffic to continue the pursuit.

I had less than a kilometre to decide between south on the 416 or continue west on the Queensway. I cut across four lanes of traffic: horns were blaring, brakes were applied, tires squealed, and silent curses could be lip-read from the drivers I'd cut off.

The slow, meandering on-ramp to the 416 tilted to the left. At the apex, I hugged the inside curb and pressed hard on the accelerator. My banged-up sports car lived up to its storied reputation and didn't miss a beat. The engine revved, what was left of the tires gripped the road, and I was joining the southbound traffic well above the speed limit.

The road lowered, following the descent of the hill from the 417 and merged on the left side with the traffic coming from the west. All traffic was now heading south. I had time to look behind me to see if the Volvo had escaped the rear-end collision or had decided simply to abort the mission.

Nothing!

I reached for Galen's phone that I thought was on the passenger seat, blindly sweeping my hand between the bolsters, then into the crevice. The phone was not there. I glanced down to the floor on the passenger side. I was looking for a small, black, mobile phone lying on a black carpet hidden in the shadows of the dash and the centre console. My speed didn't justify a hand search or more than a quick glance.

I wanted to call 911 myself but hoped my erratic driving had caused enough problems to make other drivers call.

A quick glance over my shoulder convinced me that the green Volvo was nowhere in sight. Two exits lay ahead, Hunt Club Road, and Fallowfield Road just a few kilometres farther on. *Should I exit and return to the police station or continue south on the 416 and leave Ottawa behind?* I thought to myself.

I had already passed Baseline Road, but had to decide fast, as I passed the sign indicating that Hunt Club Road was just ahead. I was sure Galen and the police would want to debrief me on the shooting and speeding on the Queensway. Decision made. I slowed to sixty kilometres per hour, indicated my intentions to exit, not knowing if any of my rear lights were still functioning, and took the Hunt Club exit.

Just then, my head snapped back as my car was rear-ended. The impact sent the car hurling forward, my foot slipped off the brake. The seat belt held me in place, pulling tight over my chest. I found the brake, slowed the car, and quickly collected myself as

I looked back, fearing the green Volvo had returned. My car was rammed again, causing more pain as I fell forward and the shoulder strap dug deeper. I didn't have time to react. Looking in the rear-view mirror, a white sedan kept up with the assault. Another full rear impact pushed my car closer to the ditch. I stepped on the clutch, put the stick in first gear, and floored the accelerator. Nothing!

"Fuck!" I must have stalled the car during the last collisions.

My head snapped back as the white car slammed the rear of the Porsche again. The Porsche started to slide sideways on the loose gravel. Pressing down hard with both feet on the brake pedal did nothing to stop the car from sliding farther toward the edge. The momentum pushed my car into a blue directional billboard. The sound of snapping posts echoed louder than the sounds of tires dragging in the gravel. The bright blue billboard telling drivers where the closest hotels were in the region came crashing down onto my car`s windshield, fracturing the glass into tiny spider webs. I looked up to see the logo for Days Inn resting on the windshield. Again, I felt the impact of another direct hit.

I stepped hard on the clutch, turned the key and the engine roared back to life. I pushed the stick back into first, let the clutch out and stepped hard on the gas. I had lost all sense of direction. Each hit had pushed or spun my car in different directions, but all I wanted was to put space between me and the white car.

The Porsche's tires spun in the gravel. The needle of the tachometer spun wildly up then down, then up again. The billboard slipped off the windshield giving me a clear view of my path ahead. The highway lay before me. The culvert wasn't deep. The tires pushed against the gravel, found dry grass, caught traction, and propelled the car toward the south lanes of the highway. Just as soon as my car started gaining speed, it stopped cold. With a thundering crash, the low front end of the Porsche met the opposite grade of the culvert. The back tires kept spinning, pushing the car deeper into the small hill. I turned and looked through the shattered hatch that had its glass blown out from the gunshot on the Queensway.

The driver slowly opened his door and exited the vehicle.

"I don't know this guy! Should I know him?" I was unsure if I said this out loud or in my mind.

Panicking, I depressed the clutch, positioned the stick from first to reverse and floored it. Nothing but the sound of spinning tires! The car wasn't moving anywhere. Slowly, the rear end moved a little to one side, then the other. The stranger was less than fifteen feet away. The gas pedal was depressed all the way to the floor, but I pressed harder out of shear desperation. Closer!

"Fuck this!" I thought to myself.

I opened the driver's door, jumped from my seat, and was jolted back into the car by the seat belt. Looking down, I thumbed the red release button, felt the tension of the belt disappear, and shot out of the car. Then my world went black.

MY EYES WERE CLOSED. Bright flashes of light went off and pain raced across the back of my head. I tasted grass. I spit out dirt and debris. I reached around and rubbed the back of my head. I opened my eyes to see the undercarriage of my car. The sound of cars speeding by on the 416 could be heard in the distance. Memories flooded in: the chase on the Queensway, getting rammed from behind, attempting to flee the white car.

Without thinking, I hopped from my prone position to being on my hands and knees. I was immediately put back down in the dirt, lying on my stomach, with the weight of the attacker's foot placed firmly on my back.

"Don't look up!" The voice was steady, confident, and unwavering, without a hint of emotion.

"I am not moving."

"For a paramedic, you don't drive very well."

"Yeah, well, I don't drive the ambulance very often. I like to attend." I thought a little sarcasm might hide my fear. "Why me?" The question was short, self-explanatory. I had to know.

"Actually, you really just sort of fell into things, didn't you. If you hadn't barged into the apartment that day, we wouldn't be here. You just made the game more interesting, that's all."

"It's a game to you?" My voice rose higher, my body tensed. "You kill people and call it a game?"

"It is a game for some. Not for me. Well, Ethan, I really have come to like you. Really I have, but time is short, and I must be on my way."

There were sounds of tires stopping on the gravel shoulder, a door opening and closing, a concerned male voice calling out, "Do you need help?"

I could feel his foot twist on my back and the explosion of a gun being fired. I strained to look back as a car door closed and shoulder gravel kicked loose under the tires from the fleeing car. The pressure returned to my back.

"Time is short and I really must go." His voice never changed. It was calm, reassuring, as if he were speaking to his mother about Sunday dinner.

Across my head where the pain still throbbed, I felt a new sensation, heat. A small, hard, hot piece of metal was pushing against my skin. The stones and dirt pushed further into my skin. Without ever having held a gun, I knew the sensation of a barrel being pushed into the mastoid bone behind my right ear.

"Goodbye, Ethan. It has been a pleasure."

My eyes closed tighter, my body tensed so hard I thought I was going to piss my pants. Seconds before dying, the mind races in milliseconds with thoughts of being discovered with the front of your face blown off, mixed with grass and dirt and blood, and the coroner making a notation that the victim pissed his pants before dying. My legacy would be a notation that I couldn't hold my bladder in a moment of fear.

Those thoughts raced at speeds that are incalculable; time stops; sounds disappear; objects freeze in motion. I now understand what they mean when people say that their lives flashed before their eyes.

A gun exploded with a sound so loud it echoed in my head. Soon it wouldn't hurt anymore. Weight came crashing down on me pushing me hard against the dirt, taking my breath away. I felt warm fluid flow freely down my right cheek. My breath was gone. I tried to inhale but no air filled my lungs. I inhaled again, still nothing. I was breathing in a vacuum. I opened my eyes and saw the same picture I'd had in my mind as I lay on the ground earlier, the undercarriage of my car.

The sun lit the far side of my car, but overhead, darkness. Sounds returned. I inhaled again and my lungs pulled in warm summer air. I made a gasping noise forcing more air into my chest. It felt good. The weight on my back was heavy. Is this what death feels like? I tried to get up. The weight kept me down. I tried to look up, but couldn't see anything but darkness. My cheek was warm, wet, and I knew immediately the sensation and smell of blood. The iron smell of blood is like no other: metallic, hard, and bitter. Was it my own?

Voices were raised in the distance. They were yelling, almost indistinguishable. Then, shoes on gravel, more shouting, voices close but muffled. I pulled my arms in close to my body, palms down against the dirt and pushed up. The weight fell off my back to the left. Voices became clear. The heat from the sun returned.

"Ethan, are you okay?"

I turned to see who it was. Dan Elliott was looking down at me, gun in hand, panic in his eyes, radio chatter coming from the portable on his belt. I was alive!

Dan placed his arm under my arm and helped lift me.

"Are you okay?" he repeated.

My head cocked to one side, the ringing in my ears was louder than the noise around me. I looked back at Dan and nodded slowly. Dan helped me stand upright. I placed one hand on my car, stood tall, arched my back and squared my shoulders to work out the kinks from the weight that had just been lying on me. I looked down at the body by my feet. The driver of the green Volvo, then the white sedan, my attacker, lay bloody and motionless.

Dan said something, but I didn't hear him. My attention was focused on the man before me. Kneeling down, I pulled his shoulder upward to turn the body so I could see his face. He rolled easily. I looked at the face of a stranger, a face changed by the bullet that killed him. Grass, dirt, and debris stuck to his face from the ground where he'd fallen. Everything above his left cheek was blown outward. His left eye was missing; part of his nose remained. The edge of the skin was jagged and torn. The sphenoid plate and what remained of his brain were visible. It was then I realized the blood on my face was his. I pulled my shirt over my head and used it as a towel to wipe the blood from my face and hands. I wiped my face back and forth not knowing if I was getting all the blood off. My hands now had blood on them as well. I hated having anything on my hands. I hated touching a patient without gloves, let alone permitting myself to come in contact with a patient's body fluids.

Sounds were still muted, and the ringing in my ears persisted. There were Ottawa Police cruisers and OPP cruisers parked along the side of Highway 416. How long had I been staring at the dead man?

Dan tugged at me, turning me to look him in the eyes: "Do you want me to call EMS?"

"For him?" I yelled, then realized I was yelling.

He shook his head, "For you!"

I turned my head side to side indicating my refusal. Words echoed in my head. My head hurt, and felt like it was filled with water flowing from side to side.

"Can I borrow your jacket?" I was still yelling. Someone from behind hung his jacket over my shoulders. Before I could thank whoever it was that had lent me his coat, he had left to do something else. I took a few steps away from the scene and sat on the grass away from it, the chaos, and the confusion. Cops from both Ottawa and the OPP were busy taping off the road, talking on cell phones and radios.

I had been forgotten about already. I could have walked away, and no one would have noticed. There were more cops here than we usually have medics to cover the entire city of Ottawa. My car was without its back window, the windshield shattered, both side view mirrors had been torn off, the front bumper was hanging off, and the hood had caved in where the sign had landed on it. Both sides were dented and banged up so badly that you couldn't even tell what kind of car it was. Bright red blood splatter and brain matter showed up well on yellow paint.

"You look like shit!"

I turned to see a red-headed, fat man sitting beside me.

"I feel like shit."

"Dan told me you're a little deaf from the gunshot. The guy must have pulled the trigger just as he was shot. There's a big hole in the ground right beside where your head was."

That explained my deafness.

"You're a lucky guy, Ethan."

"Lucky. You call this being lucky?"

"Things didn't go exactly as planned, did they?"

"This was considered as one of your scenarios?"

"You gonna go to the hospital and get your ear checked out?"

"What for? I hate hospitals."

Questions answered with questions. We argued for a while about nothing, then Galen took me home. A police cruiser was still parked outside my house when I arrived.

"Can I pull the detail?" Galen asked as we walked past the cruiser.

"Sure. I'm pretty sure I can handle things from here."

Galen gave a nod to the uniformed officer seated behind the wheel. The officer understood and drove off. We stood before the door.

"Fuck off for a few weeks, eh?"

"Yah!" I wasn't in the mood to explore the matter any further.

I unlocked the door, stepped in and turned, "How did you show up so fast?"

"About five minutes after you left, I got a phone call. This guy said that you were being followed by a green Volvo. The caller said the guy in the Volvo was the guy we were looking for. How the fuck he knew blows me away. I sent the whole fucking city's black and whites after you. You left a shitload of wrecked cars on the Queensway.

"I tried calling you, but," he paused, pulled out the mobile phone he let me borrow, "you left it on my desk."

Molly walked between my legs to get outside. Snickers stood at the door and just looked out.

"Coming in?" I made the offer but wished Galen would decline.

"Nah. I have to do some more work and clean up that mess on the Queensway you left."

I stepped inside and surveyed the house. I didn't recognize it anymore. It was supposed to be our house. We were supposed to have kids, cats, maybe a dog. Now it's just me and the cats.

"Hey!" I removed the Ottawa Police jacket that I had borrowed and threw it at Galen. "Thanks for having my back."

Galen lifted his eyebrows, smirked, turned, and walked away. Molly ran past him back into the house.

36

THE TAXI PULLED UP to a house, half mansion, half resort. I didn't realize Ottawa had homes like this. I tend to forget how much money is in this town. Government, software, big business, all sorts of money floated around Ottawa.

The taxi followed the circular drive and stopped under the stone canopy that led to the solid, carved double front doors. I paid the fare and walked up steps to the doors. I was cradling a bottle of scotch that cost more than what I make in a day. Galen told me to buy a bottle of whiskey, rye, or scotch; "expensive," he said.

"Whatever you decide to spend on the bottle, double it!" His words were bouncing in my head at the cash register when I paid for the bottle. He said his poker group did not drink beer or eat pretzels. It wasn't that kind of group. I see why Galen said that.

Even the door buzzer was ornate. Gold laurels flowed around, above and below the centre white button. Even the centre button appeared to be something more than white plastic; porcelain, perhaps. I pressed the button once. Silence! Perhaps the buzzer was not working. The owner of this house did not appear to be someone who would let something like an inoperative door chime go unnoticed. I decided to wait a moment. The door opened before me. A very well-dressed lady in a white flowing gown, dangling earrings, and a shawl over her shoulders answered the door.

"You must be Ethan?"

"Yes, I am." Rather well turned-out for a maid.

"My husband said he was expecting you. Please come in." She opened the door wide and stepped to one side. I walked past her into the foyer, which was probably larger than my entire house.

"Down the hall. Follow the loud chauvinist talk," she quipped. She motioned down the hall.

I shyly handed her the bag, which even now seemed under-valued.

"Oh, that! I'm sure that is for the game tonight. New guy always has to buy the expensive bottle."

"Will you be joining us?" I knew it was a stupid question. Galen had told me it was a guy's night of poker and TV.

"Oh, no! My husband has his night, and I have mine." With that, she walked down another hall and disappeared. I walked for at least fifty feet along oak-panelled walls and tiled floors before I came to a lit room. Seated around a large table, Galen and his friends sat in large dark leather chairs. The conversations didn't stop when I entered the room. Galen gestured for me to join them.

Again, I clumsily offered the scotch in a Dollar Store bottle bag. Galen handed it to his host, who pulled it out of the bag and let the bag fall to the floor. The owner of the house scanned the bottle, turned it over, and admired the vintage. "The son of a bitch actually bought an expensive bottle."

It was then I noticed everyone was drinking beer. He got up, retrieved several glasses, and placed them on the table.

"Sit."

There was only one vacant chair. I sat without saying a word.

"Ethan, this is Judge Thomas—or, as we call him here, Bill. That's why he has the big chair, makes him feel important around us commoners. We still aren't sure if he actually wears pants under his robe."

I looked at Galen. He knew I was not familiar with a Judge Thomas.

"Supreme Court of Canada."

"Ah!"

I stood to shake his hand. "Sir."

"Son, around here, we do not stand on formality or protocol. It's Bill." He stood, shook my hand, and sat down. He opened the bottle and began to pour.

Galen went on, "You know my boss, Richard Stabenow. Around here, we call him Dick. Never ever call him Dick at the station."

"Rich." Easier to *never* call him "Dick." Richard nodded.

"I've heard a lot about you, son. You did a fine job out there. Sorry to hear about your car."

I hate being called "son." With a single, simple, and effective word, it shows who is dominant.

Galen motioned directly across the table, "Colin Peets, president of Pendergrass Software."

Colin didn't have a problem. He stood, walked around the table, retrieved a glass of my expensive scotch, shook my hand firmly, looked me square in the eye, and sipped from the glass. "Nice to have you join our group."

He was the businessman from the group. He knew his position and felt comfortable here.

"Last, but not least, Liz Matyas."

I stood and walked around the table to greet her. Galen continued, "Liz is the, well, we aren't quite sure what you do at CSIS, now do we, Liz?"

Liz stood, smiled, and extended her hand. "I am not sure what I do. Let's just say I'm in logistics."

"Liz was the one who quietly expedited the profile we got and coordinated the response from Quantico. It didn't do any good, but it was nice to have the help. She helps coordinate things from all the agencies."

I felt woefully under-qualified to be in the same room with this group. Each person was at the top of his or her respective fields, and I was . . . well, I was a glorified ambulance driver. Tom would be proud.

Introductions aside, we all took our seats and the conversation flowed as freely as the scotch and the other drinks. I was included in whatever topics were being discussed. My opinion, even if without relevance, was still considered. I was amazed at how quickly the group made me feel comfortable.

"So, how about we lose some money?" Liz rubbed her palms together briskly, but unlike the calloused hands of a worker, her hands made the sounds of oiled skin and silk brushing against each other in a light Caribbean breeze. Her evil grin offset the sound of her soft hands.

"Never trust anyone from CSIS at poker!" This came from Galen, who obviously knew her well.

Liz smiled.

"All CSIS agents lie and cheat," Judge Bill said.

After more conversation, more scotch, and a lot of money changing hands, I pushed my chair away from the table and excused myself to find the washroom.

"Front foyer, go north, third door on the right." Judge Bill never looked up from his cards.

I retraced my steps from when I first entered the house. It was at a slow pace to take in the woodwork, paintings, and furnishings. The conversation at the game table never stopped and it echoed in the wooden halls.

When I returned, the poker chips had been restacked on the table, cards sat squared into a neat stack in the centre, and everyone had taken a break. I sat down to a glass that had been refilled with my scotch.

"Did Galen ever debrief you on the case?" Richard asked.

"No, I figured in time I would get all the details. I am curious as to how you got to me so fast after I left the station."

Galen stood with glass in hand. He walked over to the liquor table and poured something clear from a decanter. He spoke as he poured.

"Within minutes of you leaving, I received a call on my cell. The caller said you were being followed by a green Volvo and that you would be killed if we didn't stop the driver."

Galen took his seat.

"We tried a trace but got nothing. Stupid fucking phone systems."

Richard smiled.

"One of the guys at the station called Dan Elliott while we traced, and he was following you from a distance back. After the first attack, Dan called for backup."

Galen drank from his glass. Everyone else paid attention.

"Prints came back on the guy Dan killed. Ex-military; most of his file was blacked out. We got a first name, Andrew, no last name, no SIN, no address, no date of birth, *nada*, zilch. Not much we could do about that. I pushed to have a few more details on this guy, but got absolutely no response. Even Liz couldn't persuade any more information from the military. I guess once they release a document, they don't change their mind.

"Our guy served in the first Gulf War. Department of Defence won't tell which unit, where he served, or what he did . . . again, zilch. So we are left with an ex-military guy with no employment record since the mid-nineties, no income statements, no tax return filed with Rev Can, nothing we can trace to his whereabouts for the last decade plus."

Galen put his glass down, pulled himself closer to the table and stacked his poker chips.

Richard continued, "We found a cell phone in the Volvo, pre-paid, untraceable. Everything in the car was generic, stuff you would find in any discount store across the country. My guess is this was not their first time. What caused one to give up the other is anyone's guess. He got tired, they argued. The leader has done it before, who knows."

"So you figure one of them gave the other up? It doesn't make sense."

Judge Bill shuffled the deck of cards without breaking his stare on Galen.

"Ante up! Actually, it does make a little sense. Think of it this way." Bill dealt the cards. "If one became a liability, made mistakes, or just pissed the other guy off, what better way to get rid of him? Call the cops with his whereabouts and let them deal with him. With his personality, you know he wouldn't go down without a fight and would probably eat a bullet anyway."

I looked around the table. Everyone had a stack of chips, white, yellow, red, and blue. Looking down before me, each stack had ten chips. I waited for others to toss in their kitty chip. One by one, a blue ten-dollar chip was tossed into the centre of the table.

"Looking back at the timetable of each incident," Galen continued, "the time of the call I received immediately after you left," he looked directly at me, "it was pretty much agreed there must have been two of them."

"Remember Ethan, we had conflicting reports on the height, weight, and appearance of the assailant in different events." He called a murder an event. "A team of two would explain why we had two descriptions."

The hands had been dealt, and I spread the five cards in my possession. What the hell was I looking at? I had never played poker before today and still had no idea what I was doing. What I knew of poker, I'd learned from watching television.

More chips flew into the circle, bids were raised and met, cards laid and requested, cards moved and repositioned according to importance in each player's hand. No one folded yet.

"So, was it a tag team thing or was one of them the leader?" Liz never took her eyes off her cards while she spoke.

"Andrew was not the leader for various reasons. The caller who told me Ethan was being followed had an air of authority when we spoke, then questioned me to make sure I got the information correct. That does not indicate someone who takes orders but rather someone who gives them."

Galen paused to study his cards.

Colin, who hadn't said a word all night, joined in the conversation. "Has anyone figured out why that one particular group was chosen? It seems odd that those people, with nothing in common, randomly selected, would be the target of these guys."

"Spree killers are usually defined by killing more than one person in multiple locations, usually on a single day. Those victims have little in common other than being in the wrong place at the wrong time. Our guys killed for fun and picked their victims out of the newspaper, tracked them down, and killed them for sport.

"These guys were killing for the thrill. No sexual gratification that we know of at the scene. It was fun: pure and simple. They got their jollies by selecting a group, tracking them down, and making a sport of it."

Galen repositioned his cards. More raising, more chips going into the pot. More curious stares as I fumbled with my cards. I added my chips into the pot.

"We are going national looking for similar incidents across the country. It is not common for killers to cross borders; so, for now, we are sticking to Canada."

"Call."

I looked up. Hands were being laid and other hands tossed into the pot without ever revealing themselves. I laid my hand before me.

"Beginner's luck!" Colin smiled and pushed the pot in my direction.

The entire time I wasn't even sure what I had done. At this

point I looked up and had to ask, "Is it impolite to stack? Do I keep them in a pile? What?"

"Stack them neatly by colour. Whoever has the biggest stack, wins. Got it?" Liz smiled.

"Got it!"

I quickly pulled the chips apart by colour and arranged them before me. One square blue chip failed to mix in with the round chips. I pulled it out and examined it. Someone had included an SD card in the mix.

"The advantage of being a judge is telling a cell phone company that the deleted message from a customer's account was vital information on a case and I needed a copy. Galen gave me your wife's information and I called the cell company and got your wife's voice mail back."

"They said it was gone." I held the SD card like someone holding a rare diamond in the light.

"Don't believe half the shit you hear from those mobile companies, young man."

I looked back to thank him. That was all that was needed.

Liz pulled the cards into a deck and started to shuffle.

"Or a CSIS agent playing poker who has control of the deck! You may walk home tonight a winner!"

About the Author

AFTER GRADUATING as a paramedic in 1983 from the Ambulance and Emergency Care Program (now Primary Care Paramedic Program) at Fanshawe College, Perry worked part time for various EMS agencies before settling in Brockville, Ontario, in 1984. He continues to work as a full-time paramedic and, with almost thirty years of experience in dealing with the sick and injured, he uses his past experiences to weave together his novels.

When not working as a paramedic, he is also the owner of Sands Canada, a medical equipment company dedicated to the pre-hospital care community. As well as retailing equipment used by paramedics and other medical responders, he and his staff design high-end medical deployment cases based on his decades of field experience.

Perry is a native of Sudbury but grew up in London and now resides in Brockville, Ontario.

All Good Things is Perry's first novel. He has finished the next novel in the Ethan Tennant series, *The More Things Change*.

TO ORDER MORE COPIES:

GSPH

GENERAL STORE PUBLISHING HOUSE
499 O'Brien Road, Box 415, Renfrew, Ontario, Canada K7V 4A6
Tel 1.800.465.6072 • Fax 1.613.432.7184
www.gsph.com